MARITAL DUTY

"Good heavens, Miranda! You're about to be married and no one ever instructed you. What will you do tonight when you're alone with Lord Huntsley?" Sara asked.

"Pretend, I suppose. I am very good at bluffing, you know that. Marital duty has something to do with kissing, I'm almost certain. How difficult can that be?"

"Well, *I* know something about it."

"You do?" Miranda looked at her friend in astonishment.

"Once, when I was walking through the fields, I saw a footman with a village girl. They were together under a maple tree. They were kissing." She lowered her voice. "But that's not all."

"What else were they doing?"

"He had pulled down her bodice and was caressing her bosom!"

Miranda recoiled. "No!"

"Yes! And what's more, I later heard that the girl was with child."

Gasping for air, Miranda clutched her shawl tightly across the portion of her anatomy in question. "Lord Huntsley will want to touch my—?"

Books by Angie Ray

Ghostly Enchantment
Sweet Deceiver
A Delicate Condition

Published by HarperPaperbacks

A Delicate Condition

 ANGIE RAY

HarperPaperbacks
A Division of HarperCollinsPublishers

This is a work of fiction. The characters, incidents, and dialogues are products of the author's imagination and are not to be construed as real. Any resemblance to actual events or persons, living or dead, is entirely coincidental.

HarperPaperbacks *A Division of* HarperCollins*Publishers*
10 East 53rd Street, New York, N.Y. 10022

Cover illustration by Bob Berran

First printing: November 1995

Printed in the United States of America

HarperPaperbacks, HarperMonogram, and colophon are trademarks of HarperCollins*Publishers*

❖ 10 9 8 7 6 5 4 3 2 1

Special thanks to
Peggy McCallum
Barbara Benedict
and to my three friends
(who prefer to remain anonymous)
who said this plot was absolutely believable.

A Delicate Condition

1

She looked just as a bride should on her wedding day.

Staring at the image in the mirror, Miranda felt as though she were looking at a stranger. Her white satin dress, with its festoons of lace and roses around the hem and pearls sewn into the bodice and sleeves, was elegant and stylish. Her red-gold hair, usually so untamable, was arranged in a coronet of braids and covered by the lace-edged veil. It made her look refined, regal even. She appeared much older than her nineteen years—poised, mature, sophisticated.

So why did she feel as though she was about to be sick?

"You're going to be married," she told her reflection firmly. "And you're going to be very happy."

Her stomach churned.

Fortunately, before she could think any more about how happy she was, the door opened behind her and a voice with a slight lisp asked, "Miranda Rembert, are you talking to yourself?"

Miranda turned to see a heart-shaped face with a halo of brown curls peeking around the bedroom door.

"Sara!" Without a thought for the delicate satin and lace wedding gown, Miranda rushed over to hug her friend. "Oh, I'm so glad to see you!"

Laughing, Sara returned the embrace. "Silly, let me look at you." Stepping back, she surveyed Miranda from head to toe. The twinkle in her brown eyes was replaced by an expression of awe. "Miranda, you look absolutely *stunning.*"

"Do I?" Involuntarily, Miranda glanced toward the mirror. "But never mind that. Come sit down and tell me how you managed to convince your aunt to let you come."

Unmindful of her billowing blue skirts, Sara plopped down on the bed. "My aunt decided that her heart was strong enough to do without me for one week while I tended my mother's sickbed."

"Your mother's sickbed?" Miranda perched next to Sara and clutched her arm. "Mrs. Rowan is ill? Oh, Sara, I'm so sorry. I hadn't heard."

"Probably because she's in her usual good health." Sara smiled, revealing a slight gap between her two front teeth. "I fibbed."

Miranda tried to look suitably shocked, but she couldn't help smiling. "Sara, you shouldn't have."

"Yes, I should. What else could I to do when my best friend is going to marry a man I've never heard of?"

Miranda's smile faded. Her gaze wavered before Sara's suddenly stern expression. "I suppose I should have written you."

"You most certainly should have! I almost needed one of Aunt Gerta's pills for heart palpitations when I received the wedding invitation. Who is this Viscount Huntsley? Couldn't you have written a line or two to tell me about him?"

Miranda rose and stepped over to her dressing table. "I'm sorry, Sara. I wanted to write, but I didn't know how to explain in a letter."

Frowning, Sara trailed after her. "What is there to explain? How did you meet him?"

"His father and mine are old friends, apparently." Miranda picked up one of her elbow-length lace gloves and pulled it on. "Papa invited Huntsley to visit a few months ago."

"And he fell in love with you at first sight?"

"No." Carefully, Miranda pushed down the fabric between each of her fingers. "Thelma said his finances are not too healthy and that my dowry will be an enormous help to him."

Sara's brow puckered. "But you're in love with him, aren't you?"

Miranda slipped a pearl button into its tiny loop of fabric. "Not exactly."

"Not exactly?" Sara leaned forward, trying to see her face. "What do you mean, not exactly? Oh, Miranda, surely you haven't agreed to marry for some mundane, practical reason? Not when we always swore we would never marry for anything but love!"

"I said that before my father remarried and brought home a new wife." Miranda tried to force another button through a loop, but it resisted her efforts.

Sara's frown deepened. "Has Lady Rembert been cruel?"

"Oh, no. No, not really. It's my own fault, actually." She wrestled with the button as she tried to explain. "I feel . . . uncomfortable around her."

Sara stared at her in disbelief. "So you decided to get married? Miranda, when are you going to stop being so impulsive?"

"I was not being impulsive. I thought it all out very carefully. My options are very limited—either marry or live here for the rest of my life. I would much rather marry."

"That makes sense," Sara admitted reluctantly. "But why not go to London for the Season and find a man you could love?"

Moving to the window so she could see the button better, Miranda said, "Thelma has never moved in fashionable circles and has no connections there. And you know how isolated it is here. I don't think there is an unmarried male within a hundred miles. Except for Mr. Pelham."

"Mr. Pelham?"

"The new vicar. He came here after you went to live with your aunt." Miranda gazed out the window toward the distant church steeple for a moment before returning to her task. "He is very handsome."

"Miranda!" Sara squeaked in alarm. "Are you in love with this Mr. Pelham?"

Startled, Miranda looked up from the stubborn button. She laughed, a slight heat rising in her cheeks. "Of course not. Not really. Well, perhaps just a little. He is so *very* handsome, you see."

"Then why aren't you marrying him?"

"I might have if he had ever mustered the courage to propose." Her brows drew together. "I think Thelma may have said something to discourage him. She told *me* that I was in the throes of a silly infatuation and that I should forget about Mr. Pelham because Papa would never countenance the match. I vow, I was half-tempted to propose myself and elope. But then Lord Huntsley arrived, and he was—"

She broke off, biting her lip.

"Lord Huntsley was what?" Sara's brown eyes were alight with curiosity. "More handsome than Mr. Pelham?"

Miranda shook her head slowly. "No. Lord Huntsley isn't really handsome. Not the way Mr. Pelham is. But he is—" she groped for a word to explain her fiancé, "he is very compelling."

"Compelling?" Sara frowned. "What do you mean?"

"I don't know how to explain it exactly. He has a presence about him. He is very elegant. Very sophisticated. Very . . . masculine, I suppose."

Sara made a face. "He sounds rather intimidating to me."

"Intimidating?" Miranda twisted the button on her glove and gave a nervous laugh. "What nonsense!"

Sara stared at her. "You sound as if you're scared of him."

The button suddenly popped off Miranda's glove and fell to the floor. Hastily, she bent down to pick it up. "Oh, dear, look what I've done. Sara, will you sew this back on for me?" She handed the other girl the button.

Sara took the button but did not move. "You can't be scared of him. You've never been scared of anything in your life."

"Sara, I must have the button sewn on—"

Sara paid no attention. "Remember when we were nine and were lost in the forest near the graveyard? I was frightened out of my wits. But even when night fell and I swore I saw a ghost, you sat on a log singing until your father found us."

A tiny laugh escaped Miranda. "Only because I thought my singing would be sure to frighten off any ghost. I was petrified."

"What about when we were twelve and Old Miser Napworth caught us stealing his plums? He was going to cane us both. I was blubbering with fear, but you made him laugh so hard, he let us go."

"I didn't make him laugh on purpose. I was scared silly. I just hoped he wouldn't come near us if I told him we had the plague."

Sara looked unconvinced. "Then what about when you were fifteen and your mother fell ill? You managed Black

Down Abbey single-handedly for two years until she passed away. And you still would be if your father hadn't remarried."

Her smile fading, Miranda walked back to her cluttered dressing table and searched for a needle and thread. She didn't want to think about those two years. She had never been so terrified in her life.

Sara touched Miranda's arm. "*Are* you scared of Lord Huntsley?"

"Of course I'm not scared of him." Miranda picked up a needle and spool of thread. "It's just that he has a very odd effect on me."

"An odd effect? What do you mean by that?" Sara's eyes widened. "Has he kissed you?"

Miranda shook her head. "He has been the perfect gentleman."

Sara frowned in disappointment. "Then what is it? You are confusing me, Miranda." She held out her hand for the needle and thread. "Speak plainly for heaven's sake."

Wordlessly, Miranda gave the needle and thread to Sara. How could she explain Lord Huntsley's effect on her when she didn't understand it herself? She only knew that when she first met him, she had forgotten all about Mr. Pelham. And when he was in the room, it was difficult to look at anyone else. And that whenever she was near him she was inexplicably tongue-tied. "It's—it's just difficult to know what to say to him sometimes."

Sara slowly stitched the button into place. "But how can you be happy if you can't talk to him?"

"I am sure I will become more comfortable with him. That's all I want, Sara, to be comfortable with him. And for him to be comfortable with me."

Sara, looking doubtful, helped Miranda pull on her second glove and button it. "How can you make him comfortable?"

"I will be like my mother was, sweet and gentle—"

"Sweet and gentle? You?"

Miranda barely noticed Sara's unflattering disbelief. "I want my marriage to be like my parents'." She remembered the evenings her father and mother had spent together. Sir Cedric had been so gentle and considerate of his invalid wife. He had often read to her or played cards with her or just sat and talked to her.

An image rose in Miranda's mind of Huntsley, sitting next to her and laughing as they played whist and discussed the weather. She smiled dreamily. "They were so happy together. Papa worshiped Mama. He called her his angel—"

The door opened again, and Lady Rembert, her buxom figure lavishly displayed in a purple bombazine dress, bustled in.

Miranda's pleasant daydream vanished. She stared at the older woman, feeling the same jolting shock she always did whenever she saw her stepmother. Thelma, with her black hair and well-padded hips and bosom, was the complete opposite of Miranda's golden-haired, delicate and dainty mother. What on earth did her sweet, gentle father see in this woman?

Thelma's sharp brown eyes studied Miranda for a long moment, then shifted to Sara. "Hello, Sara. How is your aunt?"

"Her palpitations are much improved, Lady Rembert, thank you," Sara murmured.

"That's good to hear." Thelma's gaze returned to her stepdaughter. "You're very pale."

"Am I? Perhaps because of the cold." Miranda picked up a white silk shawl that was draped over the dressing table chair and wrapped it around her shoulders.

Thelma frowned. "I don't think it's the cold, I think it's that dress. The white satin makes you look like a wax doll. I wish you had listened to me and bought the cream satin instead." The brackets around her mouth deepened. "But I suppose it's too late to change now. Perhaps some rouge would help."

She marched over to the dressing table and rooted through the clutter until she found a small container of bright pink rouge. "Ah, I thought I had given you this. It should do the trick."

"I don't think that particular color is very becoming to me," Miranda said politely.

"Nonsense. I wear it all the time and have received many compliments on my youthful bloom."

"The pink clashes with my hair," Miranda insisted.

"You are too sensitive about your hair. Some people think red-gold hair is attractive—even though it isn't very fashionable. But now that you're going to be married, you can wear caps to hide it. I will give you one if you like."

Miranda gritted her teeth. "No, thank you. And I would prefer not to wear the rouge."

Thelma pursed her lips, but after a moment she shrugged. "I suppose it doesn't matter. Brides are always pale." She replaced the rouge and picked up a cut-glass bottle of rosewater. "Are you wearing any scent? If you perspire, perfume will help mask the odor."

Sara made a choking noise.

Miranda took the bottle from her stepmother and returned it to the table. "I will not perspire."

Thelma picked up the bottle again. "You cannot be certain of that. It's natural for a bride to be nervous. Why, even at my age, when I married your father, I perspired quite profusely—"

"Perfume gives me a headache." Miranda said. The whole conversation was giving her a headache. "Didn't you say it was time to leave? Perhaps we should go downstairs—"

"Not yet. I must speak to you first." Thelma paused, a

slight flush rising in her normally sallow cheeks. Glancing at Sara, she said, "Would you please go see if the carriage is ready yet?"

"Of course, Lady Rembert." With a speculative stare at Miranda, Sara left.

Thelma waited until the door closed behind Sara before speaking. "Please sit down, Miranda. I have something very important to discuss with you."

Reluctantly, Miranda sat down on the dressing table chair. "Yes, Thelma?"

To Miranda's surprise, Thelma's gaze skittered away from hers. She smoothed a bit of lace on Miranda's skirt and frowned at the veil. "I don't know why you chose that veil. A hat would have been much more becoming."

"It's my mother's veil," Miranda said automatically, watching in wonder as Thelma fidgeted with the watch pinned to the bodice of her purple dress.

"Oh, is it? It's not what I would have chosen, but I suppose I can see why you would want to wear it. It does hide quite a bit of your hair—"

"Thelma," Miranda interrupted, growing alarmed at her stepmother's unusual vacillation. "Is something wrong? Has something happened?" A thought struck her and she clutched her shawl. "Good lord, has Lord Huntsley not shown up?"

"What? Oh, good gracious, no. He's waiting at the church. No, I need to speak to you on another matter entirely." She cleared her throat. "A matter of utmost delicacy."

Confused, Miranda repeated, "A matter of utmost delicacy?"

"You are very young, Miranda. And you have led an unusually sheltered life here at Black Down Abbey. I know you will find this hard to believe, but I remember when I was young and ignorant like you."

Miranda's grip on the shawl tightened.

"Which is as it should be for a young lady," Thelma added. "But I must warn you, that is, I must *explain* to you about—" she took a deep breath, "about your Marital Duty."

"Marital Duty?" Oh. Oh, *no*. Miranda's cheeks grew hot. "You don't have to—"

"Yes, I do." Thelma squared her plump shoulders. "Your father asked me to."

"Oh. Well, it really isn't necessary. What I mean to say is . . ." Miranda forced a laugh. "I already know all about it."

"You do?" Thelma sounded half-disbelieving, half-hopeful.

"Yes," Miranda hurried to assure her. "Mama told me before she died."

"She did!" Thelma's face settled into its usual disapproving lines. "Hmmph. Most girls are not told about such things until their wedding day. But perhaps it's just as well . . . that is, do you have any questions?"

Miranda shook her head vigorously.

"That's good." Thelma tweaked the lace on Miranda's dress again. "Just remember to obey your husband and watch that temper of yours and you will do fine." She glanced at the watch on her bodice. "Now I'd better go see what's keeping the carriage—"

She broke off as a quick knock heralded Sara's return.

"The carriage will be ready in ten minutes," Sara announced.

"Ah, excellent. Thank you, Sara. I, uh, I'd better check on Sir Cedric, then. As soon as you're ready, come down, Miranda." Thelma fled the room.

Sara stared after her in astonishment. "What was that all about?"

Miranda picked up her fan from the dressing table. "She wanted to tell me about my Marital Duty."

"Your Marital—" Sara's voice broke off and her eyes widened. She crept closer. "What did she tell you?" she asked in a loud whisper.

"Nothing. I told her I already knew all about it."

"Miranda Rembert! You know all about it and you've never told me?"

Sara sounded so indignant, Miranda couldn't help laughing.

"You dreadful tease, tell me at once," Sara demanded.

Miranda's laughter faded. Looking down, she toyed with the ribbon on her fan.

"Miranda? Miranda!" Sara's voice was full of sudden comprehension and awe. "Did you lie to Lady Rembert?"

Miranda tilted her chin. "Yes," she said defiantly. "And so would you if you had to listen to someone tell you how young and ignorant you are."

"Good heavens." Sara was stunned. "But what will you do tonight? When you're alone with Lord Huntsley?"

Miranda's chin lowered a notch. "Pretend, I suppose." Forcing herself to shrug, she said, "I am very good at bluffing my way through situations, you know that. Marital Duty has something to do with kissing, I'm almost certain. How difficult can that be?"

"Miranda." Sara stared at her with knitted brows. "*I* know something about it."

"You?" Miranda looked at her friend in astonishment. "Did your mother tell you something?"

"No, no. You know how strict she is. But at Aunt Gerta's, I was walking through the fields one day, and I saw a footman with a village girl. They were together under a maple tree. They were kissing." She lowered her voice. "But that's not all."

Miranda could barely hear Sara's whisper. She leaned forward. "What else were they doing?"

"He had pulled down her bodice and was caressing her bosom!"

Miranda recoiled. "No!"

"Yes! And what's more, I later heard that the girl was with child."

Miranda, gasping for air, clutched her shawl tightly across the portion of her anatomy in question. "Lord Huntsley will want to touch my—?"

The door burst open. With a start, Miranda turned. Thelma stood in the doorway.

"Miranda! The carriage is ready! Hurry!"

Miranda, still reeling from shock, allowed herself to be hustled downstairs and into the carriage.

Lord Huntsley would want to touch her *breasts?*

A short while later, Miranda stood at one end of the long church aisle, shivering. Because of the cold, she tried to convince herself. It *was* cold. The chill from the ancient flagstones seeped through her silk slippers, and her breath made white puffs in the frosty air. The scent of damp stone tickled her nose—the result, no doubt, of a leak in the church's high-timbered roof.

She wished she had chosen velvet instead of satin for her dress. And long, tight-fitting sleeves instead of short, puffed ones. She wished she had worn three petticoats instead of one, and her flannel drawers instead of the flimsy, silky pantalettes. She wished she was at home, in the parlor, sitting by the fire, instead of here in the cold, damp church about to be married to a man who would want to touch her breasts. . . .

"Psst! Psst! Miss Rembert!"

Miranda glanced around and saw that the door to the vestibule was slightly open. The vicar was beckoning to her.

She looked at him uncertainly. He beckoned again, his big blue eyes pleading.

Obeying the silent summons, she walked over to him. He

pulled her into the room and shut the door. "Thank heaven!" His golden curls were tousled as if he'd been running his fingers through them, and his angelic eyes were fraught with worry. "Miss Rembert, I must speak to you!" Mr. Pelham whispered as he grasped her hands.

He looked so worried, she automatically returned his clasp. "What is it, Mr. Pelham?" she whispered back.

"Miss Rembert . . . I knew it was impossible . . . Your stepmother made me see how foolish I was being . . . It is only my foolish heart that dared to reach for the stars, my foolish heart that has watched and yearned . . . Miss Rembert—Miranda—I must tell you . . . I love you!"

"Good heavens!" Miranda said blankly.

"I tried not to but I know you felt it too. How often did our gazes meet in silent longing, our hearts pining for what could not be? Oh! The torture of watching you every Sunday sitting in church, your face like that of an angel. My heart succumbed to the tender lure of love."

"Mr. Pelham, please!" Miranda protested, trying to withdraw her hands. "I am to be married in a few minutes."

His grip tightened. "Yes, I know. I am sorry. I tried to keep silent, but the love in my heart is too strong to be restrained. Especially now, when you are about to be married to that—that womanizer!"

"Womanizer?" Miranda repeated.

"Please, forgive me for mentioning it. It is only that my love for you is so pure, so holy, I can not bear to think of you being forced to submit to the carnal desires of that man—"

"Ahem."

The slight cough made Mr. Pelham stop in midsentence. He stared over her shoulder at someone behind her.

Slowly Miranda turned and saw a tall, dark figure lounging in the doorway.

"Pardon me," Alexander Setton, Viscount Huntsley, said as he gazed upon their clasped hands. "Am I interrupting?"

2

Huntsley's tone was polite, but there was something forbidding about his entire aspect. Perhaps it was because his coat and trousers, as coal black as his hair, emphasized the width of his shoulders and the length of his legs, making him look very broad and tall. Or perhaps it was because his white waistcoat and snowy cravat made him appear so sophisticated and elegant. Or perhaps it was because his light blue eyes surveyed them with a coolness that was almost frightening.

Mr. Pelham released her hands as if they were hot coals. "N-no, no, of course not," he stammered. "I-I-I was just offering a few words of prayer to Miranda—to Miss Rembert, I mean. I-I . . . Please excuse me!" He fled the room.

Huntsley, his eyes still cool, arched a brow at Miranda.

"He—he wanted to wish me well," she said, trying to sound nonchalant.

"If he wished you any more well," Huntsley drawled, "I might have to challenge him to a duel."

She laughed weakly. "You mustn't joke about such things."

He stepped closer, some of the stiffness easing from his shoulders. "Miranda," he said softly, "is something wrong?"

Lowering her gaze, she noticed his hands with their long, slender fingers. "Wrong?" she repeated, hating herself for the quiver in her voice. "I don't know what you mean."

He stepped forward again so that he was standing directly in front of her. "Is there something you wish to tell me?"

"No, nothing," she insisted, looking everywhere except at him.

"Miranda," he said, his voice a little grim, "are you in love with Mr. Pelham?"

Her gaze flew to his, then fell. "Of course not," she said, a blush rising in her cheeks. "You had better go, my lord. You shouldn't be here. It's bad luck for the groom to see the bride before the ceremony."

"I don't believe in superstitions." His eyes narrowed. "You wouldn't lie to me, would you, Miranda?"

She gave an artificial little laugh. "Certainly not, my lord."

His cool gaze studied her for several moments longer. Then, he sighed. "In a few minutes we will be married. Don't you think you might call me Alex?"

"Of course . . . Alex. But you really must go now."

"Must I?" He smiled, one of his rare, beautiful smiles. "But I haven't told you yet how incredibly lovely you look."

The blue of his eyes deepened suddenly, and he looked at her in an odd manner which made Miranda think of what Sara had said. The muscles in her stomach clenched tightly. Involuntarily, she took a step back.

The look in his eyes faded and a faint frown creased his brow. "Miranda—"

But before he could finish, the door opened again and her father peered in, a worried expression on his usually placid face.

"Ah, there you are, Huntsley," Sir Cedric said. "The vicar is ready to begin."

Alex's hesitation was barely noticeable. "Very well," he said. He turned back to Miranda. Watching her from beneath heavy eyelids, he raised her hand and pressed his mouth against the thin lace of her glove.

With another slow smile, he released her hand, then quickly strode through the door.

Miranda stared down at her hand. Underneath her glove, her skin was burning.

"Miranda?" her father said.

Feeling slightly dazed, she looked up.

He smiled at her, his round blue eyes kind and gentle. "Everyone is waiting."

She followed him from the vestibule and took her place at the end of the aisle. Sir Cedric smoothed his wispy gray hair, tucked her arm through his, and nodded to someone at the front of the church.

A loud chord of organ music boomed up to the rafters.

The guests in the pews rose to their feet. Fifty pairs of eyes turned to stare at her.

Miranda froze. Her breath made funny little gasping noises. Sir Cedric patted her trembling fingers, and stepped forward.

Her feet refused to move.

Sir Cedric pulled gently on her arm and she stumbled forward.

Panic surged through her as he half dragged her down the aisle.

Her knees were buckling by the time she reached the front of the church. She straightened her legs, locking her knees.

Mr. Pelham looked dolefully at her. He cleared his throat.

"Dearly beloved friends, we are gathered here to join together this man and this woman in holy matrimony . . ."

Her stomach churned.

". . . An estate not to be taken in hand unadvisedly, lightly, or wantonly, to satisfy men's *carnal lusts* and appetites like *brute beasts* that have *no understanding* . . ."

She pressed her clasped hands against her stomach. *Dear Lord. I can't be sick. Not here. Not now.*

". . . But reverently, discreetly, soberly . . . duly considering the causes for which matrimony was ordained . . ."

Breathe. Breathe deeply.

". . . For the procreation of children . . ."

Don't breathe so fast. Stay calm.

"And for the mutual society, help, and comfort that the one ought to have of the other, both in prosperity and adversity . . ."

Oh why did I agree to this? Sara was right. I am much too impulsive. . . .

"Wilt thou have this man to thy wedded husband? . . . Wilt thou obey him and serve him . . . ?"

Obey and serve him?

". . . Love, honor, and keep him in sickness and in health? And forsaking all others, keep thee only unto him so long as you both shall live?"

"I will," she croaked. *I will not faint.*

Huntsley lifted her hand. "With this ring I thee wed. With my body I thee worship."

I will not faint! I will not faint!

Alex touched the ring on each of her fingers and slipped it onto the fourth. Mr. Pelham stared at her gloomily. "Those whom God hath joined together, let no man put asunder."

Miranda looked up into her fiancé's—no—into her *husband's* face.

There was a roaring noise in her ears. She thought she would swoon. Was she having palpitations like Sara's aunt? She couldn't breathe. If the palpitations didn't kill her, asphyxiation surely would.

Dear heaven, what have I done?

3

What the hell have I done?

Alex stared down into his bride's face. Her eyes were wide and green and . . . terrified.

He sighed silently.

He should never have agreed to this, he thought, holding her trembling hand gently as he pretended to listen to the interminable prayers that followed. He should have stuck to his refusal even to meet her. He should have ignored his father's persuasive arguments and his mother's tearful reminders of his duty, and listened to the inner voice of logic that had warned him to stay away from Black Down Abbey and Miss Miranda Rembert. But the appeals and the tears had increased until he agreed to go, and once there, the warning voice had grown fainter and fainter until, without thought for the consequences, he'd proposed.

The warning voice was blaring at full trumpet now. It had started when he walked into the vestibule and found Miranda with that weasely little vicar, and it continued to sound all through the wedding feast that followed the ceremony.

Alex sat at his bride's side, watching her pick at her food, wondering if he should have questioned her more closely about her relationship with the vicar. Especially considering what her stepmother had said after his proposal.

"I should warn you that Miranda was slightly infatuated with the vicar a few months ago," Lady Rembert had confided. "But I told her Sir Cedric would never approve the match, and that brought her to her senses."

The warning should have brought *him* to his senses.

But it hadn't. Instead, he had watched Miranda closely for a week, looking for signs of infatuation. He had not seen any, not even when they attended church together and the vicar prosed on about the evils of carnal lust. So, he had dismissed the notion that she might care for Pelham.

Now, seeing her so impossibly stiff and nervous, he wondered if he had been too hasty.

Was her tension due to shyness or reluctance?

"Would you like some of this hen?" he asked, offering her a slice of the succulent bird.

She shook her head.

"Some of the peacock, then?"

"No, thank you," she said, pushing the creamed celery around her plate. "I'm not very hungry."

Alex frowned, but a burst of laughter at the end of the table distracted him.

"This is a magnificent bird," a slurred voice announced. "It deserves a toast."

Alex groaned silently, recognizing the voice of George, his sister Selina's husband.

"You're right, George," another voice agreed. "We must honor the bird!"

Alex groaned again as his sister Petronella's husband, Preston, rose drunkenly to his feet. Whenever Preston and George were together, they drank too much and became a little too crude for mixed company.

Preston clanged a knife against his glass, almost knocking it over. "A riddle for everyone," he announced solemnly, raising his glass.

> "Can you name the proud bird that no one dare mock?
> The men admire him
> The maids desire him.
> 'Tis the peacock, the peacock, the peaCOCK!"

The men, who had been imbibing rather too freely, roared with laughter. Except, Alex noticed, Mr. Pelham— his pasty little face wore a disapproving frown.

"What about the hen? We can't forget her!" George stumbled to his feet. "I wish to make a toast to the peahen!" Swaying slightly, he sang out:

> "And here's to the peahen
> With its tender nest.
> It tempts all men
> With its delicate BREAST."

Alex felt Miranda stiffen beside him. Glancing at her, he saw she had flushed very red. He looked around the table, searching for a sober face.

His gaze fell upon his old friend, Daniel Hamilton-Smith. Daniel met his eyes steadily, then nodded.

Rising to his feet, Daniel cleared his throat. In a calm, clear baritone that quieted everyone, he said, "I am a soldier, not a poet, but considering Huntsley is such a good friend, I will make an effort." He held up his glass.

> "Let us spread these glad tidings far and wide.
> Good fortune to Huntsley and his bride—"

"Now take her home for a good *ride!*" George bellowed.

The men howled. A babble of voices rose and the chaos was complete.

Alex frowned. As if his bride wasn't skittish enough. . . .

"Would you like to leave?" he asked her in a low voice.

She glanced up at him, her eyes full of relief. "Oh, yes! I need to change, but it will only take a few minutes."

He allowed her to leave first, hoping the wags wouldn't notice her departure.

They didn't. They were too busy drinking and shouting out their bawdy compositions.

A few minutes later, Alex rose casually to his feet. He slipped out of the dining room into the hall and closed the door on the festivities. He strode toward the front door.

The dining room door opened behind him, admitting a blast of rowdy laughter, then closed again, shutting out the noise.

"Alex, wait!"

He turned to see Daniel behind him. Alex stopped and said wryly, "I thought I'd better get Miranda out of there before everyone frightened the wits out of her."

"Wise decision," Daniel said. "I just wanted to wish you good luck."

"Thank you. And thank you for your attempt to intercede in there."

Daniel grinned ruefully. "I'm just sorry I wasn't more successful. George and Preston are quite a pair."

Alex felt a grin tug at the corner of his own mouth. "Aren't they? I only hope Miranda and I can make our escape before they realize we've gone."

"You're driving in the carriage?"

"Of course."

Daniel frowned. "Do you think that is wise? You know that you—"

"Hush," Alex said, hearing a rustling on the staircase. He looked up and saw Miranda descending, dressed in a green-and-blue plaid dress. The subdued colors set off her hair to perfection. His gaze lingered on her hair. He imagined it spread across his pillow and Miranda looking up at him with that sweet combination of shy nervousness and half-understood awareness.

The door to the dining room burst open and the noisy merrymakers streamed into the hall. With hugs and laughter, they bade the newlyweds farewell.

"Good luck," Daniel murmured, following Alex as he escorted Miranda outside and handed her into the carriage.

"Thank you." Alex shook hands with his friend, then climbed in after Miranda. He barely had time to settle himself before he heard the crack of a whip. With a lunge, the carriage moved forward. He looked at his bride and saw she was staring at him with wide, fearful eyes.

Alex sighed.

He had a feeling he was going to need all the luck he could get.

Rain pattered against the roof of the carriage. Although it was still an hour or more until dusk, the inside of the vehicle was already dim and gloomy.

Miranda peered uncertainly at the shadowed figure across from her. She wished she knew him better. If she did, perhaps she would feel more comfortable, less uneasy. He was gazing out the window, his hand resting on the window ledge. She could see the dark outline of his long fingers. A strange tingle shot through her breasts, and she crossed her arms protectively over her chest, heat rising in her cheeks as she remembered what Sara had told her. How could she possibly allow such an intimacy?

"Are you cold, Miranda?"

Startled, she looked up. In the dusk, his eyes were unreadable. "Just a little."

"Would you like another blanket?"

"No, thank you."

"You're certain? I would hate for you to catch a cold."

"I'm fine, really."

His gaze drifted down to her arms clutched across her chest. A rather sardonic smile curled his lips. "Will you stop looking so nervous if I promise not to attack you in the carriage?"

Flushing, she lowered her arms. "I'm not nervous," she lied. Hoping to divert his attention, she asked, "How long until we arrive at the inn?"

"An hour or two."

An hour. Or two. If she were lucky. Only two hours until . . .

She forced a bright smile to her face. "I thought the wedding went very well, didn't you?"

"Mm. It might have helped if Mr. Pelham were a little more proficient at his lines. I thought he was going to choke when he read the line 'With my body, I thee worship.'"

With my body, I thee worship.

Miranda's throat felt suddenly dry. She had never really understood the significance of those words, never really thought much about them. Now they took on a whole new sinister meaning. "He hasn't been a vicar very long. He's very young."

"I noticed. He hasn't learned the trick of hiding his emotions. It's rather disconcerting to have a man of God making eyes at one's bride."

"Making eyes?" She blushed. "Oh, no. I'm sure you are mistaken."

He stared at her for a long moment. "Am I?"

"Yes, of course." Speaking about the wedding had been a mistake, she realized. Frantically, she cast about in her mind for some other topic of conversation, but none occurred to her. Finally, in desperation, she said, "At least it was a beautiful day for a wedding."

As she spoke, the carriage rolled through a puddle, and mud splattered against the window. She stared at the dripping brown globs.

"Wedding days are always beautiful to the bride and groom," he said blandly.

"Er, yes, that is what I meant." Keeping the smile pinned to her face, she said, "I enjoyed meeting your family."

"Did you?" He directed an inscrutable glance at her. "I must apologize for the behavior of my brothers-in-law at the feast."

She shook her head. "You are not responsible for their behavior. And besides, I didn't mind Preston's toast." She hadn't cared for George's, about the peahen, but the one about the peacock had been innocent enough. "In fact, I liked it. The guests thought it very amusing, too."

He stared at her, rather strangely, she thought, but didn't reply.

Determined to keep the conversation going, she said, "Your parents were very kind. Your father was quite pleasant, and your mother was . . ." She paused, trying to think of a word to describe his mother. "She was very gracious."

"My mother is always gracious," he said dryly.

"Is she? How nice." Hastily, she continued. "I liked your sisters very much, too. Especially Petronella. She told me all about her little boy. I hope she will visit us."

"I am certain she will. She is all agog to see Ribblebank Manor."

"So am I." She peered through the deepening shadows. "What is Ribblebank Manor like, my lord?"

"My name is Alex, remember?"

"Oh, yes. Alex." She had to force herself to say his name. "Alex" seemed too familiar, too intimate. "Will you tell me about Ribblebank Manor?"

"As I remember, it is very small—only six bedrooms." He paused a moment, as if expecting her to make some comment.

When she was silent, he continued. "My father inherited it when his uncle died some three months ago. And now he has given it to me as a wedding present. It's been over twenty years since I was there, and I have only the vaguest memories." He turned his gaze toward the window, staring out at the dark, misty landscape. "I do remember the dogs, though."

"Dogs?"

"Yes. My granduncle raised dogs—the finest hunting dogs in Berkshire. He was very proud of them. The last time we visited, my mother objected to their presence in the house, or some such thing, and my uncle threw us all out. Told us never to darken his threshold again, etc., etc. He loved those dogs."

"Do you think there are still dogs there?"

"I doubt it. They were probably sold off after my uncle died." He shifted on his seat, and his knee came into contact with hers.

She jumped. Quickly, she moved her legs to make room for his, then rushed into speech. "What a shame. I like dogs. They are so cute, and Papa wouldn't let me get another one when my terrier died because Thelma is allergic to dogs. If the dogs are still there, I wouldn't mind keeping them. If you want to, that is—"

"Miranda—"

She stopped babbling and looked at him.

He opened his mouth to continue when a gust of wind shook the carriage and a new spate of rain rattled against the windows. An odd look passed over his face and his jaw tightened. "Never mind," he said, turning toward the window again.

Silence fell, and this time Miranda did not try to break it. Sitting quietly in her corner, she stared out her own window and tried not to think of what lay ahead. She wished she could stay in the carriage forever, driving through the rainy night, and never arrive at the inn.

Her wish wasn't granted.

Less than an hour later, several buildings flashed by her window and the carriage slowed. Miranda glimpsed a Tudor-style building before the carriage turned and passed under an archway into a narrow courtyard. The rain was falling heavily.

The carriage stopped and a hostler, holding an umbrella, opened the door.

Miranda stepped down, and her boots sank into mud. Gathering her cloak about her, she hurried across the courtyard, dimly aware that there was a surprising number of vehicles in the small area. Their owners were probably waiting for the rain to clear, she thought as she and Huntsley stepped through the doorway into a room with old rough-timbered walls and ceilings.

She paused, and Huntsley stopped at her side. "Your face is wet," he said softly, looking down at her.

"Is it?" she asked foolishly.

Nodding, he pulled out a handkerchief and gently dabbed at her nose and cheeks and chin.

Miranda held her breath, her cold skin suddenly growing warm and flushed.

"My lord, my lady! Welcome to my humble inn!" The innkeeper bustled forward to greet them, an obsequious smile on his face.

Alex turned to the short little man. "The private parlor, if you please."

An uneasy expression spread over the innkeeper's round features. "'Tis late, my lord. I thought perhaps the rain would delay you. Your rooms are ready, though. Would you like to retire immediately?"

Huntsley glanced at her. "Miranda?"

She shook her head vigorously.

He turned back to the landlord. "No, thank you. A light supper, if you please."

The thought of food was not appealing, but at least it would delay the moment when they went upstairs, Miranda thought. She noticed a bill of fare hanging on the wall listing Swanston Lea lamb and asparagus. Her nausea returned.

"Certainly, my lord, at once!" the landlord was saying. "Er, would you like a tray in your room?"

To Miranda's relief, Huntsley refused.

"No. The parlor will be fine." His foot tapped impatiently.

The landlord wrung his hands. "Oh, my lord! I am so sorry! But he insisted! I had no choice. . . . It is so late, I thought perhaps you would not show. And he was so insistent!"

Huntsley's brows snapped together. "Am I to understand that you've given the private parlor I reserved to someone else?" He sounded coldly ominous, and the innkeeper stuttered helplessly.

"I—I—I—"

"I'm afraid the blame is mine, dear boy," a languid voice interrupted. Miranda turned to see a shadowy figure standing in the doorway of what must have been the disputed parlor. The figure straightened and moved into the light. Miranda stared in fascination.

He was a gentleman of astonishing appearance. He wore a dark green coat and a bright yellow-striped silk waistcoat. Frothing lace formed a jabot and spilled from the cuffs. Immaculate black breeches hugged his well-formed legs. Suspiciously stiff and shiny black locks were arranged in a series of perfect curls across a white brow. He also sported a beribboned cane in one hand and twirled a quizzing glass by its riband in the other. Holding the glass up to one heavy-lidded pale green eye, he inspected the trio before him.

"Lud, what a fuss," he drawled. "I'm sure I would never

have appropriated the room if I'd known 'twas yours. Certainly I relinquish all claim."

Huntsley's eyes were suddenly cold and hard. "You are too kind, de Morieux."

"You are correct as always," replied de Morieux. Alex stiffened and the stranger smiled slightly. "But I do insist."

Huntsley did not return the smile. "Then of course, I accept. On this occasion, your insistence is quite welcome."

It was de Morieux's turn to stiffen. The men's gazes met and clashed, and a thread of tension crackled through the air.

Then the stranger's eyelids drooped, and he turned his attention to Miranda. For a moment his gaze met hers and she noticed that in spite of his foppish clothes, his eyes held a dangerous glint. He smiled, and two sharp incisor teeth gleamed, giving him a wolfish appearance.

"Huntsley, you sly fellow, you must introduce me to this charming lady."

Miranda's eyes widened a trifle before Huntsley stepped in front of her, blocking her from de Morieux's view. "I don't think that would be wise. Please excuse us, Your Grace."

The stranger bowed as Huntsley pulled her into the private parlor.

"Who was that?" Miranda asked, looking over her shoulder. She caught a glimpse of the man still standing by the stairs, idly swinging his quizzing glass and staring after them.

"No one of importance," Alex said, shutting the door firmly.

No one of importance? Miranda could not believe it. Alex had called the stranger "Your Grace" which meant that the man must be a duke or an archbishop—and judging by his clothes and manner, she doubted he was an archbishop. Was he a duke, then? And why had the two men seemed so antagonistic toward each other?

She wanted to ask, but the tight line of Alex's mouth and jaw discouraged questions.

Her curiosity about the stranger faded, however, when a timid knock heralded the arrival of their food, forcing her to focus on the more important issue of how to make the meal last as long as possible.

She picked at her lamb and pushed the asparagus around her plate. She poked at the cream cake until it dissolved into crumbs. But all too soon, the dishes were removed, the table cleared, and there was nothing else to do.

Taking a deep breath, Miranda looked up at her husband.

He stared back at her for a long moment. He set down his wineglass and rose from his chair.

"It's time for us to retire."

4

Miranda's breath caught as he loomed over her. She had known him three months, but she felt as though she was looking at a stranger. Why had she never noticed before how hard and determined his jaw was? His mouth was a straight, firm line; he rarely smiled. His nose had always been just a nose; now its bold arch seemed vaguely threatening. So did his hair. The color of polished ebony, it was combed back, the curl restrained, giving him a harsh air, a harshness echoed by the slant of his eyebrows. Had his brows always been so dark and so heavy? And his eyes—she had thought they were an ordinary light blue. She didn't remember them being so dark, so intense.

She was supposed to allow this man—this *stranger*—to touch her breasts?

She had thought she could go through with it, but she couldn't. She just couldn't.

"Miranda?"

She didn't move from her seat. "There . . . there is something I want to say to you first."

His brow arched. "Yes?"

"We are both new to the state of marriage."

"Yes?"

"The stress of the wedding has taken its toll on both of us, I'm sure."

"Yes?"

"We . . . we haven't known each other very long."

He frowned. "What are you trying to say, Miranda?"

"I thought it might make it easier—for both of us—if you were to wait awhile before you . . . you know."

"No, I'm afraid I don't."

"Before you—we—perform our Marital Duty."

He choked a little. "Perform our Marital Duty?"

"Yes." She grew more confident when he didn't immediately refuse. It hadn't occurred to her before, but perhaps he was as uneasy about the idea of touching her breasts as she was. Why, the very thought probably embarrassed him as much as it did her! "I thought we could wait awhile until we know each other better and are more used to each other."

"I see." His expression was unreadable. "And how long do you wish to wait?"

"I thought perhaps . . . three months?"

A log on the fire snapped and cracked loudly in the sudden silence. Outside, a carriage drove by, the harness jingling and the horses' hooves *clip-clop*ping on the cobblestones. Somewhere inside the inn, a strident voice called for the landlord, and a door slammed shut.

Unable to look at him, Miranda stared at her clenched fists in her lap. Her stomach twisted itself into knots. Was he going to refuse? She didn't know what she would do if he did. She didn't think she could bear it.

"Three months?" His voice was as imperturbable as ever. "I suppose I can wait three months."

For a moment, everything whirled and spots of light

danced behind her eyes. Then, everything righted and cleared as relief rushed through her, making her feel giddy. She looked up with a brilliant smile. "Oh, thank you, Alex! I am sure it will be much better this way. You won't be sorry."

"Won't I?" he murmured, his gaze lingering on her glowing face. "I'm afraid I already am."

Lying on his back in his lonely bed a few hours later, Alex stared up at the shadowy ceiling of his room, trying not to think of his bride in the next room.

He was failing miserably.

Sighing, he rolled over and closed his eyes. He had known, ever since he first met her and saw the sweet innocence shining from her eyes, that he would have to be extremely gentle with her. And he had been. He had been the perfect gentleman all through the courtship. Hell, he hadn't even kissed her when he proposed.

But he had known she would be worth the wait. He just hadn't planned on waiting *this* long.

He moved his head, trying to find a more comfortable spot on the pillow. He supposed it wouldn't kill him to wait a few more months. It would be worth it if it meant that she would come to him willingly, without fear. He wanted her eager, not trembling and frightened.

Nor did he want her thinking of another man.

He frowned a little, remembering how cozy she and Pelham had been in the vestibule together. She had denied she was in love with the vicar, but in the carriage she had blushed vividly when Alex mentioned his name.

He didn't doubt his ability to make Miranda forget about the vicar, but it wouldn't do to force the issue.

No, he had made the right decision—he knew that. He only hoped that being noble would somehow help ease the ache in his groin.

So far, it wasn't helping at all.

Groaning, he buried his face in the pillow and tried to go to sleep. It wasn't easy. He tossed and turned most of the night and woke up with a bear of a headache. Peering into his shaving mirror and seeing his bloodshot eyes, Alex thought he looked like death warmed over.

Miranda, on the other hand, when he escorted her down to the private parlor for breakfast, looked happier and perkier than he'd ever seen her.

"I can't wait to see Ribblebank Manor," she said with a gratingly cheerful smile as she poured herself a cup of tea and buttered a piece of bread. "Did you notify the servants that we would be arriving today?"

"Yes," Alex said tersely. He took a drink of the hot black coffee he'd ordered. It tasted like tar. He took another long drink.

"Do you know the housekeeper's name?"

Alex looked at her over the rim of his cup. "Why do you want to know the housekeeper's name?"

"So I may greet her properly, of course."

"I believe it is Mrs. Driscoll." He swallowed some more of the coffee.

"Do you know any of the other servants' names?"

"The steward is Yeager. I expect the butler's name is Bomford, since I seem to recall my granduncle saying something about the Bomford family serving as butlers since the manor was built. Do you wish to know the names of the cook and the maids as well?" he asked sardonically.

"Yes, I do," she said immediately, smiling brightly.

He set his cup down. "I'm afraid I do not know."

"Oh. I suppose I will have to wait until we arrive."

"Yes, you will, won't you?"

She caught his sarcasm this time. He regretted it immediately when she turned hurt, questioning jade-green eyes toward him.

"I'm sorry, Miranda," he apologized in a more pleasant voice. "I didn't sleep well last night."

"You didn't?" she asked in surprise. "I slept like a baby."

Alex gritted his teeth. "We had best be on our way," he said. "We still have a long way to go."

"Yes, of course. The rain has cleared. It is a beautiful day for a drive."

An image of the small, confined carriage entered his brain. He made an instant decision. "I hope you don't mind, Miranda, but I intend to ride today."

"Of—of course I don't mind," she said, the smile fading from her face and the uncertainty returning to her eyes.

Alex felt guilty, but he didn't change his mind.

He could only endure so much.

The carriage rolled along the road under fluffy white clouds in a bright blue sky. A few green buds poked up bravely from the rain-washed earth, but Miranda didn't notice. She sat in the carriage, staring blindly at the empty seat across from her, wondering what had gone wrong.

She had been so happy this morning. For the first time since meeting Alex, she'd felt at ease with him. She had been bursting with questions about Ribblebank and had been looking forward to breakfast.

But Alex had acted very strangely throughout the meal. He had been quite unlike his usual kind and patient self. He had almost sounded *sarcastic* a few times. And then he had decided to ride!

She didn't know what to think. Was he angry at her? If so, she didn't know why. She wondered if he was upset about the Marital Duty business. Surely not. He would have said something if he was. Wouldn't he?

She wished she understood men better. She wished she understood *Alex* better.

With only her own troubled thoughts for company, Miranda found the journey long and tedious. She tried to sleep for a while, curling up precariously on the narrow seat, but a jolt of the carriage sent her tumbling to the floor.

After that, she leaned back in her corner, dozing fitfully until they arrived at Ribblebank Manor.

It was too dark to see the house clearly, and Miranda was physically and emotionally exhausted, but she perked up a little as she entered her new home.

The interior was lit by only a few candles, and the first thing she noticed was a distinct canine odor. The second was the four or five dogs leaping about excitedly. One jumped up on her, leaving muddy paw prints on her skirt, and the butler, surprisingly young for such an august position, flapped his elbows in a most undignified fashion as he attempted to shoo the animal away.

The rest of the hastily assembled servants seemed strangely unorganized. The fat and fluttery housekeeper clutched her cap and apron as though she feared they might fly away. The whipcord-thin cook looked sullenly at the floor. The two maids giggled. When they were finally in line, Miranda said a brief word to each one. Alex only nodded distantly.

Exhausted, Miranda decided to wait until tomorrow to inspect her new home. Alex escorted her to her bedroom door, and bid her good night, his expression as cool as when he'd spoken to the servants. She bit her lip as he walked away. What could be the matter with him?

It wasn't until she was lying in bed, unable to sleep in spite of her weariness, that an idea occurred to her.

Perhaps it was the stress of the wedding finally catching up to him.

That must be it, she thought in relief. Why, she had been rather out of sorts herself.

Her eyelids drooped and a smile curved her lips. Now

that they were at their new home, they could both relax. Tomorrow, Alex would no doubt be his usual kind and considerate self.

The sound of barking dogs dimly registered as she yawned and snuggled into the bedclothes, but she was too tired to pay much attention.

Tomorrow would be better, she thought drowsily, closing her eyes.

She drifted off to sleep promising herself that she would be a good wife. And that she would be sweet and gentle. Like her mother . . .

5

Miranda woke slowly, reluctantly, to the sound of barking dogs. Looking at the clock on the table beside her bed, she groaned and pulled a pillow over her head in an effort to shut out the noise. In the confined breathing space, her nose started to twitch.

It was the same smell she had noticed last night.

She could still hear the dogs. Had they been barking all night, she wondered, pulling the pillow more tightly against her ears. Or was this their usual practice at seven o'clock in the morning?

"Aow! Aoow! Aooow!" howled the dogs.

As if in response, Miranda's stomach growled. She remembered that she had only picked at her food last night. In fact, she had eaten very little yesterday, and now she was voraciously hungry. Sleep forgotten, she tossed the pillow aside and sat up.

Immediately, she noticed the smell again. She slid out of bed and walked around the room, sniffing, trying to locate the source of the odor. After a few minutes of vigorous sniffing, she gave up, and walked over to pull back the drapes and open the windows. Sunlight streamed into the room, and Miranda gasped with delight.

Her room was on the northeast corner of the house, and the windows framed a magnificent view. To the north stretched the gentle landscape of the upper Thames valley. She could see for miles. The meadows, fields, and woods spread out like a tapestry, and the river wove a bright silver thread across the scene.

To the east, she looked down on the gardens of the manor. She could not see any discernable pattern; the flower beds looked neglected. In the distance, past more fields and some magnificent hedgerow elms and oak woods, stood a mansion. She smiled happily.

Her smile faded when she turned to survey her room. The bright sunlight highlighted the air of decay. The crimson damask bed curtains were faded and torn, as was the mock India wallpaper. The mahogany dressing bureau lacked a drawer. Miranda walked over to an escritoire and opened the fall front writing board. One of the brass brackets was broken.

She rang for her maid, who entered shortly with a bowl of water and a sour look on her face.

"What's wrong, Alice?" Miranda asked as she hurriedly washed her face.

"Nothing, miss—my lady, I mean." The maid helped Miranda into a warm, blue wool dress. With a disdainful sniff, she added, "It just isn't what I'm used to, that's all." She refused to elaborate, and Miranda was too eager to go downstairs to question her further.

Miranda walked down the stairway, admiring the fine carving on the bannister. Its beauty was marred, however, by the dullness of the grimy wood and by the broken dog gate that hung askew at the bottom of the stairs. The—green?—carpet that graced the hall was badly stained and covered with dog hair.

In the hall, she found the butler on his hands and knees, his face pressed to the floor as he groped under a table.

"Bomford!" Miranda exclaimed. "What on earth are you doing?"

The butler jumped to his feet. His light brown hair was mussed, and a smudge decorated his cheek. "I—I beg your pardon, your ladyship. Some—some ladies left their cards yesterday, and I cannot find them."

Miranda assumed he meant the cards and not the ladies, although judging by what she had seem of him, she would not put it past him to lose a whole flock of women.

"I see. Well, keep looking."

He started to crouch back down when she remembered to ask, "Have you seen Lord Huntsley?"

Bomford snapped back to attention. "He has already ridden out, your ladyship."

"I see." Her smile wavered. "I suppose I will have breakfast by myself, then. In the dining room."

"At once, your ladyship."

Entering the dining room, she glanced about. Briefly Miranda noticed the smoke-blackened ceiling and the unattractive blue-green paint on the walls.

She served herself from the sideboard and sat down at the table. She popped a bite of beefsteak into her mouth, chewing thoughtfully. It was very tough, so she had a long time to think.

She had hoped to spend the day in Alex's company. If she was to be a good wife to him, she was going to have to overcome the silly nervousness that assailed her whenever he spoke to her. Spending more time with him might help.

Now, she wasn't quite certain what she should do.

But perhaps he would be back shortly. While she was waiting, maybe she could explore the house.

She swallowed the stubborn piece of meat with some difficulty and decided not to eat the rest of her beef. She inspected her other choices: a half-cooked rasher of bacon bubbling with grease and two thick slices of bread and butter. She opted for bread and butter, and washed it down with a great quantity of tea before summoning the housekeeper to accompany her on a tour of the rooms.

The house was not inspiring. Most of it showed signs of occupation by dogs. Indeed, she discovered several of the black, brown, and white beagles engaged in various pursuits during her tour. One was chewing on a book in the library. Others were sleeping in the guest beds. No wonder the place had such a pervasive smell, she thought. Evidence of poor household management lurked in every corner.

Miranda was delighted.

She might not know much about men, her husband in particular, but she did know about household management.

Standing in the doorway of another ramshackle bedchamber, Miranda decided she had seen enough and turned to the nervous housekeeper. "I think this has been a bachelor household for too long," she said cheerfully. "Don't you agree, Mrs. Driscoll?"

The housekeeper twisted a corner of her apron between her plump fingers. "It hasn't been easy keeping house with them animals roving about."

Miranda eyed her curiously. "Why didn't you evict them after his lordship died?"

Mrs. Driscoll looked shocked. "I couldn't do that, my lady. His lordship specifically ordered that the dogs be allowed to do whatever they wished. I couldn't go against orders."

"I see." Obviously, Mrs. Driscoll needed a great deal of supervision.

Miranda opened her mouth to tell the housekeeper to have the maids start cleaning at once, but then she hesitated. Should she talk to Alex first? He might have some particular wishes. Perhaps she would discuss the whole

matter with him—it would give her something to talk to
him about. She glanced at the dilapidated bedroom again.
But perhaps she should make up a list of necessary tasks.

"I must check with Lord Huntsley, but I think he will be
happy to approve any decisions we make." She counted off
some of the more pressing needs. "The rooms all require a
thorough scrubbing, the chimneys need to be cleaned, and
the furniture repaired. Can you think of anything else?"

The housekeeper nodded eagerly. "The linens should be
checked, for one, and the carpets need cleaning—except for
the one in the hall, which needs burning—and the stillroom
needs restocking, and—"

Miranda laughed. "Not so fast, Mrs. Driscoll. Let us go
downstairs to the library, where I can write all of this down."

A few hours later, Miranda, seated behind the desk in
the library, leaned back in her chair and studied her list. It
was very comprehensive, and she was quite pleased with
herself.

Restoring the house would be a challenge, but it was one
she welcomed. She couldn't wait to show Alex her list. He
would be quite delighted when she told him her plans. She
smiled happily. He was sure to think her a very good wife
indeed.

Alex rode into the stableyard at dinnertime in a black
humor. He had ridden out that morning, intending to take
just a short ride, but he had stopped at a cottage when he
saw a tenant farmer loading up his family and belongings in
a wagon. With barely concealed hostility, the farmer
explained that he couldn't pay the rent. Upon further questioning, Alex discovered that not only was the amount
excessive, but that this was the third time in a year that
Yeager, the estate agent, had raised the rents. The farmer,
his wife, and their three small children had nowhere to go.

Appalled, Alex told them to stay while he looked into the matter. Much to his embarrassment, the woman burst into tears and thanked him repeatedly. The farmer, although more dignified, also expressed his gratitude.

Alex had remounted and ridden farther, finding more and more signs of neglect. The roads were in poor repair. Two farms were untenanted, the cottages falling apart. He discovered a flock of sheep wandering through a hole in a fence and a small pear orchard that was completely overgrown. A dairy farm that seemed comparatively prosperous was the only bright spot. Everything else was a mess. Not at all the scene he'd expected to present to his bride.

Things couldn't be worse, he thought bleakly as he entered the house.

He was wrong.

Seeing Miranda at dinner, smiling shyly at him, caused his body to react in a way he would have thought impossible given his state of fatigue. She was wearing a creamy-white dress, almost the same hue as her skin. He couldn't tear his gaze away.

"I talked to Mrs. Driscoll today. . . ."

She continued speaking, but he didn't really listen. Instead, he watched the candlelight glinting off the red-gold of her hair and the flutter of her long, dark lashes. They made lacy shadows on her clear, smooth skin and seemed to point to her mouth.

Shifting uncomfortably, he ate a bite of pheasant. It wasn't very appetizing. He washed it down with wine and turned his gaze back to Miranda, just in time to catch a glimpse of her white teeth as she placed a bite of meat between her lips. Her lips were full and shiny, and as he watched, her tongue slipped out to lick them. He immediately imagined her tongue flicking out to meet his own.

"We made a list. . . ."

Hastily, he drank some more of the wine, cursing himself

for his wayward thoughts. After the long miserable day, he should be thinking not of Miranda, but of bed—

An image flashed into his brain of his bed . . . and of Miranda, naked and eager, waiting for him there.

He thrust back his chair, the legs screeching against the oak floorboards. If he didn't get out of there quickly, he was going to carry her upstairs and make love to her—

"Alex?" She was looking at him in astonishment.

"Please excuse me, Miranda," he said. "I have some work to do. I must look over the estate books." Without waiting for a reply, he strode to the door.

"Alex, wait!"

His hand on the knob, he paused. He looked over his shoulder and saw that she had risen to her feet. Her dress clung to the soft curves of her figure.

He closed his eyes for a moment. "Yes?"

"You haven't told me what you want me to do."

He grew still. "What I want you to do?"

"Yes." When he didn't reply, she added, "About the house."

His grip on the doorknob tightened. The *house?* What the devil was she mewling about? Something to do with the house? "Leave everything to Mrs. Driscoll."

"But Alex, I think she might need some direction."

Oh, hell. Now he understood. Miranda did not have any experience managing a household. Which meant that he had the house and the servants to worry about, too. Just what he needed. Well, the house would have to wait. For now, the estate was more important. "I am satisfied with the way Mrs. Driscoll is handling everything for now," he said curtly, then turned on his heel and left.

Miranda stared after him in astonishment. He wanted her to leave everything to Mrs. Driscoll? She sank back into her chair. Surely he could not be serious. Hadn't he noticed what a shambles the house was?

He must have. She bit her lip. Perhaps he had spoken without thinking. Perhaps he was tired from his long ride. Perhaps she should have broached the subject of the house another time.

Perhaps you should have told him what a boor he is.

Miranda suppressed the rebellious inner voice sternly. She wasn't going to allow herself to become angry over such a trifle. She must try harder to please Alex. But how?

Gloomily, she looked down at the remains on her plate. The smell of cheap tallow candles lay heavy in the air, masking most of the unpleasant aromas that arose from the dish. She took a bite of the stringy fowl, wondering what abuse it had suffered to make it so unpalatable. Why was the food so terrible? Alex had eaten almost nothing.

A thought occurred to her. She knew her father's temper often relied greatly on the state of his stomach.

She brightened. The food was a problem that could be easily resolved. She would talk to Mrs. Rouse tomorrow.

Perhaps a well-cooked meal would improve Alex's disposition.

6

The next morning, Miranda descended a narrow flight of stairs to the tiny, cramped kitchen to speak to the cook. Mrs. Rouse listened with her arms folded across her nonexistent bosom as Miranda gently suggested that she try to improve the meals.

"I noticed last night that the meat was a bit tough," Miranda said tentatively, ducking her head to avoid hitting it on a rack of pans hanging from the ceiling.

Mrs. Rouse nodded grimly.

Miranda tried to smile encouragingly. "Perhaps if you used a different cut of meat, the stew would be more palatable."

"Aye, indeed it would," came the sour response. "Iffen I had the budget for it." She turned to stir something in a pot hanging over the fireplace.

"Mrs. Rouse, are you saying you do not receive enough monies to purchase proper provisions?"

A succinct nod was her answer.

Miranda laughed in relief. "If that is all, then of course I shall speak to Lord Huntsley about increasing the food allowance. Tell me how much you need."

The pinch-faced cook named an amount that sounded reasonable to Miranda. "Of course I must discuss it with my husband, but I see no reason why he shouldn't approve the expenditure."

Much mollified, Mrs. Rouse admitted she would be "fain if your ladyship could do something about these dogs. I don't hold with dogs in the kitchen, I don't."

"Of course," Miranda said again. She was delighted. That had been much easier than she expected. Now all she had to do was talk to Alex. He was in the library, she knew, but she decided not to interrupt him. She would wait until dinner—the food on the table would surely drive her point home better than anything she could say.

Alex frowned down at the ledger. If only his uncle had kept receipts! The records were a mess, but one thing was clear. The ledger stated that the money received for the tenant farm was half what the farmer had indicated.

Obviously Yeager, the estate agent, had been lining his pockets. Now Alex would have to discharge him and run the estate without any help at all until he could arrange to hire a new steward. Damn the cur for his greediness!

At least he saw no evidence that the rest of the staff was dishonest. Expenses for the household were very low, almost negligible. Thank God he wouldn't have to hire a whole houseful of servants. At this point he was grateful for even small mercies. Heaven knew he needed a few.

His head began to ache. His uncle's affairs would take weeks, if not months, to straighten out. Especially since he himself had so little knowledge of estate management.

Worst of all, if his calculations were correct, it would take a great deal of money to rectify the situation. Money that he did not have. He thought fleetingly of Miranda's dowry, then shook his head. Her dowry would only be a drop in the bucket. And besides, he had determined from the outset that he would not use her money. The idea that he must rely on his wife for support was repugnant to him. No, he could do this himself—he *would* do this himself— but money would be tight. He would have to watch expenses carefully.

His lips tightened. His granduncle Quentin, like most of the Settons, seemed to have a talent for mismanaging money. Alex's father had spent most of his life restoring the family fortune that had been depleted by the first earl's profligate spending. Now it looked as though he, Alex, would have to repair the damage caused by the first earl's brother.

The task was a monumental one. He would have to toil harder than his tenants for the next few months, but at least the work would keep his mind off his beautiful, desirable wife.

But then again, he thought later that night at dinner, maybe it wouldn't.

His weariness disappeared and his blood surged when he saw the pale blue dress she was wearing. It revealed and concealed in the most tantalizing way. Although the gown was almost girlish with its ruffles and bows, it clung to her breasts and waist lovingly, making it difficult for him to tear his gaze away.

"I spoke to Mrs. Rouse today. . . ."

He tried to listen to what she was saying, but her dress tormented him. He hated its high neck. She should wear only low-cut gowns so that he could see the hollow of her neck, the smooth skin of her shoulders. His gaze drifted down the long sleeves to the tiny pearl buttons at the cuffs. He imagined undoing those buttons and pressing his lips against her wrist. He wanted to see as much of her skin as possible—he wanted to see *all* of her skin.

"It's been a problem for her, you see. . . ."

His gaze was drawn by the fiery red-gold crown of her hair. It was coiled at her nape, the weight of it looking much too heavy for her slender neck. He tried to imagine it hanging down her back. How long would it be? Past her shoulders? To her waist? It would look like silk spread out across his pillow.

"I think her request is not unreasonable. . . ."

He forced himself to concentrate on his food; it was tasteless. All he wanted to taste was Miranda—her smooth skin, her shining hair, her rosy lips . . .

"If you will increase the household allowance, I will be able to rectify the problem."

The word "allowance" caught his attention. "I beg your pardon?"

"I need money for the house, Alex."

He frowned. Dammit, the last thing he needed was to spend more money.

"Please, Alex . . ."

Her jade-green eyes had golden flecks in them, which glowed brightly as she pleaded. He had a sudden urge to tell her he would empty the estate coffers, mortgage the house, and sell the clothes off his back if she would just come upstairs with him to his room.

"Alex?"

He looked at her innocent eyes and nearly groaned. He could just imagine her reaction if he said such a thing. She would be shocked, horrified. Frustration ate at him. "I'm afraid you will have to make do with what you have," he managed to say.

"But, Alex—"

He could not bear to listen to her pleading. "That is my final word on the subject," he said coldly.

She sat very still, her head bowed. Then, with great dignity, she rose to her feet. "If you will excuse me, my lord, I find I am rather tired. Good night."

Alex watched the sway of her hips as she stalked from the room, almost bumping into the butler as he brought in the dessert course.

"My lord!" Bomford exclaimed, staring after Miranda. "Shall I return the dessert to the kitchen?"

Alex stared at the deflated soufflé.

"Yes," he said morosely, sinking into his chair. "And then bring me the brandy."

While Alex was drowning his sorrows in brandy, Miranda was fuming upstairs in her room.

Leave everything to Mrs. Driscoll, she thought furiously as her maid helped her change into a nightgown and wrapper. *Make do with what you have.*

How could he be so unreasonable? Didn't he see that the house needed cleaning, the servants direction, and the food a miracle? Was he blind? Why wouldn't he listen to her? Was he deaf?

What else could a good wife do?

That is my final word on the subject.

"Final word—ha! Who does he think he is?" Miranda muttered.

"Beg pardon, my lady?" Alice stopped brushing Miranda's hair to look at her inquiringly.

"Never mind, Alice. You may go."

Silently, the maid put down the brush and departed, but Miranda barely noticed. She rose to her feet and paced around the room, her hair swirling.

Who *did* he think he was to order her around like that? The king of England? The czar of Russia? The sultan of Arabia?

She didn't know, and at this point she didn't care. She hadn't complained when he chose to ride instead of driving with her in the carriage to Ribblebank Manor. She hadn't complained when he'd abandoned her to her own devices for the last two days. She hadn't even complained about this wreck of a house. But now her patience was at an end. She wasn't going to stand for it anymore, she thought as she stalked to the door.

And she was going to go tell him so right now.

7

The first person Miranda saw in the hall downstairs was Bomford. He goggled at her nightgown and wrapper, his mouth gaping and his eyes as round as shillings. "My lady!"

She barely spared him a glance. "Where is my husband?"

"He—he's still in the dining room, my lady. But I wouldn't go in there if I were you."

"Oh?" She laughed angrily. "Why not?"

"He is not in his best humor. He has been, um, er, imbibing for the last hour."

"Drinking!" Another fault to add to his growing list.

"Oh, please, my lady!" Bomford's elbows flapped anxiously. "Do not judge him too harshly."

"Why shouldn't I?" she demanded, marching toward the dining room door.

"I, er, I know it's not my place to say, but—but his lordship is a fine gentleman!"

Miranda stopped and stared at the butler in astonishment. "Oh? What has he done to give you such a high opinion of him?"

"Everyone on the estate has a high opinion of him," Bomford said simply. "He's only been here two days, but he's done the one thing that could win their trust."

"The one thing? What was that?"

"Fire Mr. Yeager."

"Fire Mr. Yeager! The steward?"

Bomford nodded. "No one's ever liked him. They've blamed him for the evictions and the poor state of their cottages. His lordship has promised to work very hard to set things to rights. My mother sings his praises."

Miranda was beginning to feel like a parrot. "Your mother?" she echoed.

"Yes. She is a widow and lives in the village with my sister. I have been supporting them, but my wages were barely enough to pay the rent for their cottage. Today his lordship announced that he was lowering the rents, and he brought bags of seed for everyone. He even helped unload the wagons himself, heaving the sacks out along with the other men. He's not afraid to get a little sweat on his brow like some gentlemen are."

"Bomford," Miranda said slowly, "is the estate in a very bad way?"

He nodded vigorously. "Yes, indeed, my lady. But all of us have faith in his lordship."

"I see. Thank you, Bomford."

He stood there awkwardly.

"You are dismissed, Bomford."

With a reluctant glance at the dining room door, he crept away.

Miranda stood in the middle of the hall, still stunned by Bomford's revelations.

She had never thought about what Alex must have found on the estate. She had been too wrapped up in her own problems with the house to consider the tenants and their farms.

Guilt swept through her. The estate was in dire straits and she had been nagging him about petty domestic problems. No wonder he was short-tempered! A wife was supposed to support and aid her husband, not add to his burdens. She had displayed a lamentable lack of patience and understanding.

She glanced toward the door. She would make it up to him, she vowed silently, moving forward slowly.

She would do everything in her power to help him.

Sprawled in his chair, Alex stared gloomily down at his glass of brandy.

He was going to have to talk to her. Living in the same house with her, seeing her sweet loveliness everyday, and not being able to touch her was driving him insane. Why had he been such a fool as to agree to wait three months?

Three months! Only a few days had passed and already he felt as though he'd waited an eternity. The waiting was killing him.

He swallowed the rest of his brandy and lifted the bottle to pour himself another glass. His brows drew together as the dregs trickled out. Damn! Had he drunk the whole bottle already? He was turning into an accursed drunkard. He was really going to have to talk to Miranda.

A light tap sounded at the door. Frowning, he glanced up as the door swung open.

Miranda stood framed in the doorway. In a nightgown and thin silk wrapper, her hair flowing down her back. He blinked, wondering if he was having a vision.

"Alex, may I talk to you?"

Her voice was soft as rose petals. His hand shaking, he set the brandy bottle down and rose to his feet. The room spun crazily and he shook his head, trying to stop the spinning. "Of course." His voice sounded hoarse. He cleared his throat.

She stepped forward. "I realize I have been a little unreasonable."

Her movement caused candlelight to shimmer along the silken skein of her red-gold hair. He had wondered how it would look, but nothing he imagined had prepared him for the reality. All crimson and amber and gold, it flowed over her white silk wrapper like a molten river of fire. "No, Miranda."

"Yes, I have been."

His gaze flickered to her mouth as she licked her lips. Mesmerized, he watched her tongue lave the sweet fullness.

"I didn't realize how difficult this has been for you and I want to make it up to you."

"Miranda . . ." He could think of a hundred ways for her to make it up to him. To start, she could untie the frivolous pink ribbon at her collar and take off that robe . . .

"I want to be a good wife to you."

. . . and the nightgown, too. "Miranda . . ."

She moved forward, her smile slow and warm, as sweet and inviting as mulled wine. "I want to please you."

"You do." *Lord, how she pleased him.* He held out his hand to her.

She placed her palm in his. "I will do all the work."

Her hand was small and soft. His ring was on her finger. The gold band was really too heavy for her delicate hand, but it marked her unmistakably as his. His hand tightened on hers. "I don't think of it as work."

She smiled tenderly. "All that heaving and sweating? Of course it is work. It is only fair that I do my part."

"Miranda," he said huskily.

"I like things clean and fresh."

He became aware that his appearance was less than pristine. Hastily, he dropped her hand and tugged at his rumpled cravat and straightened his wrinkled coat.

"Of course, it will take time, Alex. But I want more than anything to do my part."

Unsteadily, he raked his fingers through his hair, trying to comb down the unruly curls. "You shall, my darling, you shall."

She laid her hand on his chest and smiled up at him. "I'm certain I'll be able to do it all myself."

His fingers stilled in his hair.

She was still smiling. "I won't have to bother you at all."

He lowered his hand to his side. "You won't have to bother me at all?"

"No, I will do it while you're busy with estate business."

"Miranda," he said, forcing himself to sound casual. "What are we talking about?"

She looked at him, her innocent green eyes full of surprise. "Why, the house, of course."

The house. The *house!* "I thought I told you to leave everything to Mrs. Driscoll," he said tightly.

"She cannot handle everything, Alex. I am more than willing to take on these duties, believe me. I do think the dogs will have to go. And Bomford is no help. I have to figure out some way to deal with him. He is terrible at his position—"

"There has always been a Bomford at Ribblebank Manor," he interrupted through gritted teeth. "I will not permit you to interfere with the staff. As for the dogs—Ribblebank has always been known for its beagles. They are part of it. I certainly don't intend to change that just because you're too fastidious to endure a little dog hair. Now, unless you are prepared to fulfill the one 'duty' that you are uniquely qualified for, I suggest you get the hell out of here."

Miranda's mouth fell open. "But, Alex—" She stopped abruptly, staring at his burning eyes, the tight line of his mouth, and his clenched fists. Her mouth snapped shut, and without another word, she turned and left the room. In the hall, she clutched the skirt of her nightgown and ran up the stairs. She did not stop running until she reached the safety of her room.

Once there, she stood in the middle of the room, shaking, trying to regain her composure.

It wasn't easy. She had never seen him look so ominous, or sound so menacing. What had he meant by that remark about fulfilling the one duty she was qualified for? He couldn't have meant what she thought he meant. Surely he would never be so . . . so *coarse.*

But what had made him so angry? She replayed the conversation in her mind and could find nothing exceptional in it. In fact, at first he had seemed very receptive to what she had to say. When she entered the room, he'd even looked pleased to see her, immediately setting down the bottle of brandy.

The brandy. Of course. Bomford had warned her. Alex had been drinking. *Heavily.*

No wonder he'd been so unreasonable. No wonder! The liquor had obviously made him irrational.

And once again she was the victim of his foul temper.

Her lips tightened. This was the last straw. She had gone to him in good faith, putting aside her own considerable—and not unjustifiable—anger to offer him her support. And what was the result? He told her she was too fastidious about a little dog hair.

A little dog hair!

Why, there was enough dog hair in the house to supply a wigmaker for a year!

She glared at the floor as if she could see Alex in the dining room below her. "You're a drunkard and a lout, Alexander Setton!" she cried out loud.

Her fists clenching and unclenching, she moved to the writing desk. A little dog hair! She had been right the first time—Alex was completely unreasonable! Why wouldn't he listen to her? The servants were virtually incompetent, the food inedible, and the condition of the house gave new meaning to the phrase "going to the dogs."

She sat down at the desk and opened the fall front. Its single bracket creaked loudly.

She had wanted to be a good wife to him. She had wanted to be sweet and gentle. But Alex was obviously too pigheaded to appreciate such qualities. As far as she was concerned, his rude behavior made him undeserving of a wife with those virtues and he would be well served if she abandoned them.

She breathed deeply.

Unfortunately, she was dedicated to the precepts of sweetness and gentleness. In spite of his boorishness and his brainlessness, she would not lower herself to his level. To the best of her ability, she would remain true to the standards set by her mother.

She pulled a piece of paper out of a drawer and placed it on the skewed writing board. Carefully, she sharpened a quill and dipped it in an inkwell. Then she began to plan how she would sweetly and gently make Alex's life as miserable as possible.

8

Miranda put her plan into action the next day.

While Alex was out making rounds on the estate, she seated herself behind the desk in the library and summoned the housekeeper. In a short while, Mrs. Driscoll stood before her, twisting a corner of her apron in her plump fingers.

"Mrs. Driscoll," Miranda said. "I wish to begin the improvements we listed a few days ago. I want you and the maids to start scrubbing the house from top to bottom."

"Certainly, my lady," Mrs. Driscoll said.

"In fact, now that I think of it, I want you to hire a few more servants. Is that possible?"

"Oh, yes, my lady! I can think of several likely village girls. But . . ."

"But what, Mrs. Driscoll?"

"I thought you said his lordship wouldn't approve any expenditures."

No, he definitely would not. But Miranda didn't tell the housekeeper that. "Don't worry about Lord Huntsley, Mrs. Driscoll," she said firmly.

"But won't he be upset?"

Yes, Alex would be upset. In fact, he would very likely be enraged.

She smiled cheerfully. "Hire two footmen and another maid. If necessary, we will assign them tasks which will not bring them into contact with Lord Huntsley. That will be easy enough. He spends most of his time outside or here in the library, and since I don't wish you to clean the library—"

"Not clean the library?" Mrs. Driscoll repeated doubtfully.

"Those are my orders, Mrs. Driscoll. Neither are you to clean his lordship's bedchamber."

Miranda smiled blandly at the housekeeper's incredulous expression. "My husband detests having anyone interfere with his things."

Mrs. Driscoll left, fingering her apron again, and Miranda returned her attention to her list. She checked the housekeeper's name off and read the next name: Bomford.

Miranda frowned. She had a feeling the butler would be more of a challenge than Mrs. Driscoll.

Bomford, in violation of the high code of butlering, frequently allowed his emotions to show. Often his mouth would gape and his eyes goggle, and he had an unfortunate tendency to stutter and flap his elbows. Miranda tapped her pen on the desk as she considered how to utilize his, er, special talents.

Rather than summon him to the library, she decided to seek him out. Her search led her to the pantry, where she found him polishing the silver. Her appearance so startled him that he knocked over the jar of plate powder resting near his elbow.

"My lady!" Blushing to have been discovered in his shirtsleeves, he scrambled to retrieve his coat. "I beg your pardon . . . excuse me, please . . . that is, I must . . ."

Miranda smiled soothingly. "Please, calm yourself. I only

came to tell you of some changes and to ask you to carry out a few tasks for me."

While he thrust his arms into his coat sleeves, she told him about the new servants. "You will need to consult with Mrs. Driscoll regarding their duties," Miranda said. "Now, about the dogs—"

"The dogs?" Bomford spoke as if he'd never heard of such an animal.

"Yes, the dogs. From now on, they will be allowed only in the library and his lordship's bedchamber. You understand?"

Bomford goggled, which Miranda took as an affirmative. He goggled even more when she instructed him to move the stained and flea-infested Aubusson carpet from the hall into the library.

"Shall I have it cleaned first, your ladyship?"

"No." Miranda smiled sweetly. "Lord Huntsley prefers it the way it is."

"But—but . . ."

Miranda had a burst of inspiration. "Bomford, I have a special task for you, a very important one."

His objection to her previous order died on his lips. Excitement lit his eyes.

"I want you to be Lord Huntsley's special . . . er, attendant. He is working very hard, you understand, and needs frequent help. Therefore, when he rings for a servant— other than his valet—you shall attend him. If he is in the house, be sure to stay close by him."

"Very well, my lady. I will go look for him now." He puffed out his chest and hurried away.

Thoughtfully, Miranda watched him go. Only a saint would be able to endure Bomford's constant attendance.

Fortunately, Alex was no saint.

With a happy smile, Miranda began to hum.

*   *   *

After firing Yeager, Alex's work had increased tenfold. In the past week, he had gone to market to buy seed, hired workers to rethatch cottages, and ordered flint and gravel to repair roads. He had interviewed tenants, counted sheep, and read every farm journal he could find. And without fail, every morning at eight, and again after dinner, he worked on the ubiquitous accounts.

He detested the accounts.

Slamming the ledger closed, Alex leaned back in his chair and closed his eyes. Although he had made some progress, the books were still a mess. Why hadn't his granduncle seen what Yeager was doing? He supposed he shouldn't be surprised. Uncle Quentin had only ever been interested in his dogs. Almost certainly the old man would have been easy prey for an unscrupulous steward.

He rubbed a weary hand across his brow. His head ached, partly from doing numerous calculations, partly from anger at his granduncle, and partly from the unpleasant closeness of the library.

What the devil was that smell? he wondered. Sharp, sour, with a strong ammonia scent, it overpowered even the odor of the cheap coal on the fire.

His gaze wandered over the seven dogs resting in various parts of the room. A suspicion rose in his breast. Surely they were housebroken.

Why were all these dogs in the library, anyway? Two or three house dogs were fine, but allowing untrained animals the run of the house was a mistake. He would have to impose some kind of rules for the dogs. Miranda had tried to suggest something of the sort, he knew, but he had cut her off.

He rose to his feet, and the dogs immediately followed suit. He opened a window and returned to his seat. The dogs settled back into their comfortable positions.

Alex shivered as a cold wind blew in. Huddling over the desk, he opened the ledger again.

He was in the middle of adding a long column of figures when the door flew open and Bomford came in.

"Your lordship . . . oh, your lordship! The window is open! I will close it for you at once!"

Distracted, Alex lost his place. With a silent curse, he looked up at the butler. "I prefer it open," he snapped. "What is it you want?"

"I, ah, I was just checking to see if you needed anything, your lordship."

Alex clutched his pen tightly. This was the third time in the last hour Bomford had come into the room for no apparent reason. "As I told you before, Bomford, I will ring if I need anything." He rapped out the words sharply. "Don't interrupt me again."

Bomford's throat worked convulsively. "Of course. I beg your pardon. I didn't mean to interrupt. I shall leave at once—oh, but what is that book doing on the table?" He picked up a book from a table by the sofa. "I can't believe one of those lazy maids didn't put this away. You may rest assured, your lordship, that I will speak to them."

Tsking and clucking, the butler returned the volume to the bookshelf. "Don't hesitate to ring if you need anything, your lordship. I will be right outside the door." Bowing awkwardly, Bomford left.

Alex glared after him. He was trying to be patient with Bomford. He knew the butler was supporting his mother and sister. But really, the man was a total idiot. For some reason the servant had been dogging his steps the last several days. Every time Alex turned around, he bumped into the dolt. He wished now he hadn't been so adamant about having a Bomford for a butler. He hated to admit it, but Miranda had been right about the servant.

Miranda. He had not seen her all week except at dinner, and then she was always stiff and reserved. A niggling guilt tweaked him. He should not have spoken to her the way he had.

At least she appeared to be keeping herself busy. He knew she was overseeing the servants, but he had decided not to object. Actually, he was glad to see the maids cleaning and polishing the various rooms. He looked forward to having both his bedchamber and this room thoroughly scrubbed.

Absentmindedly, he scratched his wrist and frowned at the floor. He had never noticed before how filthy the carpet was. In fact, he could have sworn the carpet in this room was blue and gold instead of green and gold. But of course, with all the dirt, it was difficult to tell what color it was.

He would have to thank Miranda after this room was cleaned. Perhaps he would even tell her at dinner how he appreciated all the work she had done. Except in one regard—and that was his own fault for agreeing to it—she was turning out to be an exemplary wife—industrious, quiet, obedient.

A knock at the door interrupted his thoughts. Leaning forward over the ledger, he called out impatiently, "Yes?"

Bomford came in. "Your lordship, I just wished to inform you that you have less than an hour until your appointment with the new tenant Mr. Bott. I thought you might like to be reminded."

"Thank you, Bomford," Alex said through gritted teeth. "I believe I will go and change now."

At this point, he thought as he mounted the stairs two at a time, he would do just about anything to get away from Bomford.

That same morning, satisfied with the progress being made on the house, Miranda decided it was time to speak to Mrs. Rouse.

She descended the steep stairs to the kitchen and found

the cook elbow-deep in bread dough, the scent of yeast and flour in the air.

"Good morning, Mrs. Rouse." Miranda ducked under the pans and eyed the cook a trifle warily. For all her slightness, the woman was pummeling the dough with a great deal of force.

"Mornin'" was the taciturn reply. She flipped the dough, and a cloud of flour rose up.

Miranda sneezed. "I wished to speak to you about your request for more monies," she said. "Unfortunately, my husband has some strict notions about economy."

The cook divided the dough into four pieces and continued to knead.

"I'm still hoping to convince him to increase the food allowance, though." Miranda stared at Mrs. Rouse's sharp profile. "Since he seems to find what you've been cooking perfectly acceptable, I thought perhaps you could continue to prepare his meals just so. But for me, and the rest of the household—"

The cook turned her head and met Miranda's gaze.

"—for the rest of us, I thought you could, er, try some new recipes."

Mrs. Rouse methodically covered the dough with some towels, then wiped her bony hands on her apron. Something that could have been a smile lifted the corners of her mouth. "I understand, your ladyship."

"I'm glad you do, Mrs. Rouse," Miranda said, smiling also. "I only hope his lordship will understand as well."

Alex returned to the house at dinnertime, hunger gnawing at him. Usually he ate sparingly of the unappetizing fare provided by Mrs. Rouse, but tonight he was hungry enough to eat anything.

Intent on the prospect of food, he nodded absentmindedly

at a maid he passed in the corridor. To his surprise, she flushed and ducked into one of the rooms. Frowning, Alex stared at the closed door. What was wrong with the girl?

Perhaps she was shy, he thought, dismissing her from his mind. He continued on his way to the dining room.

Miranda was waiting. She smiled cheerfully at him across the table. That was unusual enough to make him stare at her. She turned her head slightly towards the door, revealing her charming profile. Her nose had just the hint of a tilt.

He forgot all about Miranda's nose when the door opened and Bomford brought in two bowls. His own nose twitched and his mouth began to water. One bowl was placed before Miranda. He could see the steam rising from what looked like some sort of broth. He sniffed the delicious aroma of thyme, parsley, and cloves wafting down from Miranda's end of the table.

Alex barely waited for the butler to put the bowl down before he picked up his spoon. He was about to scoop up a spoonful, when he stopped, staring down at the unappetizing glob in his bowl. He looked questioningly at Miranda.

"I had to have Mrs. Rouse prepare some special dishes for me since I have a delicate stomach," she explained sweetly. "Certain foods disagree with me."

He wished he could claim the same, he thought, looking down at the unidentifiable slop in front of him. He spooned a large, cold lump into his mouth.

It tasted even worse than it looked. As far as he could tell, it was made of flour, water, and some soggy vegetables.

"Is something wrong, Alex?"

Alex managed to swallow the lump of soup. "No. Why do you ask?"

"You appear to be in pain."

Hell yes, he was in pain. He was dying of hunger. "Not at all." He forced himself to take another spoonful and almost gagged. God, it was awful.

"Alex, the earl and countess of Briarwood have invited us to dinner tomorrow night. Shall I accept?"

"I suppose we must." he said reluctantly. The Briarwoods were the highest-ranking family in the area. It would be unpardonably rude to refuse the invitation. He just hated to waste a whole evening socializing when he had so much work to do.

On the other hand, he thought as he took another bite of soup, it might be worth going just to get a decent meal.

For the next course, Bomford brought in two covered platters. When Miranda's was uncovered, a roast leg of pheasant was revealed. Even across the length of the table it looked tender and juicy. Fork in hand, Alex leaned forward as the butler placed the other platter in front of him and removed the cover with a flourish.

"What the hell—?" Alex scowled at the same reheated mutton he'd had all week, then glared across the table at his wife. "I want the pheasant also."

"I'm sorry, Alex," Miranda answered. "Mrs. Rouse said her budget does not allow her to dress a whole pheasant."

He slammed down his fork. "You will inform the cook that from now on, she will serve the same meal to both of us."

Her slim arched brows rose. "But the expense—"

"I will authorize the expense," he growled. Damnation, he would mortgage the estate for some of that pheasant. He reached for his wineglass, then paused when he saw Miranda's long, dark brown lashes sweep down, concealing her expression.

"As you wish," she responded demurely.

He stared at her for a long moment. With her bowed head and lowered eyes, she looked young and sweet and virtuous. The picture of an obedient wife.

Shaking his head, he drank a deep draught of wine before picking up his fork and manfully taking a bite of the mutton.

He must have imagined the very odd gleam he thought he had seen in those innocent green eyes.

*   *   *

The next day disaster struck along with a new storm. The seed for the spring planting arrived, only it was wheat instead of the hops he had ordered. Alex spent a wet frustrating day, tracking down the seller and arranging for the correct load to be delivered.

He came home drenched and muddy, and headed straight for the stairs only to be blocked by Bomford.

"My lord! Thank heaven you're home! Did you forget that you and her ladyship are to dine with Lord and Lady Briarwood tonight? You have barely three hours to prepare!"

"Thank you for reminding me, Bomford," Alex said, gritting his teeth. "Now step aside before I freeze to death in these wet clothes."

Bomford was instantly all concern. He trailed at Alex's heels, up the stairs and down the corridor to the bedchamber. "My lord, shall I order extra coal for the fire? Shall I have Cook prepare a concoction to ward off a chill? Shall I—"

Alex slammed his bedroom door closed in the butler's face. Shivering, he wondered what the penalty was for murdering a servant.

He glanced around the dim bedchamber. There was no sign of his valet, so he stripped off his coat himself and was about to toss it on the bed, when he heard a soft whine.

Stopping in his tracks, he stared at the sight on the bed.

A beagle, its newborn litter surrounding it, rested comfortably in the middle of his bed. The mother was busily washing the pups with her tongue. She looked up, and her tail thumped against the soiled cover a few times before she went back to her task.

After a few moments of stunned immobility, Alex strode to the bellpull and yanked ferociously.

Within seconds, Bomford appeared.

"Remove these animals at once," Alex snarled.

"Y-y-yes, my lord," the butler stuttered, looking very worried. He then proceeded to exclaim, "Shoo! Shoo!" and flap his elbows in a most ineffectual manner.

"For God's sake, go get a basket or something to carry the pups," Alex snapped.

"Of course, my lord, at once! Oh dear! I tried to tell her ladyship you wouldn't like it . . ."

Alex froze. "Lady Huntsley told you to bring this dog here?"

"Yes, indeed! She said you were so fond of the dogs, you would want them to be as comfortable as possible. I tried to explain to her, but she insisted your bed was the perfect place."

"I see." Cold anger filled him. That conniving little—

"Oh no, it's n-not what you think," Bomford stammered. "I mean, I'm sure she meant it for the best. Why, she's very concerned for your comfort . . . telling Mrs. Rouse to prepare special meals for you just as you like them and having me attend you specially."

"Is that so?" Alex smiled with an effort. "Where is my wife, Bomford?"

"Ah, er, in the stillroom, I believe."

"I think I will pay her a visit. I really must 'thank' her for her efforts on my behalf."

Alex strode from the room, leaving Bomford goggling.

9

The door to the stillroom crashed open, causing the bottles on the shelves to rattle. Miranda, sitting at the long worktable, looked up in surprise.

Alex stood in the doorway, his black hair plastered to his head, his shirt and waistcoat soaking wet.

"My dear wife, how very industrious you look."

There was a silky threat in his voice. She swallowed, then tilted her chin up. "Is something wrong?"

"No, not at all. I just wanted to thank you for your 'industry' on my behalf."

Miranda looked down at the yellow powder she was grinding with a mortar and pestle. "I don't know what you mean," she said haughtily.

"Don't you? Dogs in my bed, specially prepared meals, even a special servant to attend me. Tell me. What have I done to merit such 'special' treatment?"

Indignation swelled her breast. "I have followed your wishes, my lord. What is your complaint?"

"You dare ask me that?" He strode forward. Bracing his

hands on the table, he leaned forward threateningly. "There's a pack of whelps in my bed and you dare ask me that?"

"I tried to speak to you about these matters! You did not seem interested. If I was forced to resort to more extreme measures, you have only yourself to blame."

"Do I? I think I can very easily find someone else to blame—my sweet little wife who promised not so long ago to obey and serve me."

"How can I obey and serve someone who has less sense than a baboon?" She gripped the pestle, resisting the urge to throw it at him. "Oh, I wish I'd never married you!"

"You wish you'd married that sniveling little vicar, I suppose."

"Yes, I do! He was kind and considerate and—"

"And I doubt he would know what to do with a woman."

"You're wrong! He knew exactly what to do!"

"Oh?" Alex's eyes narrowed and his voice grew dangerously quiet. "And what was it he did?" His gaze fell to her breasts.

She could not miss the implication. Blushing furiously, she retorted, "He treated me with respect." She picked up a small bottle and poured its contents over the yellow powder. White acidic fumes immediately ascended.

Alex jumped back, his eyes watering from the pungent smell. "What the devil is that?"

"Oil of vitriol," she said coldly. "I'm making aromatic vinegar. It's used to purify rooms. I hope to kill some of the fleas."

"Well, put it away, dammit—"

The door crashed open again.

Bomford entered, his hair on end and his coat askew. "My lord! There you are! You only have two and a half hours until it's time to leave for dinner at the Briarwoods'. Shall I summon your valet for you?"

Alex did not move for a moment. Then he smiled pleasantly at the butler. "Bomford, if you barge into a room again without knocking I am going to get out my hunting rifle and shoot you."

Bomford's jaw dropped. His eyes huge, he stared at Alex's smiling mouth and eyes. Abruptly he turned and fled.

Miranda jumped to her feet. "Was that necessary, Alex? He was trying to be helpful and you've scared him out of his wits!"

"He never had any wits to begin with," Alex snapped. "Don't try to change the subject, Wife. I demand an explanation."

Miranda lifted her chin again. "The explanation is very simple. I refuse to endure your boorish behavior any longer. I am fed up with your insistence on wallowing in this filthy house, your unreasonable outbursts of anger, your excessive and intemperate drinking—"

"Are you quite finished?" His voice was soft.

She kept her chin high. "Yes, for now. If we didn't have a dinner engagement, I'm sure I could go on for hours. But I must change."

She made her way around the table, only to stop when she realized he was blocking her path to the door. "Step aside, please," she said haughtily, standing a safe distance from his dripping figure.

He didn't move.

His eyes were icy blue. She recognized the anger in them, but there was some other emotion there too, something she had seen before but didn't quite understand. Whatever it was, it never failed to make her nervous.

She swallowed. Deciding it was easier to go around him, she stepped to the side, skirted his tense figure, and stalked to the door.

"Miranda . . ."

She paused in the doorway, the hair on the nape of her neck prickling.

"This discussion isn't over yet. Not by a long shot."

Holding her head high, she left the room, the smooth menace of his voice ringing in her ears.

Alex stared broodingly across the dim carriage at his wife as they drove to the Briarwoods' later that evening. She was attired in the pale blue gown that set off her hair and skin beautifully, but her expression was as chilly as the gown. She gazed out the window as if there was something utterly fascinating about the stark, moon-swept landscape.

He was content not to speak. Although more than an hour had passed since their argument, he still did not quite trust himself. The image of her standing defiantly before him remained fresh in his mind.

He had wanted to silence her bold tongue. He had wanted to sweep her into his arms, carry her upstairs and punish her for her impudence—only the punishment he had in mind would be very pleasurable. After he was done with her she certainly wouldn't be prating about that damn vicar.

His fists clenched as he remembered her words about Pelham. It was fortunate he was not a jealous man—and that Miranda was so damn innocent—or he would suspect there had been more between her and the vicar than he'd been led to believe. It was also fortunate that Pelham did not reside in the vicinity, or Alex would have sought out the little weasel and pounded him to a pulp.

The carriage bounced and swayed as it turned a corner. Alex, his jaw tightening, glanced out the window and saw they were approaching the Briarwood mansion.

The house was of yellow brick with a magnificent, sweeping set of stone steps leading up to tall doors flanked by pillars. The doors were opened by the butler, an individual of infinite graciousness, who admitted them into the entry hall. A beautiful crimson-and-gold oriental carpet and a magnificent staircase with a painted mural on the wall immediately caught Alex's attention. Remembering Bomford's flapping elbows, the flea-infested carpet in the library, and the broken dog gate still hanging on the staircase at Ribblebank Manor, he frowned.

Miranda, looking around the magnificent hall, frowned too, and a renewed surge of anger swept through her. Although Ribblebank Manor would never look like the Briarwoods' home, it could at least be clean and well kept. If only Alex wasn't so unreasonable! She had to force herself not to glare at him as the butler led them into another beautiful room where the earl and countess were waiting.

"Welcome to Briarwood Hall," the earl said, coming forward to greet them. He was a large, bulky man with white beetle brows and a warm smile.

Miranda, liking him immediately, smiled back.

Lady Briarwood's black eyes sparkled as she greeted them also. She was tiny compared to her husband, but her perfect posture made her seem taller, and her elegant lavender dress and snow-white hair gave her an air of dignity. Her smile was friendly, and Miranda, who had been a trifle nervous about meeting her, relaxed.

When the men had walked over to the sideboard to pour themselves a glass of brandy, the countess turned to Miranda and said, "I am especially pleased to meet you, Lady Huntsley, because I was acquainted with your maternal grandmother."

"Were you?" Miranda asked in surprise. "I never knew her, but my mother told me a little about her."

Lady Briarwood smiled. "Yes, Marie was quite a character. She caused scandal after scandal, but she was so charming, no one cared in the least. Except for that last one, of course, when she ran off with a married man and was killed in a carriage accident."

Miranda's eyes widened. Her mother had said that

Grandmother Marie died in a carriage accident—but she had failed to mention the lover. In fact, according to her mother, Grandmother had been the model of propriety. "Did you know her well?" she asked, hiding her shock.

Lady Briarwood nodded. "We were very close, as a matter of fact. We came out the same season." The older woman studied Miranda. "You have something of her looks. She was very beautiful."

Miranda blushed. "Why, thank you, Lady Briarwood."

"My dear," Lord Briarwood said, returning with a glass of brandy in his hand. "Have you heard? Huntsley has discharged Yeager."

Lady Briarwood raised her brows. "No, I hadn't heard. That's excellent news indeed. I never liked that man." She looked at Alex inquiringly. "Who have you hired to replace him?"

"No one yet," he replied.

"I can recommend a new agent if you're interested," Lord Briarwood offered.

"I would be very interested," Alex said.

Lord Briarwood provided the man's name and an impressive list of qualifications. "He's a cousin of my agent," the earl said as they went into the baronial dining hall and sat down to dinner. "He should do a good job for you. Unlike your granduncle's man."

Alex, his gaze fixed on an approaching servant carrying a platter with a roast on it, said absently, "Uncle Quentin didn't pay much attention to estate matters."

Lord Briarwood nodded. "He was really only interested in his dogs."

"One slice or two, my lord?" the servant murmured.

"Three." To the earl, Alex said, "Did you know my granduncle well?"

"No, not really. I bought a dog from him on occasion, but he never visited or entertained, as far as I know. Of course he had been especially reclusive the last month before he died, when he was in deep mourning."

About to take a bite of the roast, Alex paused. "Mourning? For whom?"

"For Bessie."

Alex frowned.

Lord Briarwood's eyes started to twinkle. "His favorite hunting dog," he elaborated.

Alex's gaze met Miranda's. She lifted a napkin to her mouth.

"Ah, that Bessie," Alex said expressionlessly. "I believe my uncle was a trifle eccentric in his later years."

Miranda nearly choked on her roast.

Alex placed a bite of the meat in his mouth. An expression of extreme bliss appeared on his face. He did not participate in the conversation for the next few minutes.

"Huntsley, would you like me to see if our cook has a cousin also?" the earl asked.

Alex had to finish chewing before he could speak. "I beg your pardon?" he said, a slight frown creasing his brow.

Lord Briarwood was watching him with an amused smile. "You seem quite famished. Perhaps you would like me to see if our cook has a cousin also."

A dull flush rose in Alex's cheeks. He slanted a glance at Miranda, who bit back a smile.

"No, thank you," Alex replied, recovering quickly. "My wife has everything under control. Don't you, darling?"

"Yes, indeed," she said sweetly. "Except, perhaps, for the butler." She turned to Lady Briarwood. "Bomford is not quite up to snuff, but he is devoted to the Setton family. Especially to Alex. He follows him everywhere."

It was Alex's turn to choke on his roast.

Lady Briarwood looked back and forth between Miranda and Alex, a perceptive gleam in her eyes. "Perhaps our butler could give him a hint or two."

"Oh, no, Lady Briarwood, we couldn't impose—"

"We accept," Alex said firmly.

Lady Briarwood smiled. To Miranda she said, "It's no imposition, dear. Figgley has this house organized like Wellington's troops. A few hours here and there won't affect his regimen. He will welcome the challenge, I am sure."

"It will certainly be a challenge," Alex muttered.

Miranda pretended not to hear him. "Then of course we accept," she said to Lady Briarwood. "Alex and I greatly appreciate it."

Lady Briarwood laughed. "It is a pleasure for me to be able to help Marie's granddaughter. Don't ever hesitate to come to me for assistance if you need it."

"Thank you, Lady Briarwood," Miranda said demurely. "I will remember that."

Several hours later, Alex sat in a corner of the carriage watching Miranda again. But this time she wasn't cold and silent. Instead, she was laughing and chattering about the evening at Briarwood Hall. Her anger from the afternoon had completely vanished.

So had his, actually. At some point during dinner, he had suddenly seen the humor of the situation. She had, too. He remembered the moment when their gazes met over the table. Her eyes had been full of laughter. He, too, had been hard-pressed not to laugh out loud.

After that, she had been more relaxed than he'd ever seen her, and he was reminded of the first time he'd met her, when he caught a glimpse of a sweet smile in her eyes that had quite literally taken his breath away.

Tonight, that smile had been there again, and he hadn't been able to tear his gaze from her.

Watching her now, in the dim light of the carriage lamp,

Alex remembered the litter of puppies in his bed and thought wryly that perhaps she wasn't quite as sweet as she appeared. But strangely, he didn't mind at all. In fact, now that he'd gotten over his anger, he felt oddly exhilarated.

"I do hope Lady Briarwood's butler will be able to help Bomford," she was saying. "And if you hire the new steward, things will be much better."

"Will they, Miranda? Does that mean I won't be finding any more dogs in my bed?"

Her gaze flew to his. Then she lowered her lashes. "I'm sorry about that," she murmured, not sounding very repentant.

"What possessed you to do such a thing?"

Her lashes flew up. Her eyes sparkled with indignation. "You can ask that? When you refuse to let me improve the house and you never listen to me?"

He frowned. He knew he had not always listened to her complaints. How could he listen when all he could think about was taking her to bed?

"Are you still angry at me?" she asked.

He stared into her eyes for a long moment. "No, Miranda."

No, he wasn't angry, he thought, watching her from beneath lowered lids. Because now he had a solution to his problem. He was surprised he hadn't thought of it before.

All he had to do was seduce her.

10

Alex put his plan into action the next evening at dinner.

"The dining room looks very nice," he said, surveying the freshly painted pale blue walls. The smell of paint still lingered in the air.

"The workmen labored all day yesterday," Miranda replied. "They cleaned the ceiling, too."

Alex glanced up at the previously smoke-blackened ceiling. The cleaning had revealed some very fine molding. "A vast improvement," he commented. He took a bite of the minted lamb on his plate. "The food also shows a miraculous improvement."

"Does it?" she asked innocently, a smile playing about her lips.

"Mm-hm." He took another bite. "I wrote to the steward Lord Briarwood recommended."

Miranda sipped her orgeat. "I hope he will come,"

"So do I. I never realized managing an estate was so much work." In a casual tone, he added, "I also made arrangements to sell off the dogs."

She looked at him, then quickly lowered her gaze to her plate. "Oh?"

"Only if you have no objections, of course."

The smile tugged at her lips again. "I would like to keep one or two . . . for pets, you understand."

"I suppose we could keep a few of the newest litter. Having been born in my bed, they're practically family."

She appeared to have some difficulty swallowing, but after a moment managed to say, "I would like that."

"Excellent. Tell me, what did you do today?"

Her smile widened. "I had the servants clean your bed-chamber and the library."

He laughed.

Miranda's breath caught at the sound. She hadn't heard him laugh since they'd come to Ribblebank Manor. She wished he would laugh more often. And smile, too—the way he was smiling at her now, with a light in his blue eyes that made him look warmer, more approachable.

He had changed since yesterday. The stiffness had gone out of his shoulders and his eyes had lost that brooding look. She knew the exact moment the transformation had taken place—last night at the Briarwoods', when the earl had mentioned old Bessie. She had suddenly been struck by the ridiculousness of their whole situation and had been hard-put not to burst out laughing.

Had Alex experienced a similar revelation? Watching him laugh now, she suspected he had. But would it make any difference? Had anything really changed? Had *Alex* really changed?

"Miranda," he said, putting down his cutlery and wiping his mouth with his napkin, "What do you do after dinner?"

"I usually sew in my bedroom."

"Ah. What an industrious wife I have. I thought I might read in the library this evening. Would you like to bring your sewing in there?"

He wanted to spend the evening with her? This was definitely new. "If you want me to."

His eyelids lowered for a moment. "I definitely want you to."

"Very well. But I warn you, there's not much of a selection of reading material. Your granduncle apparently had a fondness for Gothic romances. There isn't a farm journal in sight."

"I like Gothic romances."

"You do?"

"Certainly. Miranda, I was wondering . . ." He smiled intimately at her.

She looked at him a bit warily. "Yes?"

"I was wondering if perhaps you would read to me. After working all day, I find it very soothing to be read to."

Read to him? He wanted her to *read* to him?

"Oh, *yes,* Alex! I would love to read to you!"

He really had changed.

Over the next several days, Miranda continued to be amazed by the change in Alex. Instead of his usual surly and withdrawn manner, he was charming and affable, telling her how he spent his day and inquiring after hers. She told him about the work on the house and reported on Bomford's progress—a subject Alex seemed very interested in.

Although he still worked long hours, he no longer disappeared after dinner. Instead, he spent every evening with her in the library listening to her read.

The evenings in the library were everything she had once dreamed of—quiet times spent together in pleasant companionship. Alex was the ideal husband: kind, considerate, and—of course—gentlemanly.

By the end of the week she was so comfortable with him

that when he joined her in the library that evening and sat on the sofa next to her, resting his arm along the back, she didn't think much about it.

She opened the book to where she had stopped the previous night, eager to read more because the last chapter had ended with the Evil Duke telling Lady Clarissa that he wanted her. Miranda was hoping that the next chapter would be a little more specific about what the Evil Duke "wanted"—she had a dark suspicion that he wanted to touch Lady Clarissa's breasts.

The chapter started with Lady Clarissa swearing never to give in to the Evil Duke's lust. Miranda applauded this high-minded sentiment, but her opinion of Lady Clarissa suffered a setback when the Evil Duke managed to lure her to his castle.

"And the Evil Duke said, 'Now you're mine, sweeting. Ere you depart this castle, your virtue will be no more!' 'Oh, pray, kind sir, do not ravish a poor helpless female,' Lady Clarissa pleaded. But the Evil Duke only laughed chillingly."

Miranda slapped the book down on her lap. "Well, why did the silly chit go with him in the first place? It was obviously a trap!"

Alex replied with a straight face, "She believed the Evil Duke's story that her husband was injured."

"Hmmph. I can only feel the utmost disgust for such a poor sort of female. To believe such a ridiculous story, and then to moan and sigh when he meant to ravish her, instead of doing something to purpose."

"How would you react if you were faced with imminent ravishment?"

"Why, I—" She turned her head to find his face very close to hers, his gaze dark and gleaming. The book slid from her lap and fell to the floor. She tried to lean forward to pick it up, but his hand slid into the curls at the nape of her neck, preventing her. She looked into his eyes again, seeing the black pupils and the band of blue around them. She couldn't seem to breathe. His face came closer, closer, until it blurred, and instinctively she closed her eyes.

Her heart was beating very fast as she felt the light pressure of his mouth on hers. She hadn't been sure what to expect, but she had been afraid that kissing might be unpleasant. She was happy to discover that it wasn't. In fact, it was rather enjoyable. The kiss made her feel warm and happy.

The pressure deepened a little. She felt the same tingling in her lips that she sometimes felt when he touched her hand or shoulder. The sensation was quite pleasant. The warmth inside her increased. She felt . . . *close* to Alex. Very, very close. But there was none of the wicked lust that the Evil Duke had displayed. She relaxed. Alex was her friend. She could trust him—

His tongue traced the seam of her lips.

Her eyes flew open, the gentle, pleasant sensations fleeing. Shock raced through her. She put her hands against his chest and pushed.

He released her instantly. He smiled at her, but his voice sounded a little strained when he spoke. "It's late, Miranda. Perhaps you should go to bed."

Her hands were still braced against his chest. Hastily she lowered them and rose to her feet. "I think you're right. Good night, Alex." She hurried out of the room.

Alex stared after her.

Then, for the hundredth time that week, he cursed himself for being such a damn gentleman.

11

He had kissed her.

Sitting in the library the next morning, Miranda found it impossible to concentrate on the menus lying on the desk in front of her. Her gaze kept wandering to the sofa.

It looked so innocent with its new royal-blue velvet upholstery. She could scarcely believe what had taken place on that plush fabric.

He had pressed his tongue against her lips. His *tongue*! She couldn't believe he'd done something so repulsive. Why, her mouth was still tingling with disgust!

At least, she thought it was disgust. She wasn't quite sure. The sensation of his tongue on her lips had been very odd. It was a little like being tickled. But she hadn't wanted to laugh. The feeling had been . . . uncomfortable.

Closing her eyes, she pressed her fingers against her mouth. Perhaps she should talk to him. Tell him she didn't mind him kissing her as long as he kept his tongue to himself—

A loud cry penetrated the thick walls of the library.

"I won't! I won't!" she heard a high voice scream.

Alarmed, she rose and went into the hall to investigate.

Alex's sister Petronella stood there, mounds of baggage stacked around her, trying unsuccessfully to quiet a small tow-headed boy. With a sigh of exasperation, she pushed an inky black curl off her forehead before catching sight of Miranda.

"Miranda! How are you? It's so nice to see you again!"

A shrieking wail drowned out Miranda's reply. Petronella turned back to the child and said, "Edward, you bad boy! Be quiet! If your Papa were here, you would get a whipping for being so naughty!" This did not induce the child to reduce the volume of his protests, and Petronella's voice turned coaxing. "Look, Edward, this is your new aunt Miranda. Can you say, 'How do you do?'"

Edward turned a freckled tear-streaked face toward Miranda and said, "You're a nasty lady, and I don't like you!" Then he stuck his tongue out as far as it would go and crossed his eyes.

Miranda tried to hide her shock. Was this the sweet child Petronella had described to her less than three weeks ago? Before her horrified gaze, Edward lay down on the floor and gave vent to a full-blown tantrum.

Miranda was nonplussed. She had not been around children much, true, but in the books she had read they were always respectful and mannerly. Edward fit into neither of those categories. He was nothing like the smiling cherub she had imagined.

Raising her voice in order to be heard over the screams, she said, "It's nice to see you again, too, Petronella."

A gray moth of a woman stepped forward. Deep circles under her eyes attested to the fact that the poor creature was Edward's unfortunate nurse. She spoke diffidently. "If you please, my lady, perhaps if Master Edward could have a bite to eat in the kitchen. He refused to eat at our last stop, and I think some food might improve his temper."

"Please, take him to the kitchen and feed him as much as you can," Miranda said hastily.

Edward and his nurse went off to the kitchen, and Miranda, much relieved, escorted her sister-in-law to the sitting room. Petronella shook out her red skirts and sank into an overstuffed chair with a deep sigh.

"Thank you, Miranda. I was about ready to admit myself to Bedlam."

"Is Edward ill?" Miranda thought maybe that would explain the child's abominable behavior.

"Oh, no. He suffers from the Setton curse. He is subject to travel sickness," she explained, when Miranda looked at her blankly. "He is just tired and hungry, I'm sure. And this is a new nurse. She is virtually incompetent. Edward screamed for the last hour in the coach, and she just wrung her hands, and sighed, and did nothing! I vow, I was ready to fire her on the spot and let her down in the middle of the road!" Petronella threw her hands up in disgust, before continuing.

"Preston and Mama and Papa are following. I set out a few days early, because I knew Edward would need a break. And besides, I thought this would be the perfect opportunity for you to meet Edward."

"Oh. Yes," Miranda said. Of course she was happy to have Alex's family visit. She had met them only briefly at the wedding and she welcomed this chance to become better acquainted with them.

But having a houseful of guests meant she would have less time alone with Alex. With so many people around, she doubted he would have an opportunity to kiss her again. Which might be just as well. She certainly didn't want him to kiss her in that shocking manner again.

At least, she didn't think she did.

"Would you care for refreshment?" Miranda asked.

"Tea would be lovely, thank you. And then I think I will go to my room and lie down. My head is pounding most dreadfully. Edward screamed for the last two hours in the carriage. . . ."

While they were drinking their tea, Alex returned. Petronella jumped up and flew across the room. "Alex!" she cried, hugging him tightly. "You look wonderful!"

Alex's expression softened as he gazed down at his sister. "So do you, Nell. How's that young scamp of yours?"

Petronella rolled her eyes. "Recovering from the ordeal of travel. He screamed for three hours before we arrived. Other than that, he's fine. Growing like a weed. You won't believe how tall he is. Everyone thinks he's six instead of just four. I have my hands full, let me tell you. He's been so excited about visiting you." She sat down and picked up her cup of tea. "I promised Edward you would give him a ride on one of your horses. You will, won't you? He's very upset about leaving his pony at home. He's going to miss it terribly while we're in London."

Alex purloined a biscuit from the tea tray and popped it into his mouth. "Why on earth are you dragging him to London with you?"

Petronella sighed and set down her cup. "Mama insisted. She said she couldn't bear to be parted from him for three whole months." An uncertain frown puckered her brow. "I'm not sure she will enjoy having him in the same house with her, though."

"I imagine once he kicks up a rumpus a few times, she'll want you to pack him off to the country with his nurse." His eyes narrowed. "Am I correct in assuming that Mother and Father are following you?"

Petronella nodded.

"Are George and Selina and their children coming, too?"

"No, just Preston. Didn't Mama write you?"

"No, she did not."

"Oh, good gracious!" Petronella's eyes grew round. "You didn't know we were coming? We're on our way to London and Mama thought this would be a good chance to visit and see how you and Miranda are doing. I'm sorry, Alex. Are we imposing? Do you and Miranda want to be alone?"

"Whoever heard of newlyweds wanting to be alone?" Alex asked sardonically.

Petronella frowned. "Well, some newlyweds do. Preston and I—oh, you are funning me, aren't you? Do you want us to leave?"

"You're always welcome here, Nell." Alex glanced at Miranda. Something in his eyes made her blush and lower her gaze. A note of resignation entered his voice as he added, "And I suppose this is as good a time as any."

Miranda spent the next day with Petronella. Her new sister-in-law was cheerful and friendly and chattered constantly, rarely requiring any response. With a few questions here and there, Petronella could talk for hours. Miranda learned quite a bit about Alex in the process.

"Papa is quite the best father in the whole world," said Petronella over breakfast. "He always expected a lot of us when we were growing up. Alex was his pride and joy, even though Thomas was the elder. Alex could do anything, according to Papa. When he was ten, he stole Papa's fishing pole and caught a fish that weighed almost as much as he did. I was only eight at the time, but I still remember how stern Papa looked. He didn't get angry—he never got angry—he merely asked Alex what he thought he was doing in the most awful voice. Alex hung his head and replied that he had just wanted to catch a fish to give Papa for his birthday. Papa said nothing more, but two days later, Alex received his own fishing pole."

After breakfast, while they toured the house, Petronella talked about Lady Thurlow.

"Mama can be . . . difficult," Petronella said. "And she

always seemed to be harder on Alex than on Thomas and us girls. She still talks about the time when the boys were in shortcoats, and she had beautiful matching outfits made up for Thomas and Alex and her, complete with bonnets and fans. Thomas wore his and never said a word, although he was almost eight at the time. But Alex, who was only six, traded his outfit with one belonging to the gardener's son. He appeared at dinner in a pair of filthy, ragged breeches. Mama was furious, but Papa sided with Alex. After that, Thomas and Alex no longer wore petticoats."

Petronella giggled, then grew pensive. "I hope Edward won't be so fussy about his coats. He looks so adorable in them. He is the most wonderful boy. Did I tell you that my sister Selina has a son the same age, and Edward is almost six inches taller than he is?"

"How extraordinary," Miranda murmured, leading Petronella around the edge of the hall, where the house-keeper was scrubbing the floor, and outside to inspect the gardens.

"Yes, isn't it? He is smart, too. He said his first word when he was six months old. Everyone adores him. Mama takes tea with him every day, and he is such a little gentle-man. I think he reminds her of Thomas. Mama doted on Thomas. She was terribly cut up when he died. She's worn nothing but black ever since." A tear glimmered in her eye. Then she brightened. "But she does have Edward. And he is so sweet."

They went back inside, again skirting the hall, where Mrs. Driscoll was almost finished scrubbing. A luncheon of cold meats and dried fruit was waiting in the dining room.

"You have done wonders here." Petronella said, putting a slice of ham on her plate. "Mama told me how awful it was when Uncle was alive."

"Thank you. The estate was a mess, too. It is amazing how quickly Alex has managed to put everything in order."

"Oh, that's because of all that army discipline," Petronella said blithely.

"Alex was in the army?" Miranda almost spilled the raisins she was spooning onto her plate.

"Of course! He and Thomas were army mad. Mama didn't want either of them to join. She got her way with Thomas, since he was the heir, you understand, but Alex inveigled the purchase price out of Papa. He did well, too. He was promoted twice in the field, and received a citation for bravery."

"I didn't know." She sat down with Petronella at the table.

"He's very modest about it. He changed after the army. Before, he and Thomas were forever cutting a lark and laughing their heads off." Petronella smiled, reminiscing. "Sometimes I would say something, and they would look at each other, and for no reason at all, burst into laughter." She shook her head. "Thomas was always trying to best Alex, but he rarely succeeded. Alex was good at everything, and he was very intense about it. He didn't like to lose. Thomas shrugged it off and laughed when he lost, but when Alex lost, he sulked."

Petronella paused to take a tiny nibble of ham. "Alex and Thomas were always competing with each other. They were very close, but one or the other of them was always coming up with some ridiculous wager, some new challenge. I could never understand it. That's how Thomas died, you know. He challenged Alex to a steeplechase and fell off his horse and broke his neck."

Miranda set down her knife and fork. Although she'd known he had a brother who died, she'd never heard Alex talk much about him. Sympathy welled up in her for his loss. She, too, knew the pain of losing a loved one. "How tragic," she said quietly.

"Yes, it was," Petronella agreed. "It's been five years, but we all still miss him. I am just glad I have Edward to comfort me—"

"Mama! Mama!" a piping voice cried from somewhere outside the dining room. Miranda heard the sound of small feet running across the hall, closely followed by a shriek.

Miranda and Petronella hurried out of the dining room to find a bewildered-looking Edward staring at the shrieking Mrs. Driscoll. A trail of muddy footprints led from the front door to where Edward was standing in the middle of the newly polished hall.

It took Miranda several minutes to calm the wailing housekeeper. Petronella scolded Edward, who looked unrepentant when he finally figured out what all the fuss was about.

"I have something very import'nt to tell you, Mama," he said, tugging on Petronella's skirt.

"You must apologize to Mrs. Driscoll first, Edward," Petronella said sternly.

"Oh, all right. Sorry," he said offhandedly to the quivering housekeeper. "Now may I tell you? Uncle Alex took me for a ride on his horse and it was 'normous!"

"You may tell me all about it later, darling. Now go upstairs and find Nurse."

A definite look of rebellion crossed Edward's face, but he obeyed, dragging his feet up the stairs in exaggerated martyrdom, his face set in a deep frown. Once or twice he glanced back to make sure they were watching.

"That child," said Petronella in exasperation, her gaze following his slow ascent. "I hope his father gets here soon."

Petronella's prayers were answered. Preston Bayard and the earl and countess of Thurlow arrived that very evening.

"You've lost weight," Lady Thurlow said at dinner that night, inspecting Alex up and down over her beaklike nose. "Haven't you been eating?"

"As much as I usually do," Alex said. He placed a spoonful

of the pumpkin soup in his mouth. "Tell me, how was your trip, Mother?"

"Tolerable. At least Preston kept me company part of the way. Your father insisted upon riding for the most part, of course. This 'curse' business is most annoying. As I've said before, one need only set one's mind—"

"Miranda, Alex, you've done wonders with the house," the earl interrupted smoothly, his hooded light blue eyes calm and serene. "Last time we were here, we were practically mauled by the dogs."

Lady Thurlow shuddered. "Those dirty beasts. Jumping up on my skirts with their muddy paws. Your uncle never made any effort to control them."

"I sold them off to one of the hunt societies. They were glad to have them," Alex said.

"Good hunting around here?" Preston asked, his square face lighting up with interest.

"So I understand. I have not had the opportunity to try it yet. Coursing is very popular also."

Preston and the earl leaned forward to hear more, but the duchess said in a low yet carrying tone, "It is bad manners to discuss sport at dinner, Alex. Let us talk of something more interesting."

Everyone fell silent.

The countess looked around the table. "Please, continue your conversations," she said.

Fortunately, Bomford chose that moment to bring in a platter of poached salmon steak. Miranda looked at it anxiously. She had spent a good deal of time in the kitchen with Mrs. Rouse discussing how to dress the fish and had decided on a simple poaching sauce. To her relief, the fish looked and smelled delicious.

Lady Thurlow inspected the proffered fish with eyes as steely gray as her hair. She shook her head. "No, thank you. I do not care for salmon."

The men helped themselves to large portions.

Lady Thurlow ate sparingly of the braised leg of mutton that followed. She accepted servings of the next course of stuffed artichokes and stewed peas, but after tasting them, she laid down her fork. She said to Miranda, "Your cook has not quite mastered the art of cooking vegetables, my dear. I would be glad to speak to her if you like."

"Er, that's very kind of you, Lady Thurlow," Miranda murmured.

Preston cleared his throat. "Petronella and I have some news." He rose to his feet and went to stand behind his wife. Drawing up his stout figure, he said in a proud voice, "We're expecting another child."

A welter of exclamations and congratulations rose up around the table. Preston grinned widely, revealing slightly crooked teeth, and Petronella's extremely pale white skin turned pink. Lord Thurlow and Alex both stood up to shake Preston's hand and kiss Petronella's cheek.

"When is the baby due?" Alex asked when everyone had returned to their seats.

"In September," Petronella said. "Preston and I are most excited. We're hoping for a girl this time."

"This announcement pleases me very much," Lady Thurlow told Petronella. "I expect that we will soon hear a similar announcement from Alex and Miranda."

All eyes swung to Miranda. Blushing bright red, she clasped her hands tightly in her lap and stared down at them.

"Not yet, Mother," Alex said coolly.

"I hope we won't have to wait too long," Lady Thurlow said. "We have the succession to think of you know."

"I do know, Mother."

"Hmmph." A disgruntled look on her face, she turned to Miranda. "My dear, don't you think it's time for the ladies to withdraw?"

"Oh, yes, of course." Miranda rose hastily to her feet. "If the gentlemen will excuse us?"

With alacrity, the men stood and helped the ladies from their chairs. As she left the room, Miranda glanced back. She caught a glimpse of identical expressions of relief on the men's faces before Bomford gently but decisively closed the door and blocked them from her view.

"Your mother means well," said the earl as the butler poured wine into their glasses.

"She always does," Alex said.

"Now, Alex. Your mother may not be the most tactful person, but she does have some good notions." Lord Thurlow paused to drink some of the excellent port. "This marriage, for instance. It seems to agree with you."

"It agrees with me well enough." It would agree with him much more, he thought wryly, if his family would leave so he could continue his efforts to lure Miranda into bed.

"Arranged marriages often work out well," said Preston. "Look at Petronella and me. In spite of the inauspicious circumstances of our marriage, we couldn't be happier."

"I think it helped that you'd been in love with her forever," Alex pointed out dryly. "Even if the scandal hadn't made it necessary for her to marry you, you would have convinced her soon enough."

"Perhaps," Preston said, his expression unreadable. "By the way, I saw the duke de Morieux at a cockfight recently. He accosted me and asked me to give my regards to your bride."

Alex's brows snapped together. "That damned insolent cur."

"I thought it rather odd," said Preston. "He seemed deliberately provocative."

Lord Thurlow frowned. "You think he means to cause trouble after all this time?"

"I don't know." Preston dabbed with his napkin at a spot of food on his coat. "He doesn't bother Petronella. But then, we don't get into town very often. When we do, she avoids him like the very devil. She trembles like blancmange whenever he comes within ten feet of her." He laid down his napkin and looked at Alex. "I didn't like the way he sneered when he mentioned Miranda."

Alex's hand tightened on his glass. "He'd better stay away from her," he said quietly. "Or this time I *will* kill him."

"I would think the gentlemen would have joined us by now," Lady Thurlow said, looking up from her embroidery hoop to frown at the door of the sitting room. "I wonder what can be keeping them."

Miranda bent her head over her beadwork. "I have no idea," she murmured. She wasn't very proficient at beadwork, but she hadn't wanted to sit idly when Lady Thurlow was so industrious.

"Alex and Papa always have much to talk about." Petronella examined a loose thread on the sleeve of her red dress. "Mama, may I borrow your scissors?"

Lady Thurlow's frown deepened as she handed Petronella the scissors. "Alex is often remiss in his duty. I don't know how many times I have had to call him to task for it. It is to be hoped that marriage will have an improving effect on him." She stared pointedly at Miranda as if expecting some sort of response.

Miranda, struggling to keep her spine as ramrod straight as her mother-in-law's, smiled weakly.

"He reminds me of my brother," the older woman continued when it became evident that Miranda was not going to reply. "Geoffrey had the same care-for-nothing attitude. He always behaved outrageously, never caring for a moment that he caused Mama enormous worry. Not that Mama ever reprimanded him for showing off. She positively doted on Geoffrey—"

The door opened and Miranda looked around eagerly.

It was Bomford with the tea tray.

Miranda heaved a silent sigh. "Would you care for tea, Lady Thurlow?"

The countess blinked, then nodded, putting aside her embroidery hoop. She waited until Miranda was pouring the tea before she asked, "So, how does marriage to my son suit you?"

Miranda barely managed to keep her hand steady. She handed over the saucer and cup before replying. "It suits me very well. Alex is . . . a fine gentleman."

"Hmmph. Better less the gentleman and more the man. It is his duty to ensure the succession."

Miranda felt the heat creeping up into her cheeks again. She was relieved when Lady Thurlow turned to Petronella.

"How are you feeling, my dear?"

"Not too bad," Petronella answered. "Although my breasts are very sore."

Miranda's cup rattled on its saucer.

Lady Thurlow cast a reproving glance at her before turning back to Petronella. "Have you been ill?"

"Every day, of course. Right from the very first day. I knew immediately that I was breeding. Every morning I wake up and I have to rush to the chamber pot. I'm usually fine then, although some days are worse than others. It was the same when I was increasing with Edward," Petronella explained to Miranda. "Of course, this means I will have to be very circumspect during the Season. No dancing until dawn. And it would be very foolish to buy any new clothes." She sighed heavily, fingering her red woollen skirt, then brightened. "It will be fun anyway. It's been years since I was in London."

"Are you and Alex coming to London for the Season?" Lady Thurlow asked Miranda.

"We haven't discussed it, but I don't think so. Alex is very busy with the estate."

"You should insist, my dear. Alex needs to introduce you to the *ton*. Everyone will be very curious."

"I shall mention it to him," Miranda murmured.

"You can stay with us at Thurlow House," the older woman said, setting down her teacup. "We have plenty of room."

"Er, thank you, Lady Thurlow."

"I will be able to guide you and give you some hints on how to conduct yourself. Town manners are very different from country ones, as you will discover."

Miranda forced a smile.

"Although your manners are pretty enough, I must say. You will make a fine countess someday."

"I'm sure that won't be for a long time." Miranda glanced longingly toward the door. Where *were* the gentlemen?

"I hope you realize that there is a great deal of responsibility involved. A position to uphold." Lady Thurlow picked up her embroidery hoop again. "Of course, I will be able to help you with that, also."

For the next half hour, Lady Thurlow pointed her needle at Miranda and lectured her on some of the duties that would be required of her. She also shared with Miranda a few secrets for improving the efficiency of her household. Miranda listened frozenly. The countess then instructed her on which duties should be assigned to which servants. Miranda struggled to maintain an air of interest.

After some time, and several homilies, it became clear that the men were not going to join them. Lady Thurlow went to bed in something of a huff. Miranda and Petronella followed shortly after.

"Don't mind Mama," Petronella whispered as they walked up the stairs. "She's always like that."

12

The next morning, Miranda was about to enter the dining room when she heard voices inside. She paused, her hand on the doorknob.

"Alex, you must ensure the succession. An accident could carry you off at any time, just as it did Thomas. Then what? Cousin Dunston will inherit. Would that please you?"

"No, Mother. Don't worry, I have no intention of allowing that to happen."

"Well, then . . ."

"Then, what? For God's sake, we've been married barely three weeks. Even if she were with child, she wouldn't know it yet."

"She most certainly would. I've had four children, and with all of them I knew at once. It's impossible for you, a man, to understand, but a woman knows these things immediately."

"Mother, this is beside the point."

"The point is you must have an heir."

"The point is I will thank you not to interfere."

"Very well, Alex. I won't argue any further, for I can see you are determined to be stubborn. I will only say once more that it is your duty—"

"What exactly do you want me to do? Spend the day with Miranda in her bedchamber?"

"Alexander! How—"

"Good morning, Miranda."

The cheerful greeting made Miranda jump and whirl around. The earl stood behind her, a twinkle in his bright blue eyes.

Her cheeks, already warm from the conversation she'd overheard, grew hotter. "Oh, good morning, Lord Thurlow. I . . . I was just about to go in for breakfast."

"Let me join you, then." With a genial smile, he opened the door for her. Lady Thurlow and Alex, both looking tense, their plates of food untouched, glanced up.

"Are you ready, my dear?" the earl asked his wife. "We need to leave soon if we're to be in London by nightfall. Where are Preston and Petronella and Edward?"

"They're not down yet." The countess rose to her feet. "I hope there isn't a problem."

Please don't let there be a problem, Miranda prayed.

There was a problem.

"Petronella is very ill," Preston said, entering the dining room. "She cannot possibly travel today."

"Perhaps we should delay our departure for another day or two," Lady Thurlow said.

Miranda swallowed. "You're welcome to stay."

"My dear, why don't we go on ahead," the earl said. "We will make sure the house is opened and running properly. Preston and Petronella will have to travel very slowly, since Edward is with them." Then in a plainly audible whisper, he added, "Remember that last time we traveled with Edward? It took weeks to air out the carriage."

Lady Thurlow's beaklike nose quivered. Turning to Miranda, she said, "My dear, our housekeeper is terribly forgetful sometimes. I really must go on ahead and make sure that the linens are properly aired."

"I understand," Miranda said with perfect truth.

The earl and countess were ready to leave within half an hour. On the portico, Lady Thurlow gave Miranda a book. "This is a little present for you, my dear. I am sure you will find it useful."

Miranda looked down at the title. *The Female Instructor—A Domestic Guide.*

"Thank you, Lady Thurlow," Miranda murmured.

The countess turned to Alex. "I hope you will remember what we discussed this morning."

"Certainly I will," he said blandly and kissed her cheek. "Good-bye, Mother. Good-bye, Father."

Miranda and Alex watched the carriage drive away, the wheels kicking up flecks of mud, until it disappeared into the trees.

The tension eased out of Miranda's shoulders.

Alex heaved a theatrical sigh of relief. "Now if we can just get rid of Petronella and Preston . . ."

Miranda couldn't help laughing. "Alex!" she scolded, not very convincingly. "They *are* your family."

"Yes, and wouldn't you think they could be a little more tactful? We *have* been married only a short time." He smiled down at her in a way that made her heart flutter. "Preston and I are going to look at the south field this morning, but we will be back for luncheon. Perhaps you and I could find a secluded spot in the garden for an hour or two." He traced her jaw with one long finger. "Would you like that?"

Staring up at him, she nodded mutely.

He went off to find Preston, and Miranda walked slowly back inside. In the hall, she realized she was still clutching the book the countess had given her. Shaking herself briskly, she marched into the library and put it on the shelf, then went upstairs to check on Petronella.

"Come in," a faint voice called when she knocked at the door.

Alex's sister lay in bed, pale and hollow-eyed, her inky black hair spread out around her. A rush of sympathy filled Miranda. "Poor Petronella. Are you feeling very ill?"

"It's nothing really," the other woman said bravely. "It's something we women must endure. This is the most ill I've felt. I truly don't think I can get out of bed today." Placing a languid hand to her forehead, she drooped artistically. "Which is why I wondered if you might do something for me." Her blue eyes were bright as she looked over the edge of the covers.

"Of course," Miranda said automatically.

"You're so kind." Petronella beamed, sitting up in the bed. She was wearing a beautiful green satin robe, trimmed with row upon row of lace. "I wouldn't ask it of you if Preston had not ridden out with Alex. But we are leaving tomorrow, and I did promise Nurse the afternoon off— although what the wretched woman will do, I have no idea—and I did promise to do something special with Edward."

A deep foreboding filled Miranda. "What do you want me to do?"

"Just entertain Edward for an hour or two," Petronella replied. "Perhaps take him for a walk or something."

Or something. What on earth did one do with a four-year-old? Weakly, Miranda assented.

"Oh, thank you, Miranda!" Petronella reached over and picked up an open book that had been lying facedown on the table beside her bed. Miranda noticed a large box of chocolates resting there also. "Mrs. Driscoll should be able to tell you where he is."

Perhaps she wouldn't be able to find him, Miranda thought hopefully as she sought out the housekeeper.

She found the older woman in an upstairs bedchamber, supervising the maid cleaning the room.

"Mrs. Driscoll, have you seen Edward?"

"In the garden, my lady," Mrs. Driscoll said without hesitation.

Sure enough, Edward was there, scuffing his shoes in the dirt.

"Hello, Edward," Miranda said tentatively.

He looked up eagerly. When he saw her, his face fell. "Oh, it's you." Breaking a branch off of a bush, he crouched down and scratched the dirt with it.

Miranda gazed at him helplessly. "Your mama is ill and she asked me to look after you."

Edward's lip curled with youthful skepticism. He continued to poke the ground with the stick.

"Would you like to go for a walk? Or play a game?" she asked in a falsely bright tone.

The stick stopped its motion. "Will you play Jonah an' the whale with me?"

"Jonah and the whale?" Miranda looked at him suspiciously. "How do we play that?"

"I'm Jonah, an' I hide. You're the whale, an' you try to catch me."

Visions of looking for a small boy all morning floated through her brain. She broke a twig off the bush and tried to think of some alternative. "How do you know about Jonah?" she asked, stalling for time.

"My nurse tol' me 'bout him. She said I'm a reg'lar Jonah when it comes to causing ca-cat'rophes." His small face beamed with angelic pride. "She tol' me all 'bout him an' the whale."

"Do you know what a whale is?"

"It's a big fish. Like the ones me an' Uncle Alex catched."

An idea occurred to Miranda. "Do you like to go fishing?"

"Yes, we catches the biggest fish all the time," Edward boasted. "Uncle Alex says I will make a fine angler one day."

She didn't know anything about fishing. Speculatively, she eyed Edward. "Do you know how to fish?"

"Oh, yes. I know everything 'bout it."

"Then how would you like to go fishing with me?"

Edward leaped almost a foot in the air. "Do you mean it, Aunt Miranda?"

"Yes. What do we need?"

"Poles an' hooks an' worms."

"Worms? How revolting. I suppose Bomford can find some for us."

"Uncle Alex says dew-worms are the bestest for catching trout."

"I'm afraid the fish will just have to take whatever we have. Now come along, I need to change my dress."

With Edward jumping excitedly by her side, Miranda entered the house, praying that she was not making a mistake.

"Bomford," she called out, espying the butler trimming candlewicks. "We need two fishing poles."

Bomford straightened slowly and turned to face his mistress. This week's lesson with Lady Briarwood's butler had covered the importance of maintaining an impassive expression no matter what the provocation. Bomford had been practicing, and he barely flickered an eyelash at this request. "At once, my lady."

"Oh, and Bomford . . ."

"Yes, my lady?"

"Could you dig up some worms from the garden for us also?"

Miranda ran lightly up the stairs, fortunately not seeing poor Bomford's carefully blank expression give way to a most inelegant gape.

* * *

Upon returning to the house a few hours later, Preston went upstairs to look in on Petronella, while Alex went in search of Miranda.

She was nowhere to be found.

"Have you seen Lady Huntsley?" Alex asked Bomford, who was cleaning lamps in the hall.

"She is out, my lord."

Alex frowned. "Out where?"

Bomford pressed his elbows tightly to his sides. "Fishing, my lord. With Master Edward."

"Fishing? Thank you, Bomford." Surprised and curious, Alex walked back outside and headed for the river.

He had not realized Miranda was interested in fishing, he thought as he walked down the drive. If he had known, he would have taken her himself. It would be very pleasant to go fishing with her. There was a secluded glen he had discovered that might make a good fishing spot, although he hadn't had a chance to try it out yet.

He would have to show it to her, Alex decided, taking a shortcut through the pear orchard. The glen was very pretty and very private. They would be completely alone, free from the interruptions of servants and visitors. He would have Mrs. Rouse pack a picnic basket. And he would bring a blanket.

An image of Miranda lying back on a blanket in the secluded glen entered his brain. He imagined her hair loosened and her skirts hiked up to reveal her ankles. She would smile up at him, and he would bend over and kiss her. Not just a peck on the lips, but a real kiss, with his tongue exploring every hidden corner of her tantalizing mouth and his hands caressing every one of her luscious curves. And this time she wouldn't pull away. She'd be as eager for him as he was for her.

Caught up in his fantasy, Alex arrived at the river almost before he realized it. As he approached, he could hear Miranda and Edward talking. His steps slowed.

"Edward, wouldn't you like to put the worm on the hook?"

Miranda's pleading voice floated through the bushes. Alex moved silently forward and bent some branches to get a clear view of the pair.

Miranda was covered with mud. It was splattered all over her blue dress, caked on her shoes, and smeared on her hands. The hem of her dress was torn and soaking wet, and her hair straggled down her back. On her face was an expression of total and complete frustration.

Alex's lips twitched.

"No, Aunt Miranda." Edward clasped his hands behind his back, his eyes wide and virtuous. "Uncle Alex doesn't allow me to do that. He says I might stick myself."

Why, the precocious little liar! Alex laughed silently to himself as he waited to hear Miranda's response.

"We have to put the worm on the hook, Edward. We've been trying for an hour without it, and we haven't had a single bite." She wiped a hand across her forehead, leaving a long smear of mud.

"You do it," Edward urged. He was similarly wet and filthy, but unlike Miranda, he appeared to be enjoying himself.

Alex watched as disgust, resignation, and then determination crossed her face. She reached into the jar, pulled out a long wriggling worm, and gingerly tried to stick it onto the hook.

"Uncle Alex says you should put the hook in at the tail and the point should come out near the head."

Miranda ignored this advice. She finally managed to push the worm onto the hook and, with a look of triumph, dropped the line into the water.

"You're supposed to cast the line out to the middle an' sink it to the bottom. Uncle Alex says that's where the fish are."

"Uncle Alex, Uncle Alex," Alex heard her mutter. Then more loudly, "I tried that once, and the hook caught in the tree, remember? I don't want to have to climb any more trees, or wrestle with any more bushes. Besides, I have my own theory as to where the fish are."

Her confidence was not rewarded, for her line remained limp.

Edward peered over the bank into the water.

"Be careful, Edward! I am fishing for fish. I don't want to have to fish for little boys."

"There's lots of trout," he commented, before moving back a safe distance.

"There are? Then why haven't we caught one?" Miranda fretted.

"Uncle Alex says trouts shouldn't be catched in winter-time."

She stared at the boy for a moment. "For heaven's sake, why not?"

"Uncle Alex says that in winter, the trout are thin and have big heads and have sugs."

"What are sugs?"

"Trout lice."

"Trout lice!" She looked horrified.

"Yes. Uncle Alex says they suck the moisture from the fish."

Miranda appeared bereft of speech. Finally, in a weak voice, she said, "I don't want to hear any more of what Uncle Alex says. I just want to catch a fish."

Suddenly, the line went taut.

Miranda squealed. "I have one!"

Edward danced excitedly while she reeled in her prize. Alex craned his neck to see.

A fish—a three-inch chub—lay flopping on the bank.

Miranda and Edward stared at the fish, then at each other, then back at the fish.

"Better throw it back, Aunt Miranda. That's what me an' Uncle Alex do." The innocent voice piped out clearly. "Then he tells Mama and Papa 'bout the big one that got away."

Trying to stifle his laughter, Alex stepped out of the bushes. "Don't give away all my secrets, nephew," he said sternly.

Miranda and Edward spun around.

"Uncle Alex! Uncle Alex!" Edward ran forward and threw himself into his arms. Laughing, Alex swung him high.

When he put Edward down, he saw Miranda watching them uncertainly. He flashed a smile at her.

The uncertainty faded and she smiled back, her face glowing in spite of the mud.

Alex's breath caught and he stared at her for a moment before an insistent tugging on his coat recalled his attention. He looked down at Edward.

"Uncle Alex, we caught a fish!"

"Yes, so I see." He crouched down to inspect the chub.

Miranda, still smiling, said, "What do you recommend, Alex? Shall we throw it back?"

"Definitely," he answered. Straightening, he took off his coat. "And then I'll show you how to catch a *real* fish."

Dinner was a very merry occasion that evening. Edward was permitted to join them at the table, and Alex kept everyone in a state of uproarious laughter with his tales of the fishing expedition. Miranda, although she laughed along with Preston and Petronella, did not say much. She was watching Alex, half-mesmerized.

She had never seen him so relaxed. With a lock of black

hair falling onto his forehead and his blue eyes bright with laughter, he was extraordinarily attractive. She had never been so . . . conscious of him.

She had also never enjoyed herself so much as she had that afternoon. Alex had proved to be an excellent teacher. She had been a little uneasy at first, when he stood so close behind her, his arms encircling her as his hands grasped the rod over hers. She had held herself stiffly until she felt the first tug on the line. Then she'd forgotten her discomfort in the excitement of catching her first *real* fish. After that, she'd barely noticed his warm breath on the back of her neck as he gave directions, or his hands bracing her hips against his so she could reel in the fish, or the heat of him when he pulled her back against the length of his body to prevent her from falling into the river.

Now, for some reason, her insides were behaving in a very peculiar manner. The sound of Alex's voice made her quiver like jelly. His laughter made her blood race like the swift current of the river. And every once in a while, when he looked at her and smiled in a certain way, a glowing warmth spread through her.

The warmth stayed with her the entire evening. That night, when she went to sleep, she dreamed that Alex was kissing her, his tongue touching her lips, but this time it wasn't disgusting at all.

She was awakened from her pleasant dream by a pitiful wailing. It took her a few moments to identify the noise as a child's crying. Realizing it must be Edward, she lit a candle and stumbled out into the hall at the same time as her sister-in-law.

"Oh, I'm sorry, Miranda. Edward is afraid of the dark and sometimes he wakes up at night. That silly nurse hasn't the least notion of how to calm him. I really must find someone else." She hurried into Edward's room.

The crying stopped abruptly, and Miranda turned, ready

to go back to bed, when she caught sight of a tall figure at the end of the corridor. She raised her candle so she could see better.

It was Alex. Apparently he had also been awakened. His face was in the shadow, but he stood very still, and she sensed that he was staring at her.

She was suddenly conscious of her appearance. Her plain cotton nightgown covered her from neck to ankle, but she was aware of her bare feet peeping out and her unbound hair flowing down her back. Images from her dream flashed through her mind and for a moment she couldn't move. Then, murmuring a quick good night, she slipped back into her room.

Inside, she stood beside the door, listening.

Everything was quiet.

She climbed into bed and lay down. A long time passed before her heart slowed enough for her to fall asleep.

13

The next day, Petronella was sufficiently recovered to depart. With hugs and waves, the Bayards said farewell. Alex, watching the carriage drive away, was glad to see them go.

He was eager to be alone with Miranda again.

Casually, he stepped closer and put his arm around her shoulders. She stiffened and glanced quickly up at him, but he pretended to be absorbed in waving after the departing carriage.

To his intense satisfaction, she relaxed and continued waving.

He studied her from the corner of his eye, noticing the pale shadows under her eyes. He wondered if she'd had as much difficulty getting back to sleep as he had last night after being awakened by Edward's cries.

An image flashed into his mind of how she'd looked, standing in her bedroom doorway, her candle casting a soft glow over her. Her eyes heavy with sleep and her hair tumbled, she had looked incredibly warm and inviting. He'd wanted to go to her and lead her back into her bedroom and make love to her.

She must have sensed something of what he was feeling, because she had looked as nervous as a young doe and slipped quickly back into her room. He had taken several steps toward her door before coming to his senses and returning to his own bed.

Miranda stopped waving and glanced up at him, a smile on her sweet lips and in her gold-flecked eyes as she said something.

Tonight, he promised himself. Tonight—

"Alex?"

He brought his wayward thoughts under control. "I beg your pardon, Miranda. What did you say?"

"I said I will miss them."

He arched a brow in mock disbelief. "Even Edward?"

She laughed. "He was rather unruly, wasn't he? _My_ children won't behave like that."

"All children are like that to some degree."

She looked dismayed. "Surely not!"

Hiding his smile, Alex nodded solemnly.

"Well," she said bravely, "I still want children anyway."

He slipped his arm down around the curve of her waist. "I'm glad to hear that."

She glanced at him quickly, and a faint blush rose in her cheeks.

His arm tightened on her waist. "Miranda—"

"Ahem."

Alex turned to see Bomford standing in the doorway, his gaze fixed on a point somewhere on the horizon. "My lord," the butler said. "Mr. Vernon, the new steward, has arrived. He is waiting for you in the library."

Alex swore silently. "Ask him to meet me in the stables. And have the groom saddle two horses."

Bomford bowed and hurried away.

Alex turned back to Miranda, a rueful smile on his lips. "Duty calls."

She nodded, her eyes downcast.

He tilted her chin up and pressed a swift, hard kiss against her lips. "I will be home early," he whispered. He released her and strode off toward the stables.

Miranda stood rooted to the spot, staring after him, until he turned the corner of the house and disappeared from sight.

"You wanted to inventory the pantry this morning, my lady?" the housekeeper inquired.

"Oh, yes," Miranda said.

She followed the older woman down to the pantry and sat down on a chair with a writing desk on her lap. As Mrs. Driscoll counted the china and silver, Miranda dutifully made a note of each item, but her mind was not on the task. She couldn't stop thinking about Alex. . . .

"Seven Worcester dinner plates, eight bowls, and a cracked tureen," Mrs. Driscoll called out.

She had been startled when he'd put his arm around her shoulders, outside where everyone could see them. But she had liked it. And she had liked the light touch of his hands at her waist. She had felt warm and tingly and had wanted him to kiss her, the way he had in the library. . . .

"A green and gold tea service for twelve, no creamer."

Strangely, the idea of his tongue touching her lips was no longer quite so disgusting. She really wouldn't mind if he did it again. In fact, she was rather curious to know how it would feel now that she knew what to expect. Had he liked touching her mouth with his tongue?

"Two silver trays, two silver serving dishes without lids, and a silver brandy saucepan."

When she saw him in the corridor last night, she had almost hoped that he would follow her into her room and kiss her like that again. She had felt strangely breathless as she imagined his tongue tracing her lips. Her blood had pulsed with a restless yearning. She'd wanted to be close to him. To let him touch her breasts. . . .

"Four silver candelabra, a scrolled silver tankard . . . my lady, is something wrong? You are very flushed."

Miranda tried to control her wayward thoughts. "It's just a trifle warm in here. Look, Mrs. Driscoll, isn't that tankard very tarnished?"

A worried frown appeared on Mrs. Driscoll's plump face as she inspected the tankard. "Yes, it is, my lady. Mr. Bomford has some plate powder, but it doesn't seem very effective. I do wish we had another recipe."

Miranda remembered the book Lady Thurlow had given her—*The Female Instructor—A Domestic Guide.* Seizing upon an excuse to escape the uncomfortably warm pantry, she said, "I have a book that might have one. I will go and look right now, and we can finish up here tomorrow."

"Yes, my lady,"

Fanning her cheeks with her hand, Miranda went upstairs to the library and pulled the book off the shelf. Sitting down at the desk, she opened the volume and scanned the table of contents. She was about to turn to the section called *Useful Recipes,* when another chapter caught her eye. She flipped through the pages till she found what she was looking for.

Marital Duties of the New Wife.

She started reading the first paragraph:

It is the duty of a new wife—and indeed all wives—to be a tower—no, a steeple—of corporeal and spiritual strength. She must consider always how her actions reflect upon herself and her husband and apply herself to becoming the cheerful yet dignified,

*generous yet firm, kind yet strict mistress of the
household over which she has dominion. She must
remember always that others are looking to her to set
an example, and she must set a standard of industrious, good-natured piety that will be an inspiration to
friend and dependent alike and make her the object of
her husband's profoundest respect and admiration—*

The paragraph, full of exhortations to behave in a modest and pious manner, went on for another three pages.
Miranda skimmed the rest of the chapter, hoping to discover something of a more intimate and explicit nature, but
found only more of the same. Disappointed, she turned to
the *Useful Recipes* section just as Bomford entered with a
salver in his hand.

"Two letters just arrived, my lady."

Miranda put down the book and took the letters. "Thank
you, Bomford."

With a perfectly executed bow, he retreated from the
room.

Miranda looked at the first letter. Recognizing Sara
Rowan's handwriting, she eagerly tore it open.

Dear Miranda—

*I am in heaven! Aunt Gerta and I arrived in
London last week and it is simply divine! She seems
greatly invigorated by the town air (she's only had
three heart palpitations since we arrived) and so far
we have attended four balls, two routs, and a
Venetian breakfast!*

Sara went on for a full page describing the delights of the
London Season, including a detailed description of all the
men who had taken her driving, danced with her, and sent
her bouquets. She finished the letter with:

*There is only one thing that could make London
better, and that is if you were here. Oh, Miranda, do
you think there is any chance that Lord Huntsley
might bring you to London? Think of the fun we
could have! Will you please ask him?*

> *I remain your true friend,*
> *Sara Rowan*

Miranda smiled a little at her friend's enthusiasm. London
sounded very appealing. But curiously, she felt no great desire
to go. She was very happy here at Ribblebank Manor with Alex.

She laid the letter aside and picked up the other one. The
handwriting was unfamiliar this time. She opened it and
glanced at the bottom, gasping when she saw the signature.

The letter was from Mr. Pelham.

Biting her lip, she began to read:

My Dear Lady Huntsley—

*I hope you will forgive my temerity in writing to
you, but after all we have meant to each other I feel it
is my duty to tell you that I am leaving England.*

*By the time you receive this letter, I will be on my
way to America where I intend to devote the rest of
my life to bringing God's Word to the Savages of
Boston, Massachusetts.*

*I pray that time will mend my Broken Heart.
Perhaps one day, God willing, I will find a woman
with whom I can share a love like yours and mine—a
pure and holy love.*

*I hope that you, too, will try to forget me, and
make a new life for yourself with your husband.
Although I beg of you—do not allow his Carnal Lust
to corrupt your sweet purity.*

> *With warmest regards,*
> *J. Pelham*

As she finished the letter, her face grew warm again. Carnal lust. Dear heaven, was *that* what she was experiencing? Oh, surely not. Men were the only ones who had such feelings.

Weren't they?

There was another knock at the door. Feeling absurdly guilty, she hastily stuffed the two letters inside *The Female Instructor* and called out, "Come in."

Mrs. Rouse entered, a basket resting on her bony hip. "Here's the vegetables you was wanting to take to the new tenant, your ladyship."

"Oh, yes, thank you, Mrs. Rouse. I almost forgot. I had better hurry if I want to return in time for dinner." Miranda stood up, still holding *The Female Instructor.* She put it on the corner of the desk and hastened up to her room for her cloak.

A few minutes later, she set out, the basket on her arm.

The day was mild and balmy and the scent of freshly-turned earth was in the air. A pleasantly cool breeze tickled her face as she walked through a field. She breathed deeply. Perhaps the fresh air would help her think. She hoped so, because she definitely needed to think.

She was very confused. She had wanted her marriage to be like that of her parents'—comfortable and pleasant. And for the last few weeks, it very nearly had been. Except for his parents' visit, everything had been wonderful. But now she was afraid she was headed in a dangerous direction. The emotions she was feeling were anything but comfortable and pleasant.

Well, perhaps they were a little bit pleasant. She could not call Alex's kiss unpleasant. . . .

She climbed over a newly-built stile at the edge of the field and turned down a road laid with fresh gravel. Her boots crunched and kicked up tiny rocks as she tried to analyze her feelings. She had a terrible suspicion that they *were* carnal lust. Why else would she dream of him kissing her in that shocking manner? Why else would the sight of him in the corridor last night make her blush all over? Why else would she feel such a quivering, such a yearning, such an ache deep inside of her?

Her cheeks felt on fire. She turned her face up to the cool breeze, trying to control her unseemly thoughts. Switching the basket to her other arm, she turned down a "hollow" lane where the tree branches met overhead to form a leafy green tunnel. What was it about Alex that made her feel this way? She had never wanted Mr. Pelham to kiss her.

Guilt rose in her. While Mr. Pelham had been preparing to set off for the Wilderness to perform good deeds, nobly nursing a broken heart as he thought of their pure and holy love, she had been succumbing to the temptations of carnal lust.

As she turned onto a rutted lane leading to the new tenants' cottage, she wondered how she could be so shallow. She wished she could talk to Mr. Pelham. He would be able to advise her—he knew so much about carnal lust. It was the subject of one of his favorite sermons. She tried to remember that sermon now.

Silently, she began to recite what she recalled.

She was about halfway through when she arrived at the wattle-and-daub cottage where Mr. and Mrs. Hopp lived. She caught sight of a stout woman in the side garden, turning up the soil between rows of bright blue crocuses.

"Good morning," Miranda called.

The woman glanced up. Seeing Miranda, she heaved herself up and came forward, hastily wiping her hands on her apron. When Miranda introduced herself, Mrs. Hopp's rosy cheeks puffed out.

"This is an honor, your ladyship! Please come in."

Miranda followed her inside and sat down at a well-scrubbed pine table while Mrs. Hopp washed her hands in a basin of water and removed her apron. "Please forgive my appearance, your ladyship. Would you like a cup of ale?"

Miranda smiled. "Only if you will join me, Mrs. Hopp."

The woman poured two cups and sat down, her back very straight and her hands folded in her lap.

"Are you and your husband happy here?" Miranda asked, hoping to set her at ease.

Mrs. Hopp replied in the affirmative. Miranda continued to ply her with questions, and soon the woman was chattering away about her garden, her three sons who were killed in the war, and her husband's injury. Then she went on to tell Miranda how wonderful "his lordship" was.

"Your husband is a fine man, my lady, a fine man! He was most reasonable on the terms for the cottage and insisted on putting on a new roof before we moved in. My Tom sings his praises every night. His lordship is a fine-looking man, too. I'll wager he's a pleasure to bed with—"

Mrs. Hopp seemed to suddenly recollect to whom she was speaking. Flushing, she said, "Eh, I beg your pardon, my lady. My tongue is running away with me. 'Tis one of my worst faults, so my Tom tells me."

"Think nothing of it, Mrs. Hopp," Miranda said, trying to control her own embarrassment.

Mrs. Hopp smiled shyly. "I'd be most honored if you'd try my rabbit pie. It's famous in Abingdon—that's where we used to live—and I plan to enter one in the fair here."

"That sounds wonderful," Miranda said politely, even though she wasn't really hungry.

Mrs. Hopp bustled over to the pantry and cut a thick slice from a crusty, golden pie. She put it on a plate and placed it on the table, watching closely as Miranda took a bite.

It tasted odd. Not wanting to disappoint the kind woman, Miranda smiled and pronounced the pie "delicious."

Mrs. Hopp beamed. Miranda took a large swig of ale and forced herself to eat every last bit of the pie.

When she finally finished, she said good-bye to Mrs. Hopp and set off down the lane.

As she walked, she recited the second half of Mr. Pelham's sermon to herself.

At dinner that night, she was tense and nervous. Between her confused thoughts and the unpleasant taste in her mouth from Mrs. Hopp's rabbit pie, Miranda didn't have much of an appetite. She was glad when the meal was over.

Her tension increased, however, as Alex followed her to the library. She stopped in the middle of the room, her heart suddenly pounding and her palms growing damp.

"Would you like me to read to you?" she asked, hurrying over to the bookshelf and pretending to survey the titles.

He didn't respond, and she glanced over her shoulder. He was watching her, an unreadable expression on his face.

When he saw her looking at him, his eyelids drooped and he shook his head. "No, I don't think so. I'm so tired, I might fall asleep." With a yawn, he sat on the blue velvet sofa, leaned back, and closed his eyes.

Miranda, her heart rate slowing, stared at his inanimate figure. "What do you think of the new steward?" she asked.

Alex opened one eye and squinted at her. "He's a godsend." He allowed his heavy eyelid to shut again.

Looking at him sprawled on the sofa, Miranda grew irritated. She'd been thinking about him all day and now he was ignoring her. He couldn't even keep his eyes open!

"I visited Mrs. Hopp today," she said.

He grunted.

"She seems very nice. She gave me some rabbit pie."

There was no answer from her husband.

"I received a letter from Sara. She is having a splendid time in London."

Still no reply.

Stifling her vexation, Miranda said sweetly, "Perhaps I should ring for some tea."

"Hm? What?"

"For some tea! Alex, will you please open your eyes and listen to me?"

His eyes remained stubbornly closed. "I really don't want any tea, my dear. But I would like a glass of that brandy on the desk."

Miranda glanced over and saw a glass and a decanter on the desk's surface. A bit impatiently, she crossed the room, filled the glass, and moved in front of Alex. "Here you are."

His eyes opened and he smiled up at her. He took the glass in one hand. With the other, he reached up and tugged her down beside him.

She plopped onto the sofa. Startled, she looked at him and found his mouth very close to hers. Suddenly, her heart was racing again. "Aren't you going to drink your brandy?" she said weakly.

"Only if you will join me," he said.

She looked doubtfully at his glass. "Brandy?"

"You're a married woman, Miranda. You may drink brandy now."

"Oh. Well, yes, I suppose so. I will find another glass."

She tried to rise, but his arm snaked around her waist and held her in place. "That's not necessary. We can share this glass." He held the rim up to her lips. "Drink, Miranda."

"I don't know, Alex."

He tilted the glass and she had to swallow or the brandy would have spilled. She gasped a little at the strong, unaccustomed flavor.

"Drink some more," he urged.

She raised her hand to the glass, her fingers brushing against his. "I can hold it myself, Alex. I'm not a child."

"No, you're not," he said, releasing the glass. He watched her sip cautiously at the liquid and lick her lips.

His gaze fell to her lips.

A second later his mouth covered hers. Clutching the glass of brandy tightly in her hands, she closed her eyes.

He smelled of earth and wind and fresh air. She inhaled deeply, the scent making her head spin even more than the brandy had.

She thought he must hear the pounding of her heart, must feel the heat of the hectic flush spreading over her skin. But she felt no disgust, only the strange tickling sensation she had noticed before.

His tongue traced her lips again, more insistently this time, as if he wanted something. Again, he traced her lips, making them tingle and soften. And again, making them part.

When his tongue slipped inside her mouth she gasped, but he absorbed the sound. She tried to draw back, but he pressed closer, deepening the kiss, his tongue searching out every corner of her mouth.

His fingers began a slow, circular caress at her waist, then inched up her spine to the bare skin above the neckline of her dress. They lingered there a moment, moving in delicate patterns over her exposed skin, before moving up into her hair and tugging at her pins until her long tresses cascaded down around her shoulders.

Her back, from the base of her spine up to her scalp, tingled and pulsed and glowed.

He continued to kiss her, his mouth and tongue causing a hot rushing in her blood and a slow melting deep down in her stomach. She pressed closer and the slightly rough wool of his coat rasped gently against her skin above her low-cut dress, and his buttons pressed against the soft flesh of her breasts.

His fingers traveled back down to her waist then up her side until they were just below the curve of her breast. Her heart pounded with heavy, almost painful, beats.

He pulled his mouth away from hers and trailed sweet kisses down her jaw, to her chin, and then to her neck. His fingers moved up and brushed the neckline of her dress. Her breasts felt odd. They felt heavy, ripe, full.

The heat inside her increased. She began to tremble.

His hand slipped inside her bodice and cupped her bare breast, his thumb moving up to caress the peak.

The earth stopped in its orbit and an explosion of pleasure raced through her. She moaned.

His thumb brushed her nipple again and the earth began to spin wildly on its axis, and she was in the grip of a vertigo so sweet and so turbulent, she never wanted it to stop—

"Miranda," he whispered hoarsely against her mouth, "I want you. I want—What the bloody hell!"

Alex leaped to his feet. Miranda looked up at him dazedly, completely disoriented. Slowly, painfully, her brain began to function, and she saw he was glaring down at a wet stain spreading across his lap. His gaze rose to her hand, and she realized that she was still clutching the brandy glass—and that she had inadvertently tipped its contents into Alex's lap.

Her stomach lurched unpleasantly. Dropping the glass, she sprang to her feet also, her hand flying to her mouth. She stared at him with wide eyes.

"Alex! I'm so sorry!"

For a moment they both stood frozen. Then his mouth curved sensually. His eyelids drooped heavily. He held out his hand, his gaze dark and compelling. . . .

Her stomach lurched again. Nausea rose in her throat. Pressing her hand against her mouth, she bolted.

14

She was sick. Vilely sick.

Her face hot and sweaty, Miranda lifted her head from the chamber pot and rested her cheek on the edge of the bed. Her throat hurt, her stomach was still churning, and she felt utterly wretched.

She was vaguely aware that she'd made a fool of herself by running away from Alex, but she was too miserable to care.

She crawled back into bed and laid her weary head on the pillow. Her eyelids drooped shut. If she could just sleep, she was sure she would feel better.

A half hour later, she was bending over the chamber pot again.

She vomited intermittently all through the night. Within a few hours there was nothing left in her stomach, but the dry heaves continued.

Her maid hovered anxiously, wiping her brow and doing what she could to make Miranda more comfortable. But there wasn't much the maid *could* do. Miranda thought she was dying.

It wasn't until dawn that she finally fell asleep.

She woke several hours later. She lay there a moment, waiting for her stomach to start heaving, but it remained still. Cautiously, she sat up. Still nothing. The nausea was gone.

Relief flooded her. That emotion faded quickly, however, when she remembered what had happened last night.

Alex had kissed her and touched her breasts and it had been so wonderful that she hadn't wanted him to stop.

So what had she done?

She had spilled brandy in his lap—and gotten sick!

Burying her face in her hands, she groaned. What must he think of her?

She rang for Alice. She had to get up. She had to talk to Alex. She had to apologize.

The maid entered with a tray of tea and dry biscuits. "Feeling better, my lady?"

"Yes, thank you, Alice," Miranda said, drinking her tea thirstily and nibbling at a biscuit. "I want to get up."

The maid frowned disapprovingly. "You should stay in bed."

"Nonsense." Miranda forced herself to eat some more of the biscuit. "I am fully recovered."

To prove her statement, she swung her legs over the edge of the bed and stood up. She immediately swayed and had to clutch the bedpost to steady herself.

"Hmmph," Alice snorted. "Fully recovered, indeed!"

"Hush, Alice." Gingerly, Miranda made her way to the dressing table and sat down on the chair. "Please come brush my hair. It's a mess."

"And no wonder. You were terribly ill."

Miranda inspected her pale face in the mirror. "Yes, I was. But I really do feel much better. I wonder what was wrong with me?"

Alice brushed vigorously. "That silly housemaid thought

you were increasing, but of course I let her know she was far and fair off. That girl has fewer brains than a midge."

Increasing?

Alice continued her animadversions on the housemaid's deplorable lack of wits, but Miranda didn't listen.

Her mind whirled as she remembered Alex kissing her *and touching her breast!* And then there had been that burst of sensation. Dear heaven, how could she have been so stupid? Last night her marriage had been consummated and now she was . . .

Pregnant!

A wave of happiness engulfed her at the thought. Just yesterday she'd been thinking about having children, and now here she was pregnant!

Maybe.

"Shall I put your hair up, my lady?"

"No, leave it down," Miranda said absently.

She pressed her hands against her stomach. Did one automatically become pregnant when the consummation took place? She wasn't sure. She knew her own parents had been married for many years before she was born. Although perhaps they had waited to consummate their marriage, the way she and Alex had done.

"What dress do you want to wear, my lady?"

"Er, my white pelisse-robe, please."

She tried to recall exactly what she knew on the subjects of consummation and pregnancy. The servant girl that Sara had told Miranda about had become pregnant after letting a man caress her breasts. That was indisputable. Petronella had become sick every morning when she was pregnant with Edward; Miranda clearly remembered Preston saying as much. And Lady Thurlow had said that a woman knows immediately when she is with child.

"Your shawl, my lady?" Alice held up a blue-green paisley shawl with a deep gold fringe.

"Yes, thank you." Miranda hugged it tightly to her breasts. She did feel rather strange. But she couldn't really say that she *knew* she was pregnant.

She would have to ask someone how she could tell for certain. But whom?

Alex seemed the most obvious choice. But, oh, it would be embarrassing! He was a man. She bit her lip. Perhaps he wouldn't even know how to tell either.

A graphic memory came to her of last night's kiss. Her cheeks grew warm. A suspicion popped into her head that Alex knew a great deal about this whole mysterious business—

"Will that be all, my lady?" Alice asked.

"Yes, thank you, Alice." The maid left and Miranda stared into the mirror. No longer pale, her cheeks were rosy red. She waited until the pink faded a bit before she crossed to the door.

She would ask Alex. And she would try not to blush when she did.

For the fifth time in a row, Alex came up with a different total for the column of figures. Gritting his teeth, he dipped the pen in the inkwell and tried again.

Sixty-two plus twenty-nine . . .

Miranda had been very sick last night.

He had paced outside her bedroom door for hours, but her maid had refused to let him in. The woman had assured him that it was nothing serious and that Miranda would recover by morning.

Ninety-one plus seventy-eight . . .

The maid had proved correct. She had sent word down an hour ago that Miranda was awake and feeling much better and would be coming downstairs as soon as she was dressed.

One hundred sixty-nine plus forty-five . . .

He wanted to talk to Miranda. He wanted to apologize for swearing at her last night when she'd spilled the brandy in his lap.

Two hundred fourteen plus ninety-four . . .

He had handled the situation unbelievably badly. In the first place, he should have removed the glass from Miranda's hand, he thought with some disgust for his sloppy tactics. In the second place, he should not have leaped to his feet when the liquid had stung that most sensitive and highly aroused part of him.

Three hundred eight plus twenty-three . . .

Unfortunately, he hadn't been thinking very clearly. He hadn't been able to think at all after the first taste of Miranda's honey-sweet mouth. And her response—hesitant at first but then increasing—had sent him spinning out of control. He had been completely wrapped up in the scent of her cascading red-gold hair, in the taste of the sweet skin at the curve of her jaw and neck, in the feel of her soft, sweet breasts.

Four hundred thirty-three—

With an oath, Alex threw down the pen and rose to his feet. Restlessly, he wandered over to the window and pushed back the white lace curtain to look out at the magnificent sweep of countryside. A few dark clouds hovered nearby, but it was still a beautiful spring day with bright blue skies, newly green hills, and, far below, the Thames winding its way across the verdant landscape.

Some of the tension eased from his shoulders, and he smiled, remembering Miranda's exasperated voice pleading with Edward to put the worm on the hook. How frustrated she had looked. Frustrated and dirty and incredibly attractive.

The river glimmered and sparkled, and a poem of John Donne's popped into Alex's head:

Come, live with me and be my love,
and we will some new pleasures prove
of golden sands and crystal brooks
with silken lines and silver hooks.

His smile faded. Ever since he met her, Miranda had cast a strange spell over him. He was entranced by her mellifluous voice and bright laughter, enticed by her silken hair and skin and lips, bewitched by her sweetly shy innocence—

The door opened behind him. Still holding the curtain, he turned and saw Bomford standing in the doorway, a wide smile on his face.

"Yes, Bomford?"

"My lord, I have heard the happy news. The staff and I are delighted."

Alex arched a brow. "Oh?"

"Yes. All of us were overjoyed to hear that her ladyship is . . . ahem, in a delicate condition."

Alex released the curtain. "A delicate condition?"

Bomford beamed. "Yes. And may I be the first to congratulate you on your impending fatherhood?"

His impending *fatherhood?*

The room seemed to darken. He heard a distant rumbling, but he wasn't sure if it was thunder or the pounding of his heart. Air vacated his lungs, and oxygen deserted his brain. His blood slowed and stopped. He couldn't breathe, he couldn't think, he couldn't move.

"My lord?"

Bomford's voice broke Alex's stupor. He walked slowly to the desk and stared blindly at it.

It could not be true.

But her parents *had* been in a rush to marry her off, an insidious little voice whispered. And there *had* been the story about the vicar. Sir Cedric had assured him that nothing improper had taken place, but it would not be the first time a father had lied to protect his daughter.

His gaze fell on a book resting on the corner of the desk. *The Female Instructor.* He picked it up, remembering Miranda's earnest conversations about the house, her obliviousness to his desire, her innocent response to his kiss.

No, it could not be true.

"My lord? May I be excused?"

Alex looked up. "Yes, of course, Bomford." He set down the book.

"Thank you, my— Oh, let me put that book away for you, my lord. Her ladyship was reading it earlier."

As Bomford picked up the book, two pieces of paper floated down onto the desk.

"Leave the book," Alex ordered, automatically picking up the two sheets of paper. "You may go, Bomford."

Obediently, Bomford bowed and departed.

Alex was sitting at the desk, staring into space, when the door opened a few minutes later and Miranda came in. She looked very beautiful in a white dress and blue-green shawl with her hair down around her shoulders, but Alex felt no appreciation, no desire, no emotion at all.

She was twisting the gold fringe of her shawl between her fingers. When she saw him looking at her, she smiled, but it didn't hide the nervousness in her eyes.

His lips felt stiff. "Is it true?"

Her gaze flew to his and her fingers stilled on the fringe. "Is what true?"

"That you are with child?"

"I . . . I—" She looked away.

And she blushed.

15

He looked rather strange, she thought. He had not risen when she entered the room and he was sitting very still, his face pale, a muscle twitching in his tightly clenched jaw. Her nervousness increased. He did not look at all pleased at the prospect that she might be with child.

"Alex . . ." she said, uncertainly.

He rose to his feet suddenly, his chair crashing to the floor.

She jumped.

"Don't . . . say . . . another . . . word." Without looking at her, he strode to the door and left the room.

Trembling, she stared after him. What was wrong? She had never seen him look so frozen. Was it because he didn't want children?

No, it couldn't be that. Of course he wanted an heir. But then what could be wrong?

Her illness must be making it difficult for her to think clearly. She would have to ask him.

She trailed into the hall just as he was coming down the stairs again, wearing his greatcoat and carrying a valise.

Still without looking at her, he strode to the door.

Dumbfounded, she couldn't move for a moment. Then she cried out, "Alex! Wait!" She hurried after him and grasped his arm just as he was about to open the door.

He stopped, his muscles stiffening under her touch. He didn't look at her. "Let go of me, Miranda," he said icily.

"But where are you going?"

"To London."

"To London!" She swayed, and her grasp tightened on his sleeve. "But why?"

"Because if I have to look at you much longer, I'm going to beat you within an inch of your life."

Gasping, she released his arm and stepped back.

"And because I'm going to petition for a divorce."

A divorce? She stepped back again, her shawl sliding from her suddenly nerveless grasp. "A divorce?" She could hardly bring herself to say the word, it was so shocking. "But—but you can't!"

"You think not? Watch me, you little slut."

He opened the door and left.

Miranda stared at the closed door.

He had left her. He was going to divorce her. He had called her a *slut.*

Burying her face in her hands, she burst into tears.

Alex stood outside on the portico, staring at the traveling coach waiting in the driving rain.

His groom, covered from head to toe in a rain slicker, peered at him with concern. "I'm sorry, my lord. But I didn't think you'd want to ride in this weather."

Alex paused only a moment. Then with a muttered "What the hell," he entered the coach and collapsed on the seat. He stared out the window at the view that just a short

while ago had looked so bright—now it was bleak and gray.
His chest ached.

He could still barely believe it. He didn't want to believe
it. But her guilty blush had betrayed her. That and the
incriminating letter from her lover, Pelham.

Pelham! His hands tightened into fists on his knees.
God, he wanted to thrash that little bastard. He wanted to
horsewhip him and tear him limb from limb and leave his
carcass out for the crows. But the little weasel had crawled
off to America. Which left only Miranda for him to vent his
fury on.

Miranda. Sweet, innocent Miranda.

He drew his hand across his eyes, shuddering. How
could she have deceived him so? How could she have
seemed so naive, so shy, so pure? The ache in his chest
grew. God, what a fool he was. She had been plying her
pretty wiles, weaving a spell, until he was mooning about
like some love-struck youth and spouting the poetry of John
Donne.

He laughed harshly, suddenly remembering the last verse
of that particular poem:

> For thee, thou need'st no such deceit,
> For thou thyself art thine own bait;
> That fish that is not catcht thereby,
> Is wiser afar, alas, than I.

Thank God he had discovered what she was before her
snares had truly caught him.

The carriage lurched and he heard the crack of the
coachman's whip.

He felt queasy. He let down the window and concen-
trated on breathing in lungfuls of the cold, damp air.

The carriage dipped again, and his stomach heaved. He
croaked at the coachman to stop. He barely reached the

privacy of some bushes at the side of the road before sur-
rendering to the unpleasant effects of the Setton Curse.

Finally, his stomach stilled. He sank to the soaking grass
and leaned his head against a tree while the rain washed
down his face in icy rivulets.

He had never felt so cold and so empty in his entire life.

16

Lady Briarwood knocked briskly on the door of Ribblebank Manor.

Bomford, upon opening the door, immediately began to babble. "Your ladyship, thank heavens you're here! Did you receive my message? I know it was forward of me, but I didn't know what else to do—"

"Let me in, you dolt," Lady Briarwood snapped. "Can't you see it's freezing out here?"

Abashed, Bomford stood aside and Lady Briarwood swept inside. "Now tell me what has happened," she ordered.

Bomford wrung his hands. "It's been terrible, my lady, terrible! I don't know what exactly happened between my lord and lady, but his lordship came out of the library looking furious and went straight upstairs, packed, and stormed out of the house. That was several hours ago, but her ladyship is still crying in the library, and I don't know what to do—"

"Very well, Bomford, that's enough," Lady Briarwood interrupted. "Lady Huntsley can tell me the rest of the story. In the meantime, go tell the cook to make some fresh, hot tea. When it's done, bring it up."

"Yes, my lady! At once, my lady!" Elbows flapping, he scurried away.

Shaking her head, Lady Briarwood crossed the hall and opened the door to the library.

The forlorn figure crying on the sofa did not look up.

"Hello, Miranda," Lady Briarwood said softly.

Miranda sat up, looking startled. "Lady Briarwood! Oh, I do apologize, I really am not prepared to receive guests."

"Nonsense. I am not here as a guest but as a friend." The countess's sharp gaze inspected Miranda. The younger woman looked terrible. Her dress was crumpled, her hair hung in lank strands, and her face was swollen from crying. "My dear girl, what has happened?"

Tears welled up in Miranda's eyes. "Alex has left me."

"Good heavens! Why?"

"Maybe . . . maybe he was angry about last night." Miranda twisted her handkerchief. "I spilled brandy on him and I was sick and I ran away."

The countess arched her brows. "Those hardly sound like reasons for a man to leave his wife."

"No, but . . . Oh, Lady Briarwood, I don't know why he left me! He seemed angry about something and I was going to ask him what was wrong, but he left before I could, and now . . . and now I am so . . . so . . . ." The tears overflowed and slipped down Miranda's cheeks.

"Yes, yes, my dear, I understand." In fact, Lady Briarwood understood perfectly. Her experience with foolish misunderstandings between a husband and wife was vast.

Bomford entered with the tea tray. He glanced worriedly at Miranda, then quickly left.

Lady Briarwood poured some tea and held it out to Miranda. "Come, stop crying and drink some tea, girl. Tears serve no purpose."

Self-consciously, Miranda wiped her tear-stained cheeks and took the cup. She sipped the hot brew.

Lady Briarwood, watching her closely, nodded in satisfaction as she saw some color return to the younger woman's cheeks. "Good girl. Now, tell me what that husband of yours said to you."

"He said he intends to seek a divorce."

"Merciful heavens. Did he say anything else?"

"He called me a slut and asked me if I was with child."

"Aha!" Lady Briarwood set down her cup. "He thinks you have been unfaithful. Men often have these jealous fits. The young fool."

"Unfaithful? But why would he think that?"

"I have no idea, child. Have you been flirting with another man?"

"No. There isn't anyone to flirt with."

"Hm. Have you expressed an interest in some other man?"

"No. I don't know any other men. Except for Mr. Pelham. But he has gone to America."

"Hm. Very odd." She studied Miranda closely. "*Are* you with child?"

"I . . . I'm not sure. I might be."

"When did you last have your monthly flow?"

"A few weeks ago. Why?"

Lady Briarwood looked at her sharply. "You won't have it if you're with child. Didn't your mother explain that to you?"

Miranda shook her head.

"You poor dear child, surely you didn't go to your wedding night completely ignorant?"

"No, of course not," Miranda said hastily. "A friend explained everything to me. I-I was a little nervous, but Alex very kindly agreed to wait three months to consummate the marriage until I felt more comfortable."

"Three *months?* How incredibly chivalrous of him. Although I take it he couldn't restrain himself that long?"

Miranda looked blank.

"Huntsley *did* consummate your marriage?"

"Oh, yes." Miranda blushed. "Right here in this room."

"In this . . ." The countess rocked back in her chair.

In reassuring tones, Miranda added, "It only took a few moments."

Lady Briarwood was at a total loss for words, a rare occurrence for her. In a lesser personage, it might have been said she gaped. Lady Briarwood was nothing, however, if not dauntless, and in only slightly failing accents, she said, "Well, then. You have nothing to worry about. This will be very easy to settle. All you have to do is go to London and speak with him—"

"Oh, no! I couldn't." Tears welled up in Miranda's eyes again. "I don't think I can face him. The way he looked at me—as if he hated me—I couldn't bear for him to look at me like that again."

Lady Briarwood studied Miranda's tear-stained cheeks thoughtfully. She suspected the whole matter could be cleared up in five minutes—if she could convince Miranda to go to London. The girl appeared to have fallen into a fit of deep melancholy; she needed to snap out of it. What Miranda needed was some judicious prodding.

Lady Briarwood was happy to provide it. "So you're going to sit here crying for the rest of your life?"

Miranda looked up, startled.

"I'm disappointed in you, girl. I thought you had a bit more spunk in you. After all, who is at fault here? Who left whom?"

"Alex left me. But—"

"But what? Who called whom names and made unfounded accusations?"

"Alex," Miranda said slowly. "But—"

"Who didn't even give whom a chance to explain?"

Miranda appeared much struck. "He *didn't* let me

explain. He didn't even tell me why he thought I'd been unfaithful."

"Who has been unreasonable, ill-tempered, and bad-mannered here?"

"Alex." A flush filled Miranda's cheeks with color. "He even threatened to beat me."

"The cad! If you like, I could help you make him regret that threat—and the way he's treated you."

"You could?" Miranda looked down at the crumpled handkerchief in her hands and tried to think clearly. Did she want to make Alex regret the way he'd treated her? She thought of how coldly he'd asked her if she was with child, of how abruptly he'd deserted her without explanation, of how sneeringly he'd said, *Watch me, you little slut.*

A tiny spark of anger ignited deep inside her.

She remembered her early efforts to please him and the way he had coldly rebuffed her.

The spark flared into a small flame.

There was a pattern here—first he treated her with kindness and respect until she began to think that he cared for her, that she meant something to him—then, with diabolical cruelty, he carelessly crushed her hopes and dreams under the heel of his boot.

The flame burst into a fire.

Why was she the one sitting here crying? Lady Briarwood was right—*she* had done nothing wrong.

"What do you say, my dear? Will you come to London with me and make that husband of yours regret his foolishness?"

Yes, she wanted to make him regret what he had done. But that wasn't enough. She did not intend to go through this again. Alex had trampled on her feelings for the last time.

She straightened her spine. "Yes, Lady Briarwood, I will go with you."

"Excellent. And after he has suffered a little, you will speak to him and clear up this whole mess."

"Speak to him? Oh, no. I am through trying to speak to him. But I am certainly not going to sit around here and let him divorce me." Miranda lifted her chin.

"*I* am going to divorce *him*."

17

Miranda had always dreamed of going to London. She had never expected, however, that when she finally went it would be to obtain a divorce from her husband.

When she had first announced her intention, Lady Briarwood, looking dismayed, had tried to dissuade her, but Miranda was adamant.

"Very well," the countess had finally said. A small smile curled her lips. "Actually, it might be better this way. It wouldn't do for you to go begging to him. And at least this will be amusing."

Miranda was not certain what Lady Briarwood meant by that, but once they reached London she soon found out. She had pictured living a quiet, retired life as she went about the business of divorcing her husband. Lady Briarwood had other ideas entirely.

"If you hide yourself away, people will think you are the one at fault," the countess said at breakfast their first morning in London. "You must face them and hold your chin high."

"And if you are going to face them," the countess continued, "you must dress the part."

Reluctantly, Miranda accompanied Lady Briarwood to the modiste's. And once at the shop, she found herself forgetting her troubles as she pored over the fashion plates and debated the merits of various fabrics with Lady Briarwood and Madame Lulu. When they were done, Miranda had on order two ballgowns, one morning and three evening dresses, as well as a spencer, a pelisse, and a new cloak.

Miranda only balked when Lady Briarwood blithely told Madame Lulu to send the bills to Lord Huntsley.

"He has just settled all his uncle's accounts," Miranda objected. "I can use my allowance."

"Bah." The countess dismissed Miranda's qualms with a toss of her snow-white curls. "A husband is responsible for his wife's bills. That is the law. Besides, Huntsley deserves a little punishment for what he has done, and a man is only vulnerable in two places. The first I am sure you know—" Lady Briarwood paused, and Miranda nodded wisely as if she understood perfectly, "and the other is his pocketbook."

Miranda protested again several evenings later, when the countess made an announcement at dinner.

"I will have to hold a ball to introduce you, of course."

"But Lady Briarwood—"

"I insist, Miranda. I intended to have a ball anyway. Having you here to help me will make it much easier."

"Don't try to dissuade her, my dear," Lord Briarwood said to Miranda, a twinkle in his eye as he helped himself to a large serving of trifle. "She always wins in the end."

Preparations got underway. Naturally, additional shopping was necessary. Miranda and Lady Briarwood paid visits to the haberdashery, the bootmaker, the glovemaker, and a score of other fascinating shops.

"Now that you've acquired some fine feathers," the countess said a few days later, "it's time to start visiting the hens."

The "hens" were several of the leading women in society, and Lady Briarwood insisted that they call on all of them.

"This may not work," Miranda said a trifle uneasily, as they drove to one forbidding dame's house. "Very likely no one will acknowledge me when I'm living apart from my husband."

"Don't worry, my dear. There's bound to be some tattle, of course, but no one will dare snub you if I choose to lend you countenance. I have enough credit to pull this thing off I assure you."

And it was true. Miranda sailed through the arduous morning calls, and the society matrons smiled and nodded and never batted an eyelash at her odd circumstances.

In spite of the acceptance she received, the calls were an ordeal she did not enjoy. So it was with special pleasure that she looked forward to visits with her one friend in London: Sara Rowan.

Sara had been delighted to discover that Miranda was in town. But unlike the discreet society matrons and dowagers, as soon as Sara entered Lady Briarwood's drawing room, she demanded to know why Miranda was staying with the countess, and where was Lord Huntsley?

"He's in London also," Miranda said, smoothing an invisible wrinkle from the skirt of her pale yellow gown.

Sara, looking very dashing in a mulberry-colored dress with a matching hat perched on her stylish brown curls, sat on the sofa next to Miranda and fixed a stern gaze on her friend. "Yes?"

Miranda hesitated, then blurted out the shocking truth. "He's divorcing me and I'm divorcing him."

Sara's mouth fell open. She stared at Miranda a full minute before she finally managed to say, "But, why?"

Miranda sighed. "It's difficult to explain. I suppose it all started when I thought I might be increasing."

"Miranda!" Sara clutched her arm. "Are you truly? How exciting!"

"No, I'm not. My flow started last week, which doesn't happen when you are with child."

Sara's brow wrinkled in confusion. "How do you know that?"

"Lady Briarwood told me."

"Oh." Sara released Miranda's arm. "I see. Well, go on with your story."

"But at the time, I didn't know that, so I went downstairs to ask Alex, and he, well, suffice it to say, he accused me of taking a lover."

Sara bolted straight up in her seat.

"And he threatened to beat me."

"The beast!" The feather in Sara's hat quivered with the force of her indignation. "Is he insane?"

"Perhaps. The only other thing I can think of is that someone must have told him some vicious lies. But whatever his reason, it doesn't matter. I am going to divorce him."

Sara patted Miranda's hand. "Good for you. Although"—a hint of doubt crept into her expression—"shouldn't you talk to him first? Explain that you are innocent?"

Miranda pulled her hand away from Sara's. "You sound just like Lady Briarwood. Why should I explain anything to that overgrown ape?"

"Because it's the sensible thing to do?" Sara suggested.

Miranda tossed her head. "I do have my pride, you know. And besides—" she stared down at her hands and her voice dropped to a whisper, "he hurt me."

"Oh, Miranda!" Sara, her brown eyes growing soft with sympathy, hugged her friend. "He really is a beast."

Miranda stared at her a little blindly. "What did I do? How could he have been so cruel? I thought . . . I thought he cared for me."

Sara shook her head helplessly. "I don't know what you did. Are you sure you don't want to talk to him?"

With an effort, Miranda straightened her shoulders. "Yes, I'm sure. You don't know what it was like, Sara. He would become angry for no reason!"

"No reason?"

Miranda hesitated, but honesty compelled her to admit, "Perhaps there was a reason a *few* times. But most of the time he was completely irrational. I don't want to live with someone like that."

"Then you are right to divorce him," Sara said stoutly. "Have you talked to a lawyer?"

"Not yet. Lady Briarwood's lawyer is preparing the preliminary paperwork. She said that it may take a long time."

"Hm. What did Lord Huntsley say about the divorce?"

"Nothing. I mean, I don't think he knows about it yet. I haven't seen him. And I don't want to." Miranda frowned. "I do hope he doesn't hear about the ball Lady Briarwood is giving for me."

"Lady Briarwood is giving you a ball?"

Miranda nodded. "You will be receiving an invitation soon."

Sara clasped her hands together. "A ball! How exciting!"

"Yes, I suppose." Miranda's mouth drooped a little.

"You suppose! Miranda Rembert—I mean, Setton—don't you know how fortunate you are to be coming into society under Lady Briarwood's aegis? My aunt Gerta told me that the countess is friends with *all* of the patronesses of Almack's. Except Countess Lieven that is. But still, everyone is most in awe of her."

"Of course I am very grateful to Lady Briarwood," Miranda said hastily.

"And so you should be," Sara said. "Aunt Gerta will be over the moon when she hears about this ball. Everyone who is anyone will be there, I'm sure." Sara paused and fiddled with a button on her glove. "Miranda, I know this is dreadfully forward of me, but would you consider inviting Mr. Hamilton-Smith? You have met him, so it's not as though he were a complete stranger."

Miranda knitted her brow. "Mr. Hamilton-Smith? I don't seem to quite recall . . ."

"He was at your wedding. He is a friend of Lord Huntsley's. They were in the army together."

Miranda's heart sank. She really didn't want to invite a friend of Alex's. She opened her mouth to say no, then noticed that Sara's color was a touch high, and she was looking down at her lap.

Miranda's eyes widened. "Sara Rowan, are you in love with Mr. Hamilton-Smith?"

"Oh, no." Sara's blush deepened. "He's just been very kind to me. He saw me at Lady Garson's rout, and remembered me from your wedding. I've seen him occasionally at other assemblies."

"And?" Miranda prodded.

"Honestly, there's nothing else to tell. He used to be a captain until his regiment was disbanded a year or two ago. He's very dashing. And charming. And he's a fabulous dancer."

"I see." Miranda couldn't help smiling. "Then I must certainly invite him to the ball," she said in spite of her reluctance. She would have to pray that he didn't mention the ball to Alex.

"Oh, thank you, Miranda! You will see for yourself how wonderful he is."

"I only hope he won't be disappointed when he doesn't see Alex here."

"Oh, he has already seen him," Sara said. "They both belong to the same club. Mr. Hamilton-Smith mentioned just the other night that he had dined with Lord Huntsley."

Miranda tensed. "Did Alex say anything about me?"

"Not that I know of. Does Lord Huntsley even know you are in town?"

"I don't think so." Miranda smiled wanily. "But I suspect I will know when he finds out."

Alex knocked on the door of Lord and Lady Briarwood's town house. It was a brisk knock, determined, with a hint of anger in it. But also carefully restrained.

His mouth a tight line, his boot tapping impatiently, he waited for the door to open. When it did, he swung around, frowning fiercely, only to find himself facing his own butler.

"Bomford! What the hell are you doing here?"

"Lady Briarwood's butler felt I would benefit greatly from exposure to town life. He mentioned it to Lady Briarwood, who spoke to Lady Huntsley. The result, as you can see, is that I am here, in London."

Bomford made this entire speech without so much as a single stutter.

Alex arched a brow, but he made no comment. Instead he came straight to the point. "I'm here to see Lady Huntsley."

"The ladies are not at home, my lord," Bomford said, his expression wooden.

Alex's jaw tensed. "You wouldn't lie to me, would you, Bomford?" he asked softly.

Bomford coughed, his face slackening a little.

"Is she refusing to see me?" Alex's voice was like a whip.

"My lord, I d-don't think it is my p-place—"

"Your place is to tell me what I want to know," Alex said menacingly. "Are you forgetting who your master is?"

"N-no, my lord, of course not, my lord. But Lady Briarwood left strict instructions that you were not to be admitted under any circumstances."

"I see." A cold rage filled Alex. "Very well. Please give my respects to Lady Briarwood," he said sardonically.

Bomford nodded, his composure completely demolished.

Alex strode back down the steps and waved away his groom. He set off down the street at a furious pace.

How dare his erring wife come to London without his permission? How dare she present herself to Society as the innocent young friend of Lady Briarwood? How dare she be so bold?

Had she no shame?

His mother had been the one to tell him, of course. He wondered which of her busybody friends had imparted the news. Probably that bracket-faced Mrs. Hurley, he thought sourly as he turned a corner.

He had been avoiding his parents like the very devil, only sending a note around to Thurlow House to advise them that he was in town on some business, and giving them his direction. His mother had sent several notes asking him to call, which he had refused, pleading the press of business.

Her last note had been decidedly unpleasant.

Dear Son—

A matter which disturbs me greatly has come to my attention. One of my dear friends has informed me that she met your wife the other day when she called on Lady Briarwood. Why didn't you tell me that Miranda was in town? I denied it, naturally, only to have another of my dear friends confirm it! And then I had to try to explain why Miranda was staying with Lady Briarwood instead of with me! I felt extremely foolish and my dear friend had a very knowing look in her eye when I tried to say that Lady Briarwood was an old friend of Miranda's mother.

I am astonished that you cannot take a few minutes from your busy schedule to call on your mother.

*This lack of natural affection and feeling for my
wishes disturbs me greatly. I sometimes feel that I
should wash my hands of you if you were not my only
living son.*

> *Your devoted mother,*
> *Agatha, countess of Thurlow*

Alex's lack of natural feeling was such that he made no
reply at all to Lady Thurlow's note. Instead he had driven
straight over to the Briarwoods' house.

Only to be turned away!

Why? What did Miranda hope to gain?

He turned his steps in the direction of his solicitor's
office. Perhaps Barnes would have an answer. The lawyer
had handled the Setton family's affairs for many years. Alex
liked and respected the man.

"My lord, this is very disturbing news," the small balding
lawyer said a few minutes later. Seated behind an imposing
oak desk, Barnes pushed aside a large pile of legal docu-
ments, peered over his spectacles at Alex, and frowned.

"This completely destroys all hope of a quiet divorce,"
the lawyer continued. "The scandal will be enormous, especially in view of the king's continuing efforts to persuade
Parliament to grant him a divorce from Queen Caroline.
This is definitely not a propitious time to seek a dissolution
of your marriage."

Alex's lips tightened. "What choice do I have? I refuse to
allow Pelham's spawn to become my heir."

The lawyer placed his fingers together, steeple-fashion,
and gazed at the ceiling, apparently deep in thought. "There
are actually several options you could consider. Your wife
could go to a remote area, board with some family. When
she has the child, it could be fostered out. She could then
return home and it would be as if there had never been a
child."

"That's not good enough." Restlessly, Alex rose to his feet and paced over to a bookshelf filled with thick, leather-bound tomes. "She has deceived and betrayed me. I cannot accept that."

"My lord," Barnes said delicately, "you and Lady Huntsley have been married for a very short time, and you have mentioned this Pelham. Am I correct in assuming that the child is the product of a liaison previous to your marriage?"

Alex traced the spine of a thick red-leather volume with his finger. "Yes."

"And do you also believe your wife is by nature a loose woman or do you think that her delicate condition is the result of an unfortunate aberration on her part?"

Alex's hand dropped to his side and he frowned at the book. Had Miranda's fall from grace been "an unfortunate aberration?" He really had no idea. He did have to admit, however, that she did not behave like a loose woman. Certainly toward him she had shown no signs of wantonness. Quite the contrary, she had seemed almost painfully innocent.

Which only proved that she was an actress of considerable talent.

"I cannot trust her," Alex replied grimly.

Barnes sighed. "Have you discussed this with your parents?"

Alex turned a cold stare on the lawyer. "No, and I forbid you to say anything to them either."

Barnes sighed again. "Very well, if that is your wish. But I ask you to consider well your actions. A divorce will create the most appalling scandal; it will affect your entire family. On the other hand, if you can reach some sort of agreement with Lady Huntsley, you will be able to avoid all the unpleasantness inherent in these situations. Think about it at least," he pleaded.

Alex wanted to refuse, but he knew that the lawyer's advice was sound. Reluctantly, he nodded, then took his leave.

Heading once again for his rooms, Alex forced himself to consider Miranda's actions in a calm and reasoned manner. One question immediately leaped to mind.

Why hadn't she married Pelham?

Granted, her parents hadn't approved, but if she really loved the vicar, she could have insisted. Had Pelham only been a convenient diversion while she sought out bigger game—one with a title?

He frowned. It was difficult to believe that Miranda could be so coldly calculating. If she were, surely she would have pushed him to consummate the marriage. Then she could have tried to pass off the child as his.

No, it was much more likely that Pelham had seduced her with his pratings about "pure and holy" love.

Pelham. Alex clenched his fists. Did the sniveling little worm know Miranda was pregnant? Had she told him?

Alex's frown deepened. Miranda's pregnancy could not be very far advanced. In all likelihood, she hadn't even known on their wedding day.

So perhaps she was innocent of deliberately trying to foist her bastard on him. But how could he excuse her deceit? She should have told him about her past. He would have forgiven an honest mistake—even though the thought of her in the vicar's arms filled him with a fierce, deadly rage. Now, after all that had happened, could he really accept her back and continue their marriage as if nothing had happened?

No!

But what was the alternative?

He would have to return to Ribblebank Manor alone and never see her again.

The idea made him feel cold and hollow.

He would at least speak to Miranda, he thought. Perhaps they *could* come to an agreement. Work something out. He must talk to her.

But she had refused to see him.

His temper rose again, remembering this piece of insolence. He could not believe her audacity, he thought as he turned into the street where his small rented rooms were situated. She should be at Ribblebank Manor, awaiting his judgment. She should be on her knees, praying for his forgiveness. She should be cowering in her room, too ashamed to face the servants, let alone all of the *ton*.

He climbed the stairs two at a time. His valet greeted him at the door, a sealed letter in his hand.

"This arrived in your absence, my lord."

It was an invitation to a ball to be given by Lord and Lady Briarwood. The guest of honor, it proclaimed in beautifully wrought calligraphy, was to be Miranda Setton, Viscountess Huntsley.

18

"*Good evening, Lady Plimpton,*" Miranda said, shaking hands and curtsying for what seemed like the thousandth time.

She stood next to Lord and Lady Briarwood in their marble and rococo saloon, greeting the crème de la crème of Society and wished she were a hundred miles away.

It was a relief to see a familiar heart-shaped face in the line. Miranda clasped Sara's hand in a tight grip. Sara squeezed back, her eyes sparkling.

"Miranda, you look gorgeous!" Sara admired the gold gauze gown, with its tight-fitting, low-cut bodice. "Aunt Gerta won't let me wear anything half so dashing."

Miranda smiled wanly. "Married ladies are fortunate in that respect at least."

Sara opened her mouth to say something else, when she received a sharp nudge from behind. She looked at her aunt who was waving her fan.

"It's very warm in here," Mrs. Waterton observed. "I do hope I won't have a palpitation."

"Come, Aunt Gerta, I will find you a chair," Sara said, taking the older woman's arm. Over her shoulder, she whispered to Miranda, "I'll speak to you later."

Miranda nodded, and turned to the next person in line.

"Good evening, my dear." The countess of Thurlow, wearing her usual stiff black skirts, gave Miranda an arctic stare.

Miranda gulped. Her gaze flew to Lady Briarwood, but the older woman was speaking to someone. What had Lady Briarwood been thinking of to invite Alex's parents? Unhappily, Miranda turned back to her mother-in-law, wondering what Alex had told her. Nothing good, judging from the expression on Lady Thurlow's face.

Lord Thurlow's heavily lidded blue eyes were pleasantly inscrutable. "You look lovely, my dear," he said as he kissed her cheek. Miranda smiled shakily.

Preston and Petronella were next. Preston looked a little distant, Petronella questioning. Miranda tried not to wilt. She wanted to tell them that the separation wasn't her fault—but how could she explain to Alex's family that he thought she had taken a lover?

There was an awkward pause.

"How is Edward?" Miranda asked.

"In mischief, as usual," replied Preston, his stocky shoulders relaxing a little.

"He broke Papa's collection of glass bottles," whispered Petronella. She brushed an inky black curl off her forehead. "And he trundled his hoop right into Mama's new day dress when she was out walking. The hoop was covered with filth, and Mama was very upset. He leaves for the country in two days with his nurse. His new nurse. She's a treasure. Her references are impeccable. I had her from Lady Bigelow, whose children are now grown. And Edward adores her already. She says he is the tallest boy she has ever seen. Would you believe he has grown an inch since we saw you last?"

"Move on, girl!" came a testy voice. "Heavens, you are tedious, Petronella. No one wants to hear how tall that boy of yours is." Alex's grandmother, a tiny old woman with lips and cheeks painted a startling red, elbowed Petronella forward and peered at Miranda. "Eh, I remember you. So you're the gel who's causing such a ruckus in Agatha's household. Good for you!" she cackled. "Is that rascally grandson of mine here?"

Miranda shook her head. Preston, with an apologetic look, escorted the old woman into the ballroom.

The next hour passed slowly. The line stretched out the door and down the stairs, and still people continued to arrive. Miranda felt as though she were enduring some sort of ancient torture ritual.

Much to her relief, Lady Briarwood released her when the dancing started. Lord Briarwood led Miranda out for the first set.

"Are you enjoying yourself, my dear?" In spite of his bulkiness, he maneuvered her skillfully around the ballroom.

"Yes, of course," she replied quietly. Like most girls, she had often dreamed of attending a great London ball. In all her dreams, she had never imagined anything as magnificent as this one—the swelling strains of music, the buzz of voices, the air redolent with the scent of perfume and flowers; the enormous, sparkling chandeliers casting a diffused light on the colorful silks and satins; the mirrored walls reflecting the gaily twirling ladies and gentlemen—it was a perfect fairyland.

Miranda had never in her life experienced such a dreadful evening.

"That was a foolish question," Lord Briarwood said, peering into her downcast face. "Of course you're not enjoying yourself."

Startled, she glanced up. He was looking at her very kindly, and Miranda felt a rush of guilt. "I can't thank you and Lady Briarwood enough for your kindness," she said sincerely.

He shook his head, a half smile on his lips. "I must thank you." He glanced over to where Lady Briarwood was talking animatedly to several of her cronies. "My wife is having the time of her life. It's been a long while since she's had a cause to champion, and a young, wronged wife is just the sort of situation she dotes on." He smiled down at her. "It reminds her of herself, you see."

"I can't believe you ever hurt your wife," Miranda said.

"Oh, but I did. Not physically, but I hurt her very badly all the same." Lord Briarwood's bushy white brows drew together. "I almost lost her before I came to my senses and realized what a treasure I had."

The set ended, and Lord Briarwood escorted Miranda back to Lady Briarwood, who had a steady stream of men lined up to ask Miranda for a dance. Over the next two hours, she did not sit down once.

After the latest set of dances ended, Miranda limped to the side of the room and sank into a chair. Her last partner had trod all over her toes, and she was afraid that he had broken at least one.

She was sitting there, curling and uncurling her toes, when Sara dashed up.

"Oh, Miranda, this is the most divine party! And you are an enormous success."

Miranda smiled halfheartedly. "Is it not beyond anything? But what about you? I haven't seen you sitting out any dances."

"Yes, is it not wonderful? But come, you must say hello to Mr. Hamilton-Smith." Sara pulled Miranda across to where a gentleman with a very straight back and a very straight gaze stood talking to her aunt Gerta.

Miranda vaguely remembered him from the wedding feast.

"Lady Huntsley, it's a pleasure to see you again." Mr. Hamilton-Smith looked directly into her eyes. Miranda could see a touch of reserve there.

"And you also, sir. Although I must confess, my recollection of our previous meeting is somewhat hazy."

"That is not surprising. The feast was quite befuddling. But it was a very great privilege to be present at Alex's wedding."

"I am not certain he would agree with you, but thank you," Miranda replied, and Mr. Hamilton-Smith was surprised into a laugh.

The music for the next dance started. Miranda checked her card and realized that she had a free dance, so she made her way back to where Lady Briarwood sat.

"Ah, there you are, my dear," said Lady Briarwood. "I want to introduce you to someone. Mrs. Overfield, this is my young guest, Lady Huntsley."

Miranda murmured politely to the small, birdlike woman, whose eyes were like pale green glass beneath her faded blond hair. Something about the woman was familiar, but she couldn't decide what—until she heard an almost forgotten voice drawling behind her.

"Good evening, Lady Briarwood. May I say you look younger and more radiant than you did when I last saw you?"

Miranda stiffened, then turned to stare at the man bowing over Lady Briarwood's hand. It was the man from the inn, the one Alex had told her to avoid.

Lady Briarwood laughed at the compliment. "You young scamp. I've missed your overblown flattery."

"My lady, I protest. 'Overblown' is most unkind. Say rather, 'endearing.'"

"If you insist." Lady Briarwood looked amused. "Are you still causing trouble and worrying your poor mother?"

The elaborate folds of his cravat and his high starched collar prevented him from turning his head, but he threw a sidelong glance at Mrs. Overfield, who sat with an impenetrable expression. "It has been so long since I indulged in any exploits, that my mother tells me I positively bore her."

"Never that, Justin," Mrs. Overfield said dryly.

Lady Briarwood laughed at this nonsense, then said, "Miranda, have you met the duke de Morieux? He is a rascal, so I warn you to beware."

"Lady Huntsley and I have met." The duke's eyes glinted as he made another low bow. "May I have the honor of the next dance?"

Miranda was not certain she wished to dance with the duke but, feeling it would be awkward to refuse, she placed her hand on his proffered arm. She shivered a little when he put his arm around her and swept her into the dance.

She looked up into his face. He smiled down at her, but she noticed the smile did not reach his pale green eyes. His gaze had a calculating quality to it, and he watched her a little too closely, as if constantly judging her response.

"How I envy Huntsley," the duke said. "He has always been lucky with women."

Miranda stiffened a little, wondering just what women Alex had been lucky with. She was about to question the duke about it, when she noticed the corner of his mouth curling upward.

She bit back her question. Instead, she said airily, "He *is* very attractive, is he not?"

A slight frown replaced the curl of his lips. Shrugging, he looked away from her steady eyes. His gaze wandered around the ballroom, then stopped and returned to a point somewhere behind her left shoulder.

She craned her neck a little to see who had caught his attention. It was Petronella. As she watched, Alex's sister looked up and saw the duke. Immediately she turned pale.

Miranda glanced back at the duke. A mocking smile now curved his lips, and he nodded in Petronella's direction.

Miranda's gaze swung back to Petronella. A fiery blush had suffused her cheeks, and she was whispering in Preston's ear. With a hard look at the duke, Preston took his wife's arm and they made their way over to Lady Briarwood. Within a few minutes they had left the ball.

A flash of malicious satisfaction crossed the duke's face; his eyes gleamed and his lips parted to reveal the two sharp incisor teeth. But when he looked down at Miranda, he had the charming mask firmly back in place.

"You dance like an angel, Lady Huntsley. I'm afraid you will float away if I let go of you." His hand pressed her closer than was polite.

She pulled back. "My feet are firmly earthbound, I assure you."

His smile grew wider, and he pressed her closer still. "Such pretty feet cannot be content to remain on this unworthy ground."

Barely missing a step, Miranda trod heavily upon his toes. He winced and drew back.

"My feet are very happy where they are, thank you," she said sweetly.

The mask slipped, and he stared down at her coldly.

They danced in silence for several minutes.

"Are you enjoying London, Lady Huntsley?" The flirtatious edge and all pretense of charm were gone.

Miranda pretended not to notice. "Yes, it's very exciting. There are so many things to see and do and so many interesting people. It is a bit wearing after a while, though. I think I have visited every shop in Mayfair, and smiled at every dowager in London. Most everyone has been very kind."

"Have they? How fortunate for you." His voice was bored.

"Yes, indeed. A few people have been rude, which can be very intimidating, especially to a shy, country-bred girl like myself. Fortunately I have found a most effective way to handle such situations."

"What is that?" The duke appeared to stifle a yawn.

"Whenever someone is rude, I simply imagine he is a toad." To her satisfaction, he looked startled.

"A toad? And does your method work?"

She stared at him pointedly for a moment. Then with an innocent smile, she said, "It works beautifully."

The duke stared in disbelief for a moment, then shouted with laughter. "Are you always so impertinent, my lady?" he asked finally when his laughter had died down.

"Only when my husband has warned me someone is especially dangerous," she said tartly.

"Ah. So the virtuous Huntsley told you about my wicked ways, did he?" The faintest suggestion of a sneer marred the duke's lips. "I'm surprised then, that you consented to dance with me."

"It was rather difficult to refuse, Your Grace," Miranda said cuttingly.

In a flash, his expression altered. He acknowledged the truth of her remark with a quick grin, and Miranda found it impossible to resist smiling back.

She was still smiling when he swung her around in a wide arc, and she saw Alex glaring ferociously at her from the edge of the dance floor.

19

Miranda looked away immediately, but Alex's image was emblazoned on her brain—from the iciness of his narrowed blue eyes to the tense set of his jaw; from the rigidity of his shoulders encased in fine black wool to his tightly closed fists and his polished black shoes planted slightly apart.

Her chest tightened. Somewhere, deep inside, she had been hoping that when they met he would fall on his knees, begging for forgiveness and pleading to be taken back. She wouldn't have agreed, of course. Although perhaps she might have considered it—if he promised to beat himself with a switch everyday in penance like the monks of old; if he promised to go to church and pray three hours every morning and every night for forgiveness; and if he promised never to misjudge her again.

"Ah, the outraged husband," said the duke, turning her around again so he could see whom she was staring at. "Why is he glowering in that unpleasant fashion? You would think he would show a bit more finesse."

Miranda could not respond.

"Come," said the duke, "I've not had the opportunity to speak to your charming husband for several weeks."

Her first impulse was to tear herself away and flee to Lady Briarwood. But then she lifted her chin. *She* had no reason to be embarrassed.

Alex watched them approach. He was leaning casually against a pillar now, his arms folded across his chest, his gaze cool and remote.

"Good evening, Your Grace," Alex said formally, ignoring Miranda for the moment.

"It is, isn't it?" mocked the duke. "And what a pleasure it is to see you again, dear fellow. I've just been telling Lady Huntsley how I've missed your company."

"I've regretted your absence also." Alex brushed a speck of dust from his sleeve. "Perhaps we should set a date, and meet at, oh, say Jackson's for a friendly bout and to talk over old times."

"Can you have forgotten, dear boy?" The duke shuddered. "I abhor fisticuffs. One is likely to get hurt, and it is the very devil trying to conceal a bruise with rice powder, don't you agree?"

"One can always stay home, instead of offending polite people with one's ugly countenance."

The duke laughed. "What a delight you are, Huntsley. Really, you must let me buy you a drink next time you're at the club. Now I fear I must excuse myself as I have committed to the next set. Lady Huntsley—" He kissed her hand lingeringly, "I thank you for the dance. It was a joy beyond belief." With a brief bow, he strolled across the room to where a very pretty young lady stood waiting.

Alex straightened from the pillar and turned to Miranda. "Would you care to take a turn on the balcony, my lady?" Although he was smiling, his nostrils looked rather pinched.

Miranda swallowed.

Then, squaring her shoulders, she followed him out onto the balcony.

Alex was furious. At the duke, at Miranda, but most of all at himself for the rush of desire he had felt when he first saw her. He had quickly come to his senses, but the memory of his weakness was galling. He glared down at his errant wife. In her golden dress, with a tiara of pearls in her fiery re-gold hair, she looked elegant, stylish, and—incredibly beautiful. How dare she? He wished they were in a less public place, preferably a dark alley where he could wring her neck.

He steered her into a shadowed corner and faced her, his arms again folded across his chest. He noticed her shiver. Whether from the chilly evening air or from nervousness, he didn't know.

"What the devil are you doing in London?" he snapped.

She lifted her chin. "I have come to divorce you."

He stiffened. "*You* have come to divorce *me?* What game is this?"

"No game. I intend to divorce you for desertion and cruelty."

Alex laughed incredulously. "You little fool. It is virtually impossible for a woman to divorce her husband."

She pursed her lips haughtily. "We shall see."

His gaze was drawn irresistibly to her pursed lips. She had the most alluring mouth, the bow beautifully delineated and the bottom lip full and rosy—suspiciously rosy. Alex's brows drew together. Had she rouged her mouth?

Before he considered his action, he lifted his hand and rubbed his thumb against her lips. With a gasp, she immediately stepped back out of reach. He stared at her for a moment, seeing the flush rise in her cheeks, then glanced down at his fingers. No smudge of red betrayed her.

He lowered his hand to his side. "Miranda, I have been thinking." The cool air had made his voice a trifle husky. He cleared his throat and met her gaze again. "I have been thinking that perhaps divorce is not the answer."

Her eyes widened for a moment and her lips curved up at the corners. Her chin trembled a little. "Oh, Alex, I have thought so, too."

His gaze focused on her mouth again. "I'm glad to hear you're prepared to be sensible. A divorce would be expensive and cause a scandal. Perhaps we will be able to avoid the whole messy business. I am working on a list of conditions. If you agree to them, I will consider—just consider, you understand—dropping the divorce."

She looked stunned, he noticed. She probably hadn't expected such magnanimity.

She opened her mouth to respond, when a new voice intruded.

"Miranda! There you are. I've been searching high and low for you. Whatever are you doing out here in the dark?" Lady Briarwood's lavender skirts rustled as she swept onto the balcony, her gaze quickly scanning the scene before her. "Huntsley. What a surprise. I did not know you were out here."

In spite of her words, Alex gained the impression that Lady Briarwood had been perfectly aware of his presence on the balcony.

"In fact, I'm astonished to see you at all. I am certain you did not respond to my invitation." The countess moved to Miranda's side.

Like a lioness protecting her young, Alex thought sardonically. "An oversight on my part, Lady Briarwood. I decided to chance your displeasure in my eagerness to see my dear wife again. Please forgive my presumption."

The older woman's black eyes sparkled at this speech. She glanced between the two stiff figures, and a small smile lifted the corners of her mouth.

"All is forgiven, but now I must steal Miranda away, for her supper partner is waiting. Come along, my dear."

"Miranda?" Alex said, silently willing her to refuse to go with the countess.

"Perhaps you should call on me tomorrow, Alex." Without looking at him, she nodded regally and followed Lady Briarwood inside.

Alex stared after her, again conscious of a desire to strangle her—or kiss her until she begged for mercy.

Tomorrow, he might just do both.

It was five o'clock in the afternoon the next day, and Miranda sat in Lady Briarwood's drawing room seething.

Last night when Alex had made his "offer," she had been too stunned to do anything but quietly follow Lady Briarwood back into the ballroom. She had only taken a few steps before she came to her senses and wanted to return to the balcony to scream at him for his arrogance. Lady Briarwood had dissuaded her, however, convincing her that it was better to wait until she was calmer and could talk to him in a more rational manner.

Miranda had agreed and spent the night thinking of a hundred calm, cool, logical insults she could hurl at him the next day.

She'd had herself well under control the next morning as she waited for Alex to arrive.

Only he hadn't come.

The day wore on, and droves of people called to tell Lady Briarwood how much they had enjoyed the ball and to congratulate her on her charming guest. Miranda listened decorously to interminable discussions of who wore what and who danced with whom. And still Alex hadn't come.

By five o'clock, her anger was bubbling barely below the

surface as she remembered for the hundredth time that day everything he had said last night on the balcony.

Perhaps she wouldn't have been so angry if she wasn't so furious at her own gullibility. That was the worst of it—that she had been taken in by him again, when he had said that divorce might not be the answer.

Her foolish heart had leaped with hope. She had actually thought he was going to apologize. She should have known better. She should have known that his only thought was for his own convenience. Certainly he wouldn't want to waste estate money—and her dowry—on such a "messy business." And certainly he wouldn't want to listen to his mother harp about the "scandal" for probably the next twenty years.

Oh, no.

How much easier it would be for the craven, contemptible cad to force his frightened, helpless, penniless wife to agree to a list of "conditions."

A list of conditions!

Perhaps that was why he was so late. Doubtless he was adding a few more items to his list, maybe that she wear a veil and say "Yes, Master" whenever he addressed her. And that she sit around all day awaiting his pleasure.

She glanced at the clock. A quarter past five. She rose to her feet and paced around the room. Why on earth had she married such a lumpish, loathsome, lackwitted lout? She refused to wait any longer. She was going up to her room. If he came now, he could sit in Lady Briarwood's drawing room cooling his heels while she considered whether or not to come down.

"Lady Huntsley?"

Miranda turned to see Bomford standing in the open doorway. "Yes?" she asked eagerly.

"The duke de Morieux is below."

"Oh." Disappointed, Miranda started to say she wasn't at home when she had a second thought.

The duke. Perfect. "Show him up."

A few moments later, he sauntered in, swinging his quizzing glass and carrying a cane. He bowed with his usual flair. "My dear Lady Huntsley, the heavens have blessed me, for I find you here alone. I must have inadvertently done something good to merit such favor by the gods."

Her gaze wandering over his maroon coat and startling yellow waistcoat, Miranda smiled. "Surely you sometimes do good of your own volition."

"Not if I can avoid it. The result is always an effusion of gratitude that I find quite nauseating."

Miranda's smile faded, and she searched him with her gaze. With his cynical green eyes, stiff black curls, and outlandish clothes, he appeared the consummate hedonist—caring for nothing and no one but himself and his own pleasure. Was he really so shallow? And what had he done to make Alex dislike him so?

"Why do you and my husband hate each other?" she asked curiously.

"Hate? Lady Huntsley, you exaggerate. Hate is such a wearing emotion. Your husband and I merely feel a mild dislike for each other."

"But why?" Miranda persisted.

The duke studied his sleeve. "It is a remarkably tedious story, my dear. I would prefer not to bore you with it." Espying a speck of lint, he brushed it away. "Let's not spoil the afternoon talking about ancient history. I have something of import to tell you."

"Oh?"

"Yes. You cast a spell over me last night at the ball. Now, every moment I spend in your company strengthens the enchantment, till I begin to fear for my heart."

Miranda couldn't help laughing, but his glib flattery disappointed her. His mask was firmly in place, and he oozed insincerity. He continued for several minutes to slather her with absurd blandishments until he said, "I must confess something, Lady Huntsley."

Her brows rose. "Yes?"

"I came here with an ulterior motive."

Her brows rose higher. "Oh?"

"I came to entice you into going to a card party with me tomorrow night. Please say you will come."

Miranda hesitated. Although she found him amusing, she did not quite trust the duke.

"It will break my heart if you say no."

She laughed again. "Very well," she agreed. She supposed he couldn't do anything dreadful at a card party. And besides, she did enjoy playing cards.

"Ah, the gods are truly smiling upon me today. I am encouraged to try my luck once more: Will you go for a drive with me? I have the most beautiful new curricle outside, and it begs to have a beautiful lady adorning its seat."

Miranda hesitated, glancing at the clock. "I am expecting my husband."

"How unfortunate." He smiled, but his gaze grew cool. "Husbands always spoil everything."

A slight frown creased her brow. "What do you mean?"

"They never want to let their wives have any fun," the duke clarified. "They want to keep them locked up, usually at a house in the country."

Miranda's eyes widened and her mouth fell open. That *did* sound like Alex. She lifted her chin. "My husband doesn't control me like that."

The duke's eyelids drooped. "Then you will come?"

Miranda hesitated again. She glanced at the clock. Then, she tossed her head. She would tell Bomford to inform Alex that she was out but that he should wait. He could twiddle *his* thumbs for an hour or so.

Of course, she did not expect that just after the duke assisted her into the curricle and climbed in himself, Alex would round the corner in his own curricle and approach them. And she never dreamed that the duke, also catching a glimpse of Alex's carriage, would lift her hand and kiss it.

Alex pulled up his matched bays abruptly, causing the animals to snort and toss their heads. His jaw set, he stared at the couple in the curricle.

"Alas, dear fellow," the duke said in mock commiseration. "Your luck is truly out. I am here before you and the lady has agreed to drive with me."

"Miranda," Alex said quietly, ignoring the duke, "I told you I would call."

"No, no," said the duke. "A vague promise to call is not sufficient reason for me to permit you to steal away this charming lady."

The planes of Alex's face hardened. "Stealing is more *your* style, isn't it, Your Grace?"

Across the horses' heads, the men's gazes clashed and held. Miranda sat tensely, apprehensive of their blatant hostility. She slid cautiously toward the edge of the seat, intending to climb down.

Before she could do so, however, the duke laughed and jerked his horses' heads sharply to the right. The curricle rolled out into the road and the duke whipped up his horses. Startled, Miranda looked over her shoulder and saw Alex executing a skillful turn in the middle of the street.

"He's coming after us. You must stop," she said.

The duke laughed and urged the horses forward. But instead of turning west toward the park, he headed south on Audley Street, scattering pedestrians and street merchants in his path. He drove past a tilbury carrying an elderly woman and swung around a slow-moving barouche. Miranda turned to see if Alex was still coming after them.

He was.

He was leaning slightly forward on his seat, the reins threaded through his fingers, his mouth set in a grim line.

A sudden jolt made Miranda clutch the side of the carriage and turn back around. The wheels of the curricle had grazed an old woman's cart, sending apples spilling across the road. Alarmed, Miranda glanced back just in time to see one of the bays' hooves slip on an apple. The horse stumbled.

Alex, his hands remaining steady on the reins, held the horse up. The bay regained its footing and continued forward.

"Your Grace!" Miranda cried. "You must stop."

The duke, his pale eyes glittering and his mouth curling up at one corner, did not take his gaze from the road. "Come, Lady Huntsley, where's your sporting spirit? Don't you thrill to the chase?"

"Not when I'm the prey!"

He laughed, the sound exuberant, but he didn't slow down. The curricle barreled past the intersection of South Street with barely a pause, just as a groom was leading a horse from the mews. The man leaped back, his hands slipping from the reins.

Her heart in her throat, Miranda looked back to see the startled horse bolting across the street as Alex's carriage approached.

The frightened bays shied, but once again Alex controlled them with an iron hand, urging them onward.

Miranda's whole body sagged with relief. But the next instant she straightened and turned to glare at the duke. "I insist you pull over at once, Your Grace. Someone is going to be hurt!"

For a moment, she thought he would refuse. The curricle shot past Curzon Street and continued onto Down Street. Then the duke glanced at her, a rueful smile on his lips. "Your wish is, of course, my comm—"

A small boy darted into the street directly in the path of the curricle.

Miranda screamed.

Cursing, the duke hauled back on the reins. The horses whinnied and reared, and Miranda saw the child fall in the middle of the street before the curricle careened sideways and crashed into a wheelbarrow laden with lobsters.

The impact almost threw her from the vehicle. Her hip banged against the side of the seat, her fingers scraped painfully along the wood where she was holding on, and her hat was knocked from her head. Then everything was still.

For one stunned moment, she sat without moving. Vaguely, she realized that the wheelbarrow was smashed, lobsters were strewn across the street, and the merchant was shouting angrily.

The duke, who had also somehow managed to retain his seat, said mildly, "Dear me. I believe I have ruined my new curricle."

Dazed, Miranda nodded, then gave a small cry when she caught sight of the child, still lying in the road.

Shaking, she climbed down and pushed her way through the gathering crowd to hurry over to the boy.

"Are you hurt?" she asked, helping him stand up. Painfully thin, he weighed next to nothing and was perhaps seven or eight years of age. A sullen frown peeped through layers of dirt and grime on his face as he shook his head.

"Are you certain?"

The boy nodded and started to sidle away. She grabbed him just as two hands closed over her shoulders and swung her about. Alex, his face white, stared down at her.

"Are you all right?" he asked sharply.

She nodded, surprised by the fierceness of his question.

His gaze roamed over her. For a moment, she thought she saw a flicker of relief in his eyes, but then she was distracted by the boy squirming under her hold.

"Don't be frightened," she said trying to reassure him. "Wouldn't you like to have a doctor check you over?"

"H'ain't going to no sawbones."

"Will you at least come with me to Lady Briarwood's house in Grosvenor Square? I'll have the cook there give you something to eat. Wouldn't you like that?"

She smiled encouragingly, but the boy, with a quick twist, escaped her hold and darted into the crowd. She started after him, but before she could take more than a step, Alex made an impatient noise. His hand closed like a vise over her arm and he dragged her toward his curricle.

"Alex, wait!" she panted, half-running to keep up. "What about the duke?" She peered over her shoulder to where the duke was arguing with the lobster merchant. She saw him stop talking to look after them with narrowed eyes.

Alex abruptly stopped, causing her to bump into him. Startled, she looked up and saw he was staring down at her, his light blue eyes as icy as hailstones.

She swallowed.

"I will deal with the duke later." His hands closed over her waist. "But for now, I suggest you forget about him."

Suddenly she was flying through the air as he tossed her up into the curricle and climbed in after her.

"Believe me," he said softly, "you have other things to worry about."

20

Alex was furious.

As he drove Miranda back to the Briarwoods', he kept seeing in his mind the moment when the duke's carriage had skidded out of control. For one long, terrible moment, he had thought Miranda would be killed.

That she had survived without so much as a scratch did not alleviate his temper. If anything, her uninjured state made him even more furious. He closed his hands tightly on the reins. He was itching to beat her black and blue.

He did not trust himself to speak until they arrived at Lady Briarwood's and the drawing room door was closed behind them.

"Would you care to explain your behavior?" he asked in a deceptively calm manner, stripping off his gloves.

She sat down on the sofa not looking at him, and carefully arranged the gray skirt of her dress. "What behavior?"

"An excellent question," Alex said sarcastically. "So much of your behavior needs explanation that it is difficult to know where to begin. Why don't we start with the matter of your going out driving with the duke when I had specifically told you I would call."

"You were so late, I thought you had changed your mind. I thought perhaps you decided to go ahead with the messy divorce business."

He glanced at her sharply, but she was intent on brushing some flecks of mud from her skirt. "The next time I tell you I am going to call, I expect you to wait, no matter how late I am."

She mumbled something.

His brows drew together. "What did you say?"

"I said, Yes, Mas—my lord."

His frown deepened. "Do you also remember that I told you not to associate with the duke in any way?"

She finally looked up from her skirt. "For heaven's sake, Alex! His mother is a friend of Lady Briarwood's."

"He is not a friend of mine, however. I forbid you to have anything to do with him."

"You *forbid* me? How Gothic of you."

He slapped his gloves against his palm. "Your impertinence is not becoming. If we are going to come to an agreement, you are going to have to watch that tongue of yours, Miranda."

She stiffened and didn't speak, her hands tightly clenched in her lap. She appeared quite mutinous.

He was going to control that rebellion, he thought grimly, shoving his gloves in his pocket and pulling out the list he had made. "There are three conditions," he said tersely. "I will read each one and then you may ask questions if you have any. Is that agreeable to you?"

She inclined her head slightly.

Alex read the first condition. "Number one: You will not be alone with any man for any length of time; you will not flirt or otherwise encourage any man. You will not acknowledge the duke de Morieux in any manner whatsoever." That last part was not actually written down. He had decided to add it just a moment ago.

"Oh dear." She frowned. "This does present a problem."

Alex frowned. "Why is that?"

"There are times when Lady Briarwood leaves the house, and Lord Briarwood and I are alone. He usually is engaged in his own pursuits, and I in mine, but at times we sit down to breakfast together."

"I would not object to that—"

She shook her head dolefully. "No, no, you don't understand. Sometimes Bomford and I discuss household matters—when no one else is present! And good heavens, sometimes I cannot control myself and I *smile* at men. And then there is dancing. Dear me, I will have to think about this one. What is your second condition?" She smiled innocently.

Alex eyed her coldly. "This isn't the time for levity, Miranda."

"I am not laughing. Please, go on."

He gave her another cold stare, then read the next item on his list. "Number two: You will move to my parents' town house for the remainder of the Season. You will accept my mother's guidance and counsel in all matters."

He looked up to see her reaction.

She was still smiling. "Hm. I would like to agree to this—your mother is so warm and friendly I am sure we would get along splendidly—but I am concerned that she would feel like a prison warden. I wouldn't want to make her uncomfortable. I will have to think about this one, too, Alex."

His fingers tightened on the paper. "You do not appear to be taking this seriously, Miranda. I suggest you do so." He looked back at his list. "Number three: At the end of the Season, you will agree to go to a location of my choice, where you will remain until the birth of the child. The child will then be fostered out, and you will have no further contact with it."

Pausing, he glanced at her. She was perfectly still, like a sculpture.

"Are you finished?" she asked.

He nodded.

She rose to her feet. No longer smiling, the only color in her face was the sparkling green-and-gold fire of her eyes. "Now let me see if I understand this. If I give up my friends, my freedom, and my self-respect—oh, and my baby, too, don't let me forget that—then I will have the privilege of continuing to be your wife, which means you can call me vile names, beat me, and do whatever you like. Is that correct?" She looked at him sweetly.

"Yes. Er, I mean no . . ." Caught off guard, he stared down at her provocative face. Although she was smiling again, her eyes still snapped. With sudden clarity, he realized that she had no intention of agreeing to his conditions—and never had.

His fist crushed the paper. In one swift, violent motion, he threw it at the fireplace and stepped toward her, glaring. She immediately stepped forward and scowled right back.

Practically nose to nose with her, he said softly, "Don't be a fool, Miranda. I may not give you another chance."

With a haughty toss of her head, she started to turn away.

He seized her shoulders. "You haven't answered me. Will you or will you not abide by my conditions?"

"No, I will not." Her answer was terse.

Just like that. "That's your final word? You will not even discuss it?"

"I am more than willing to discuss our situation. You, however, are not here to discuss but to pass sentence. You even have my jailer picked out." She tried to pull away from him, but he tightened his grip on her shoulders.

"My mother is not a jailer, and my conditions are not unreasonable."

"Perhaps it is best that you proceed with the divorce, for I can see that we will never agree. To my mind, your list of conditions is the most insulting, degrading, unjust—"

"Given the magnitude of your sin, I don't think you can complain of injustice."

"I have committed no sin!"

"Can you really believe that you have done nothing wrong?" he demanded. "I suppose I shouldn't be surprised. Judging from your companions, I doubt you know what decent behavior is."

"If you are referring to the duke, then I must inform you that he has always been a perfect gentleman," she shot back.

Alex laughed harshly. "I suppose you like the way he slobbered all over your hand earlier and the way he undresses you with his eyes."

Miranda gasped. "Only a mind as disgusting as yours could imagine such a thing." Again she tried to turn away, but he held on, only letting go with his right hand so he could lift her chin.

"The duke is dangerous. Can't you understand that?"

Her mouth was set in a stubborn line. "In what way?"

Still holding her jaw, he leaned closer.

"He abducts young women. He takes his pleasure from them without their consent. Is that dangerous enough for you?" His gaze moved from her angry eyes to her mouth. Her lips were pressed together tightly, but he had a sudden memory of how they softened when he'd kissed her—eons ago—in the library. He leaned closer.

Abruptly, she wrenched her chin away and tore free from him. Her face set and angry, she walked over and pulled the bell. When Bomford appeared, she said, "His lordship is leaving."

Bomford, his face wooden, looked at Alex. "My lord?"

Alex ignored him. "I'm not leaving, Miranda, until this is settled."

She seemed to grow an inch or two.

"Must I order Bomford to evict you?"

Alex laughed. "You don't truly believe he would try any such thing?"

"Shall we find out, my lord?"

Alex looked sardonically at Bomford, wondering if the butler was idiot enough to try.

Bomford's face twitched nervously.

The thought of brawling with so unworthy an opponent was distasteful.

"Very well," he said coldly to Miranda, "I'll go if that's what you want. But I'll be back. And next time, I won't be so reasonable."

Without waiting for a response, he strode to the door and left.

Lady Briarwood was looking over her shoulder when she entered the drawing room a second later. "Your husband looks angry enough to spit," she observed, turning to Miranda. Her gaze sharpened. "And so do you."

Miranda was still so taut with anger she could barely speak. "Have you spoken with your lawyer recently, Lady Briarwood? Is the paperwork for my divorce almost finished? Do you think it's possible for him to hurry things along?"

Lady Briarwood arched a brow. "Slowly, my child. What has Huntsley done now?"

"He gave me a list of conditions which he said I must follow if he is to take me back. Naturally, we quarreled."

"Naturally. What sort of conditions?"

"He said I could not flirt or be alone with any man, especially the duke de Morieux."

"How ridiculous. Although I had forgotten there is bad blood between the duke and your husband. I wonder why?"

"I don't know precisely. Alex said that the duke is dangerous, that he abducts young women and . . . and has his way with them."

"How interesting. The duke does have a slightly unsavory reputation, but I would not have thought him dangerous. Mrs. Overfield is a good woman. I can't believe her son would seriously harm anyone."

"I think Alex was just trying to frighten me. I should have told him that I was going to a party with the duke tomorrow night. *That* would have given him something to be upset about."

"You're going to a party with the duke tomorrow night? Who is giving this party?"

"I don't know. He didn't say."

"Hm. That's odd." Lady Briarwood looked thoughtful. "Although I doubt the duke would cause you serious harm, I do not think he is above making mischief. It might be wise not to go."

Miranda pressed her lips together mutinously.

Lady Briarwood sighed. "Never mind. So, what did you say when your husband said you could not flirt or be alone with any man?"

"I said I sometimes have breakfast with your husband."

"Ha! Ha! I'll have to tell Henry that. Fancy anyone being jealous of that old goat."

"Lady Briarwood, please! I would be mortified if you told your husband."

"Oh, all right. That's a good one though. Did Huntsley say anything else?"

"He wanted me to move in with his mother so she could guide and counsel me."

"A watchdog, eh? What did you say?"

"I said I was afraid it would make Lady Thurlow uncomfortable to have to act as my jailer."

"Ha! Agatha would revel in it. So then what?"

"He said I would have to give away my baby."

Lady Briarwood's eyes widened. "My goodness. So did you inform him that you aren't with child, that you've never been unfaithful, and that he was an idiot for believing otherwise?"

"I . . . I tried. He wasn't interested in listening to anything I had to say. We were both very angry."

"Heavens, you young people are foolish," Lady Briarwood said in exasperated tones.

Miranda bowed her head, but fury still blazed in her heart. Alex deserved punishment for his arrogance.

Lady Briarwood must have glimpsed the rebellion in Miranda's face because she shook her head. But all she said was, "You and that husband of yours are well matched. You both have about as much sense as a pair of mules."

Still shaking her head, Lady Briarwood left the room. Miranda took several deep breaths to calm herself, then followed her, contemplating various ways to make Alex suffer.

Absorbed in her thoughts, she was about to go upstairs when a small figure streaked past her at a full run. Automatically, she reached out and grabbed his arm.

It was the boy the duke had almost run over.

Frantically, the boy tried to tug away, and Miranda turned to see Bomford coming after him, a menacing look on his face. She pulled the boy behind her.

"Whatever are you doing, Bomford?" she demanded.

"This—this young scalawag came to Lady Briarwood's door, bold as you please, and demanded some food. Claimed 'a lady' had sent him. As if a lady would have anything to do with the likes of him! I told him to be on his way and the little bugger bit me!" In proof, he waved his abused thumb.

"I'm sorry, Bomford. I did tell this boy to come here. I didn't realize it would be a problem." She looked down at the boy. "What is your name, child?"

"Samuel Johnson, mum."

"Well, you go with Bomford down to the kitchen, and Cook will give you some food."

Samuel looked warily at Bomford, who stared back sourly.

Samuel turned to Miranda. With a brash smile he said, "I 'us wondering, mum, if p'raps you 'ud like to 'ire me."

"Hire a dirty little ragamuffin like you?" exclaimed Bomford.

"I kin do lots o' t'ings," Samuel continued, ignoring the butler. "'Utever you wants."

Miranda was at a loss. She looked at Bomford. "Do you know of anything Samuel could do?"

Bomford shook his head emphatically.

She looked at the boy again. "What kinds of things can you do, Samuel?"

"I kin find coal, an' I kin carry packages, and I kin hold horses."

"Do you like horses?"

He nodded vigorously.

"Perhaps you can hold the horses for my guests. Would you like that?"

He beamed happily.

"My lady, please forgive me," Bomford interrupted, looking ready to explode. "But we can't have this dirty little rascal holding the horses."

"You're right," Miranda said thoughtfully. "He needs a bath first."

"A bath!" Samuel exclaimed.

"Yes. Bomford, will you please see to it?"

Miranda, her thoughts again focusing on Alex and his sins, continued on her way, ignoring the identical expressions of horror on Samuel and Bomford's faces.

21

Miranda felt nervous as she dressed for the card party the next evening. After the duke's behavior yesterday, she was not looking forward to going anywhere with him. Only the pleasant thought that Alex would be enraged if he found out convinced her not to cry off.

After her maid finished buttoning her willow green dress, Miranda picked up the matching reticule. It was stuffed with folded bills—one hundred pounds' worth—all that remained of her quarter's allowance.

The duke was prompt, and in a few minutes they were seated inside the carriage.

"I must apologize for what happened on our last drive together," he said as the carriage rolled over the cobblestones. "I hope that you were not too shaken up by it."

She couldn't see him too clearly in the dim light. "Not at all," she said coolly. "I'm sorry your curricle was smashed. Will you be able to have it repaired?"

"It's highly unlikely, but you mustn't regard it. I consider the curricle a small price to pay for the privilege of driving out with you yesterday. My only regrets are that my favorite coat was ruined—the sleeve was torn—and that our time together was so lamentably short."

She caught a glimpse of his gold quizzing glass swinging as he asked, "Was your dear husband very cross with you?"

Miranda gazed out at the passing houses. Some were dark, others had brightly lit windows. "He was a trifle upset."

In the light from a passing street lamp, she saw the duke give her a razor-sharp stare that contrasted oddly with his usually languid pose; then the carriage turned onto a darker street and she could no longer see his expression.

He laughed shortly. "How admirably discreet of you, Lady Huntsley."

The laugh made her a trifle uneasy, but she forgot about it for the moment as the carriage pulled up in front of a house. It was an unremarkable structure, no different from the other buildings that lined the street. As the duke knocked at the red baize door, she noticed a small sign that bore the discreet inscription A CLUB HOUSE.

Before she could grasp the sign's significance, the door opened a crack, then quickly swung wide. She looked a long way up to see what was surely the ugliest butler in London.

"Your Grace!" the man exclaimed. "Come in. Welcome." He held out a huge hand with large bony knuckles covered by fresh-looking scabs.

"Good evening, Argus," said the duke, handing the man his cloak and gloves. "How are the dice falling this evening?"

"Not too well for some." Argus's grin showed nearly toothless gums. "We've got a real flat at the Catch-Dolt table. He's losing the ready hand over fist."

The duke urged Miranda forward. "We shall have to avoid that particular table, won't we, Lady Huntsley?"

Another man, with waxed mustachios and a flashy

parrot-green jacket, bustled forward. "Your Grace!" he said obsequiously. "This way!" He led them to another door with a peephole, then up a narrow stairway to yet another door. This one was made of iron, and the eye that looked through the peephole inspected them thoroughly.

"Hurry up, hurry up, you imbecile!" cried the mustachioed man. "This is the duke de Morieux. Mrs. Hastings is waiting for him." The door opened slowly.

The mustachioed man pushed his way in impatiently. "We have a special table set up for you in the private parlor, Your Grace. Come this way."

Realization finally dawned on Miranda. "Is this a—a gaming house?" she whispered to the duke as they hurried down the corridor.

He looked at her with innocent surprise. "But of course. Did I not tell you? What better place to play cards?"

"But—but is it proper for me to be here?"

The duke laughed reassuringly. "Certainly. A few high sticklers might set up a screech, but many married women go to gaming houses. Now if you were a young, unmarried girl, it would be different."

Although not entirely convinced, Miranda said no more. They passed a room where she caught a glimpse of a large group of men standing around an oblong table covered with green cloth. Two dealers passed out cards and collected money from those with losing hands. A few heads turned to watch the newcomers as they walked by the doorway, but most of the men seemed intent on the play.

They finally entered a small parlor. Curiously, she looked about her. Decorated in yellow and green, the room boasted elaborately carved sofas and tables with wooden crocodile feet. A long gilded mirror hung on one wall, opposite a marble fireplace. In front of the fire, a golden-haired woman with sleepy eyes and a truly magnificent figure in purple reclined on a couch fashioned like an

Egyptian riverboat. She smiled lazily and held her hand out to the duke.

"Belle, you are as ravishing as ever," he said, bending over her hand.

"Thank you, Justin. I was so delighted when I received your note. There's no one whose company I enjoy more." She cast a seductive look at the duke and stretched her body in a way that made Miranda blush.

The woman stared with unabashed curiosity. "So this is the chick. Who is she, Justin?"

The duke took Miranda's arm and led her forward. "Lady Huntsley, may I present Mrs. Belle Hastings."

"Lady Huntsley!" Belle's eyes widened the barest fraction, which Miranda guessed was indicative of extreme surprise. Glancing speculatively from Miranda to the duke, Belle asked, "What mischief are you about, Justin?"

The duke arched an eyebrow and Belle laughed. "Very well, I won't tease you. But I must insist you let me know what game you're playing before the night is over."

"*L'ombre* is the only game I am playing tonight. Shall we begin?"

Belle nodded, a small smile on her lips. Rising to her feet languorously, she paused to arch her back, causing her full breasts to swell dangerously above her extremely low-cut dress. Unconsciously, Miranda held her breath. She exhaled on a sigh of relief when the bodice held its ground.

Through with her little exercise, Belle walked sinuously over to the card table and melted into the embrace of her chair. Miranda glanced at the duke. He was watching Belle appreciatively.

The duke moved a few steps and held out another chair. "Lady Huntsley?"

Miranda could see her reflection in the mirror behind him. Straightening her shoulders, she lifted her chin, then proceeded to walk stiffly across the room to her seat.

Several decks lay on the table, from which the eights, nines, and tens had already been discarded. Piles of counters were neatly stacked in front of Belle.

"How many counters do you wish?" Belle asked, her manner growing more brisk. "The blue are one shilling a piece, and the red are a guinea."

Miranda's eyes widened. She had never played for such high stakes. She wasn't sure she wanted to.

"Why don't you write a note for three hundred pounds, Lady Huntsley," said the duke. "That will be enough to start with." He waved his hand and a servant appeared with a piece of paper and a pen and inkwell.

Three hundred pounds! Picking up the pen, Miranda hesitated, weighing the odds. On the credit side, she liked *l'ombre*. She and her parents had played it often and she was good at it. On the debit side, she was uncertain of her opponents' skill, and she had only one hundred pounds in her reticule. If she lost, where would she get the other two hundred?

"I'll take three hundred also," the duke said.

Belle counted out the requested amount and pushed it toward the duke. Then she proceeded to count out another three hundred for herself. This done, they both turned and looked at Miranda as if to say, "Well?"

Miranda swallowed. She wanted to say no, but somehow, under their haughty gazes, her fingers began to write. Belle nodded in a businesslike manner and soon Miranda had her own neat stacks of counters. Three hundred pounds! She prayed she would not lose them.

"Do you play the *renegado* version of the game, Lady Huntsley?" Belle asked.

When Miranda confirmed that she did, they all drew for the deal. Belle won. With practiced skill, she quickly dealt out nine cards to each player. She named the trump and made her bid.

Miranda started out well, with the three matadors in her hand. The other two paid the penalty of a counter. She played her hand cautiously, counting the cards and sizing up her opponents. She won the first hand easily, and the next two also.

As the game proceeded, she won steadily, and her confidence grew. She had quickly discovered her opponents' weaknesses. Belle, surprisingly, had a good memory and counted the cards with great expertise, but she had no sense of strategy. In contrast the duke played carelessly, taking great risks and frequently forgetting which cards had been played.

Miranda soon had two rows of neatly stacked counters in front of her, totalling nearly five hundred pounds. She was excited and happy by her success, but she didn't let it distract her from the game.

"You're an excellent player," the duke said after she won a particularly tricky hand.

Miranda thought she heard a note of surprise in his voice. She flashed a smile at him. "Winter evenings were very long in Sussex."

Other than the occasional comment at the end of a hand, no one made much conversation. A servant quietly filled their wineglasses at regular intervals, but no other interruptions occurred.

The hour grew late, and still Miranda continued to win, although perhaps a trifle less frequently. Studying her current hand, she felt a surge of excitement when she saw that she had an excellent chance of taking all the tricks. She declared her intention to play for the *voll*.

"She's as lucky as Alex, isn't she, Belle?" the duke said.

Startled, Miranda looked up from her cards.

There was a pause as play was momentarily suspended. Belle looked curiously at the duke, a small smile playing about her carmined lips. Then, meeting Miranda's gaze, she said nonchalantly, "Did I mention, dear, that your husband used to play cards here occasionally? He is an excellent player also, as I'm sure you must know."

"Lady Huntsley, do forgive me!" the duke said. "I didn't mean to imply any relationship between your husband and this lady. I hope you did not misunderstand."

Miranda shook her head and the game resumed, but she had difficulty concentrating. She managed to win all the tricks in her hand, but just barely.

She lost badly in the next hand, and disastrously in the next. With appalling rapidity, her pile of counters dipped dangerously low. After a particularly devastating loss, she realized she was in danger of being done up completely. She gathered the cards for her deal, her hands trembling slightly as she remembered the note she had signed for three hundred pounds.

"Would you like to take a break, Lady Huntsley?" Belle asked kindly.

Miranda nodded thankfully. Belle pointed toward the cloak room and Miranda fled.

Alone in the small chamber, she sank down onto a divan. Her brain felt numb. She wished she had never come. She wished she had never heard of Belle Hastings and she wished she had never signed that note for three hundred pounds.

The note. Miranda tried to stifle the panic threatening to swamp her. She had to win back that note. If she didn't get it back, Alex would find out she had been here and it was suddenly very important to her that he not find out.

Alex. And Belle Hastings.

She wanted to go home, but she couldn't. Not until she bought back the note. Taking a deep breath, she rinsed her face and hands in a basin of water. The water was cool and refreshing on her hot skin. She splashed her face again, then patted it dry with a small towel.

"You will not even *think* of Alex and that woman," Miranda told her reflection fiercely. She would return to the table and play as she had never played before. She would win back the note and then she would go home.

Holding her head high, she marched back to the gaming room. She paused in front of the door, taking another deep breath. She could hear snatches of conversation inside.

"Why the devil . . . let her go . . . almost . . ."

"The poor thing . . . so young . . . shouldn't have . . . about Alex . . ."

She opened the door. Belle and the duke were standing in front of the fireplace, their backs to her, but they both turned at the sound of the door opening.

"Are you ready, Lady Huntsley?" Belle asked kindly.

She nodded and they all sat down. It was her turn to deal, so she picked up the cards and quickly passed them out.

With all her strength of will, she blanked everything out of her mind except the cards. To her grim satisfaction, she won the next two hands in quick succession.

A grueling half hour passed, and she managed to recoup some of her losses, but this time she felt no excitement. Her head pounded with the effort of thinking and not thinking at the same time.

After one especially difficult hand, Miranda paused to drink some wine. She took only a small sip, just enough to moisten her dry mouth. As she set down the glass, she noticed the duke frowning at Belle. Belle smiled slightly, then looked down as she shuffled the cards.

"Will you change places with me, Belle?" the duke asked suddenly. "I'm a little chilly, and I would like to be closer to the fire."

"Justin, you know that will interfere with the order of the deal."

"I'm willing to forego my turn. This is a friendly game, after all. Do you mind, Lady Huntsley?"

"Not at all," Miranda said. The only thing she cared about was winning back her note.

Belle looked as though she might argue, but then, with an infinitesimal shrug of her shoulders, she stood and exchanged seats with the duke.

The game took a sudden turn for the worse for Miranda. She lost steadily, no matter how carefully she played. She employed every stratagem she knew, with no success. At one point, she declared another *voll*, but then had to renounce, and was forced to double the stake.

At the same time, the duke's play improved dramatically. He continued to take enormous risks, but now they paid off. His attitude still seemed careless—he often stared off into the space behind Miranda, apparently paying no attention to the game—but he won consistently.

Her counters dwindled to one small stack.

The very next hand she suffered a *codillio,* the duke besting her and taking the last of her counters.

She bit her lip, trying to hold back her tears.

"What is the matter, my dear?" the duke asked.

She laughed a little shakily. "I'm all done up, I fear." She gestured to the empty space where her counters had been stacked.

"Nonsense. Your luck is sure to turn. It always does, and that is the only way to regain your losses."

"But I have lost all my counters."

"You can always write another voucher. Two hundred should be sufficient for you to recoup." His eyes glittered in the dim light, although his voice was businesslike. "You must not regard this small reversal. It is not as though it were a significant amount." He laughed lightly.

"Perhaps not," she said slowly. "But I think I should stop now."

There was a short silence.

Then the duke spoke cuttingly. "I'm beginning to think

you're a bit of a bore, my dear. Are you turning into a prude?
If so, perhaps we should not continue our acquaintance."

Miranda felt small and foolish, completely out of her
depth. She looked at the duke, who watched her coldly.
After hesitating a moment more, she picked up the pen and
dipped it in the inkwell. She scratched out the letters,
"I.O.U. 200 pounds." She dipped the pen in again and
started to sign her name.

The duke is dangerous.

Miranda paused as she remembered Alex's words. How
she wished she had listened to him! But she hadn't. She had
only herself to blame for getting into this mess.

And now she was the only one who could get herself out
of it.

She stared down at the piece of paper and the blot where
the ink was draining from the motionless pen.

Abruptly, she returned the pen to its stand, tore up the
paper, and rose to her feet. Looking the duke straight in the
eye, she said, "I'm sorry you feel that way. Would you
please take me home now?"

22

Alex studied the knocker on the door of his parents' town house. It was fashioned so that the top looked like a lion in full roar, ready to attack. How appropriate, he thought wryly. With considerable reluctance, he lifted the knocker and let it fall. The door opened immediately, and the butler ushered him inside.

Petronella, her stomach swelling softly under a pink dress, was just coming down the stairs. She paused at the bottom, her hand resting on the balustrade. "Alex! Are you here for dinner?"

"No, I have another engagement. I am here in answer to Mother's summons."

"Oh." She wrinkled her nose.

He smiled. "How are you feeling, Nell?"

"Well enough, thank you." She twisted a ribbon on her dress a moment, then asked, "How is Miranda?"

Alex's smile faded. "Fine. Enjoying her debut." He laughed without amusement. "And the company of the duke de Morieux."

Petronella drew back. "That awful man! I fear he means to cause trouble."

"I'm certain of it. He's certainly sniffing at Miranda's heels."

"Alex." She placed a hand on his arm. "I hope you and Miranda can work things out. I liked her very much, you know."

"Yes. So did I." He fingered his watch fob. "Don't worry. Miranda and I will reach some sort of amicable agreement."

With surprising shrewdness, Petronella asked, "But will that be enough?"

No, he thought. But to his sister, he said, "Of course. Now I had better go see what Mother wants."

Entering the drawing room a few moments later, he saw both the earl and the countess waiting for him.

Alex studied his father. Lord Thurlow was by nature a diplomat, and he usually tried to mediate in difficult situations. The earl's affability was always a direct indicator of how unpleasant an interview would be. The more amiable Lord Thurlow, the more hellish the session.

"Alex! How well you are looking, son!" The earl came forward to slap Alex on the back and shake his hand. "I hear you purchased Lord Timothy's breakdowns. Fine bits o' blood, those. I'd like to take a look at them sometime."

Alex groaned silently.

"Go ahead and sit down, son," the earl said. "No need to stand on formality here."

Alex sat down and waited.

With remarkable predictability, his mother went on the attack. "Alex! Have you no better manners than to lounge in that fashion in my drawing room? Where did you acquire your atrocious habits?"

"It must have been from me, my dear," the earl said as he shifted into a more comfortable position in his own chair. "Alex, have you noticed the new addition to my collection?"

Alex looked about the room. It was decorated in the classical style, complete with Ionic columns and Roman statues—and a collection of porcelain sculptures. He noticed a new one of a Grecian temple with a goddess adorning the top. He rose and crossed the room to inspect it. The detail was amazingly intricate. "Meissen?" he asked.

"Beautiful isn't it?" The earl beamed. "The goddess is Juno."

Juno, the special protectress of marriage and goddess of war. Alex let out a crack of laughter.

Suddenly, he felt impatient. He faced his parents, legs apart, hands behind his back. "Well?" he asked.

The countess looked at her husband helplessly, but he merely shrugged as if to say, "This was your idea, my dear."

Finding no help from that quarter, Lady Thurlow inhaled deeply. Her first words, however, were inoffensive enough. "Why aren't you living here with us?"

"I prefer my own place this visit, Mother."

She sighed heavily. "We see you so rarely, and now here is the perfect opportunity for you to visit us and what do you do? Move into some shabby lodgings! I just don't understand. Why, if you and Miranda would both stay here, you could work out your quarrel in the bosom of your family."

"That's kind of you, Mother. I will think about it."

"Hmmph." She did not look very satisfied with his answer but apparently realized she wouldn't receive a better one. She girded herself to address the real issue. "Some distressing reports have reached us."

"Oh?" Casually, he reseated himself.

"Alex," said Lady Thurlow through gritted teeth, "why is your wife residing with the earl and countess of Briarwood?"

For one insane moment, he actually considered telling her the truth, but then good sense intervened. "Miranda and I had an argument, that is all," he said quietly.

"An argument! Is that a reason for you to live apart? Why, if your father and I separated every time we had an argument, we would see each other once a year!"

"That is true," the earl agreed.

"Living apart from your wife is fanning the flames of gossip," the countess continued. "Several of my friends have told me about it."

Alex crossed his legs. "Perhaps you should find some new friends, Mother."

"This is no time to be facetious. My friends feel it is their duty to let me know what is being said. I am thankful that there are people in this world who are considerate of their duty. It is a rare quality, one to be admired." She stared hard at Alex.

He did not respond.

"I must tell you," she went on, "there has been some gossip about your wife and that . . . that man. Which isn't surprising, considering how often they have been seen together. Why, I couldn't believe my eyes when I saw how closely he held her at Lady Briarwood's ball." She closed her eyes for a moment as if she could see de Morieux and Miranda dancing right there in her drawing room. "Of course, such a disgraceful dance invites pawing. Things were very different when I was a girl—"

"My dear," the earl said, "you are drifting."

"What? Oh, yes." The countess's spine grew more rigid. "As I was saying, the duke and your wife are often seen together. He has also taken her driving, *and*"—she paused dramatically—"one of my dearest friends told me that de Morieux and your wife were at a common gaming house last night!"

Alex grew very still. *A gaming house?*

"What was one of your dearest friends doing at a gaming house?" the earl inquired innocently.

"She wasn't. Her husband's cousin, Mr. Linton, who is a

bachelor, was there. At least, so Mr. Hurley claims. It wouldn't surprise me at all to know that Mr. Hurley was there himself. I've never liked him much, and have always felt the greatest sympathy for poor Letty. Why men feel the need to attend such vulgar places is beyond me."

The earl stroked his chin. "Mrs. Hurley's husband's cousin saw Miranda and the duke de Morieux at a gaming house?"

"Yes. Mr. Linton chanced to look up just as they were passing by the doorway of the room he was in."

"Isn't it possible he was mistaken, my dear?" the earl asked.

"No," she snapped. "He was at Lady Briarwood's ball, so of course he recognized her. And he is very reliable, Letty told me. The duke and Miranda were definitely there. But that's not the worst of it." Again Lady Thurlow paused dramatically. "'Tis said the duke holds her note for three hundred pounds."

Alex gripped the arm of his chair, his knuckles turning white. There was a loud buzzing in his head that took a moment to clear.

". . . control your wife, Alex. You must make her behave. She is your wife, and it is your duty to see to her conduct. This whole situation is disgraceful. It's becoming difficult to hold up my head in front of my friends. What they must be thinking, I can't imagine. I don't know why all my children insist on causing me heartache. Even dear Thomas . . . although I think you led him on, Alex. I still remember how my heart stopped when I found you boys playing chicken in the middle of the road. That mail coach almost hit poor Thomas. And there was that time the vicar caught you and those low village boys playing kick-shins. How humiliated I was, to be sure, when Lady Putnam asked me why I allowed my sons to play such vulgar games! And then there was that time I had matching outfits for Thomas, you, and me—"

"My dear," the earl interrupted. "I think we are straying again. Alex can't change things that happened twenty years ago."

"No, but he can try harder to change what is happening now. The succession is in jeopardy, and what hope is there for an heir when Alex and Miranda are separated?" She pulled out a handkerchief and dabbed at her eyes, pausing every few seconds to see what effect she was having on her son.

"You're right, Mother," Alex said quickly. "I will take care of the matter." He made a show of pulling his watch out of his pocket. "Forgive me, Mother, Father, but I do have a dinner appointment. If that is all, I'm afraid I must run along."

Lady Thurlow lowered her handkechief. "First you must promise me that you and Miranda will move in here with us, once you are back together."

Alex hesitated.

"It is the least you can do." Her voice grew sharper. "When I think how I've worried about you, and how little I ask of you, why I would think you would—"

"Yes, yes, Mother," Alex interrupted. "That will be fine. Now I really must go."

He bowed to his visibly frustrated mother, nodded to his father, and quickly slipped out of the room. He had almost made it to the front door when he heard his name called.

"Alex, wait."

Turning, he saw his father had followed him and now stood studying him with an air of calm disinterest.

"That was rather an abrupt leave-taking."

Alex, feeling beleaguered, ran his fingers through his hair. "I'm sorry, sir. It's just that I'm having enough difficulties with Miranda right now. I don't feel I can handle Mother, too."

Lord Thurlow's gaze softened a little. "She's concerned for you. We both are."

"I know. And I am endeavoring to settle the matter to everyone's satisfaction. It just may take some time. I am discovering that my wife has an uncommonly wide stubborn streak."

"Hm. You know, Alex, as much as I dislike belaboring a point, I must agree with your mother that you need to have a care for Miranda. I'm afraid she is in over her head with the duke."

"Yes, sir, I know," Alex said, his eyes narrowing as he thought of de Morieux.

The earl gave him a piercing stare. "If I can help, let me know."

"Thank you, I will."

Alex left the house and mounted his horse. Heading toward the park, he considered what he should do about Miranda.

The obvious solution was to proceed with the divorce. She had proven herself to be unreasonable, wild, and reckless. She was defiant, contrary, and unpredictable. If he had any sense, he would be eager to wash his hands of her. And yet . . .

He turned his horse into the park, an image flashing into his mind of the first time he met Miranda at her father's house. Initially, he hadn't been impressed by the shy young girl, although with her red-gold hair, green eyes, and slim figure she was pretty enough. It wasn't until the third day of his visit, when her stepmother insisted that Miranda show their guest the garden, that he had noticed something else about her.

They had been walking in the chilly, snow-covered garden, when he said something—he couldn't remember what—that made her laugh.

He had grown still, watching her, as the golden flecks in her dark green eyes glowed brightly and the corners of her full, rosy lips curved upward. Seeing the sweet smile in her eyes and on her lips, he had known at that moment that he wanted her.

As he still wanted her.

The admission was galling. After everything she'd done, he should be eager to be rid of her. But he wasn't. Instead, he wanted to take her home to Ribblebank Manor, lock her in his bedchamber, and make love to her until she promised never again to defy him or argue with him or deny him ever again.

Coming to a clear stretch on the path, Alex nudged his horse into a trot. Actually, taking her to Ribblebank Manor might not be such a bad idea. Perhaps they could work out their problems there, without the distractions of London— and without the sly machinations of the duke.

Alex grew cold thinking again of the duke's mischief. His father was right—he had to protect Miranda from the scoundrel.

He turned down another path and urged his horse to a canter. The duke had been a thorn in his side for a long time. He never should have allowed de Morieux to escape that day ten years ago. But Petronella had begged and pleaded, and he had finally let him go.

Alex spurred his horse into a gallop, ignoring the indignant stares of the other occupants of the park as the wind whipped across his face.

While the duke had kept to himself and not bothered the Settons, Alex had been content to let him go his way. But now it was obvious that the duke was playing some new game—one that Alex had to stop before Miranda, in her innocence, was hurt.

It was time for him to teach de Morieux a lesson.

23

"*Thank you for coming out* with me, Lady Huntsley," the duke de Morieux said as they drove through the park. "I really don't deserve such kindness after my conduct of two nights ago." He glanced at her sideways, as if judging the effect of his words. "I do apologize. I'm something of a gamester myself, you see, and I got caught up in the excitement of your play."

Miranda stared straight ahead, without a reply. She felt certain that he had deliberately steered her toward disaster. Shivering, she remembered how close she had come to signing that second voucher. Three hundred pounds was bad. Five hundred would have been impossible.

Three hundred pounds. How would she ever get so much money? She had briefly considered asking her father or even Lady Briarwood, but she knew that her only real option was to confess to Alex. She would have to tell him that she needed three hundred pounds to pay a gaming debt. Three hundred pounds!

The duke steered the carriage to the side of the path to allow another equipage, moving at a brisk pace, to pass. "I tried to call on you yesterday, but your butler said you weren't receiving guests," he continued. "I cannot tell you the agonies of self-recrimination I've suffered not being able to apologize immediately. Please, dear lady, say you forgive me."

"Your message said you wanted to tell me something about my note," Miranda said coolly, ignoring his plea.

"Ah, yes." Holding the reins with one hand, he fingered the pocket of his bright yellow waistcoat. "While I was pacing my room yesterday, wondering if you would ever forgive me, I thought of a possible way to redeem myself in your eyes." He slipped two fingers into the pocket and drew out a slip of paper.

She stared at it for a moment before reaching out to grasp it.

It was her note.

The duke gave her a sidelong glance. "I bought it back from Belle and I would consider it a great favor if you would accept it as a token of my apology."

Giddy with relief, Miranda quickly stuffed the slip of paper into her reticule, then nodded coolly at the duke. She did not want to forgive him too easily. His conduct truly had been abominable.

"Thank you. I confess, I was a trifle worried about it."

"And I confess I should not have taken you there. I stepped beyond the bounds, and I deeply regret it."

She glanced surreptitiously at him. He seemed genuinely repentant. He also seemed more subdued, more respectful and sincere. Was it all an act to reinstate himself in her good graces? She decided she didn't care. The note she had spent the last two nights worrying about was now in her possession.

But the resolution of her plight did not completely relieve her mind. In fact, without the distraction of the note, her other worry loomed larger in her mind.

Belle Hastings.

Miranda remembered the woman's bright gold hair, her sinuous movements, and the lazy, good-natured worldliness in her eyes. She was beautiful, sophisticated, seductive. Everything a man could want in a woman.

Miranda stared blindly at a picturesque pond with ducks and geese. What was Belle Hastings to Alex? Everything about Belle's and the duke's behavior hinted at some secret knowledge, and she was afraid she knew what it was.

Alex had touched that woman's breasts.

"Are you comfortable?" the duke inquired solicitously.

Miranda nodded.

The duke, whose gaze was on the horses, did not see the gesture, and asked the question again.

"What? Oh, yes, yes."

He glanced at her swiftly. "Have you heard the latest about the king? 'Tis said he keeps a green silk bag which contains evidence of the queen's transgressions."

"I would think the queen could fill a sack with his." Miranda said tartly. She paused. "I have heard he has a mistress."

The duke kept his eyes on the horses. His voice, when he spoke, was neutral. "Many men keep mistresses."

"Even married men?" She inspected a small scuffed spot on one of her gloves.

"It depends on the man."

Miranda slowly lifted her eyes to look at the duke's profile. "Say, someone like my husband?"

The duke appeared to struggle with himself. "I'm not privy to such information," he said finally. "And you shouldn't worry your head about such matters. Come, have you noticed my hat? I had it from Lloyd's in Newgate Street; it's called the New Dash. What do you think of it?"

Dutifully, she inspected the hat. "It's very fine."

"Yes, it is, isn't it? I almost chose the Noble Lord, but that seemed like boasting."

In spite of her misery, Miranda felt her lips twitch.

"And then there was the Bashful; but I don't know. Somehow it seemed . . ."

"Wildly inappropriate?"

"Exactly so. How perceptive you are, Lady Huntsley."

The duke continued with this nonsense, seemingly determined to make her enjoy herself. Miranda smiled and laughed obediently, in spite of the dull ache in her heart.

She was relieved when the duke finally turned his carriage in the direction of one of the exits. As they neared it, the crush of carriages became so great that the duke had to slow his horses to a crawl.

The occupants of the other vehicles seemed much more interested in observing who was in each carriage than in the scenery. Miranda noticed several matrons whispering behind their hands when they saw her with the duke. Tilting her slightly trembling chin, she looked the other way where her gaze was caught by a small landau. Seated inside was Mrs. Overfield.

"There is your mother," Miranda told the duke.

He nodded coolly to his mother, but she didn't smile or wave or even nod back.

Miranda looked at the duke. There was a certain rigidity to his figure.

"Your mother does not look happy."

"No doubt she has been listening to gossip about me again. The rumors are enough to give any mother palpitations."

The duke's voice had a bitter edge to it, and Miranda looked at him curiously.

"How is it your mother has no title?" she asked.

"My father was already dead when I succeeded to the title," the duke replied. "It was very unexpected that I inherited at all. My father belonged to a junior branch of the family. I had no idea I was anywhere close in the line of succession. Apparently the wars and a series of accidents thinned out the heirs until only I remained."

He smiled a twisted smile.

"The timing was most fortuitous. As plain Mr. Overfield my prospects were quite limited. My father was a drunkard and a gamester who gambled away what fortune he had before blowing his brains out. The previous duke died just in time to prevent my mother and me from being imprisoned for debt. My astonishing good fortune was the talk of the *ton*. I'm surprised you did not hear of it."

He turned to look at her, still smiling. "My mother and I were suddenly inundated with visits from old 'friends' of my father's. People who had never acknowledged our existence were suddenly fawning over us." He paused to nod at another acquaintance. "After an initial period of adjustment, I grew accustomed to and accepted the privileges of rank. My mother, however, disapproves of what she calls my rakish ways. She is afraid that becoming a 'nobleman' has ruined me."

Miranda could understand his mother's worry. She was appalled by the depth of cynicism revealed by his speech. Was the *ton* really so calculating, caring only for a man's title and pocketbook? Or had the fault somehow been with the duke—perhaps the manner in which he had dealt with his sudden rank and wealth?

"No doubt you agree with my mother," he said lightly. "You have some reason to, after all. But I am now determined to turn over a new leaf in order to atone—my every action, my every word will be unexceptionable. Will that please you?"

"Actually, it sounds terribly boring."

The duke stared at her, then shouted with laughter. When he spoke, his voice was full of admiration.

"I like you, Lady Huntsley," he said. "I truly do."

*   *   *

The duke made a special effort to be as pleasant as possible as he drove Lady Huntsley home. Judging from her smiles, he was very successful. As she descended from his carriage and entered Lady Briarwood's house, he looked after her thoughtfully.

"Your Grace. Your Grace!" an importunate voice demanded. The duke turned to the small red-haired boy holding his horses.

"Shall I let 'em go, Your Grace?" the boy inquired.

The duke nodded and flipped a coin high in the air. Quick as a flash, the boy stepped away from the horses and caught the coin. With an admiring smile for the boy's dexterity, the duke set his horses for his cold, dark London town house.

A note was waiting for him there in the shabby library. His eyebrows rose when he saw the seal. Breaking it open, he quickly scanned the contents.

Your most noble grace—
  I understand you hold a certain note for 300 pounds. I wish to redeem this debt and all others I owe you. Therefore, I would consider it a great pleasure if you would meet me at Jackson's Boxing Academy today at five o'clock for this purpose. If you are unable to extricate yourself from that yellow waistcoat you so persistently wear, I shall of course understand.

                                    Yrs. &c
                                    Huntsley

The duke crumpled the missive in his fist. He stood immobile for a moment, then glanced at his watch.

Three o'clock.

His mouth a hard line, he went up to his room and rang for his valet.

Exactly one minute before five the duke sauntered into Jackson's famous academy. Alex, who had been watching the door, immediately approached him.

"My dear duke," Alex said, "how kind of you to accept my invitation."

"How could I refuse such a charmingly worded request?"

"Oh, you could have claimed you were ill or had sprained a finger. It wouldn't have surprised me." Alex held out a purse. "Three hundred pounds. The note, if you please."

"I'm afraid you are too late, Huntsley." The duke inspected his coat sleeve. "Your wife has already redeemed it."

He raised his eyes, and the two men stared at each other for a long minute.

When Alex spoke, his voice was completely devoid of emotion. "Since you are here, why don't we have a go? I have been longing to discuss some of the finer points of fisticuffs with you."

The duke was silent.

"What? No glib reply? I fear you're not quite the *man* I thought you were," Alex drawled with mock pity.

The duke's eyes were curiously blank. "I would be glad to instruct you, dear boy. I have long wanted to teach you a few lessons." He began unbuttoning his waistcoat.

Alex quickly stripped off his neckcloth.

When they were both bare to the waist, they squared off.

Two men who had just finished their own exercise and were about to leave, paused. They stood by the wall and watched as Alex and the duke circled each other.

"This looks as though it may be interesting, Barney," said the first.

"I do believe you're right Algy," said the other. "They look demmed serious."

"I'll wager a guinea on the mean-looking one," the one called Algy said, noting the ugly look in the duke's eyes.

"Done," said Barney, admiring Alex's powerful chest and shoulders and muscular arms.

Alex stared into the duke's pale green eyes, watching for a flicker that would reveal what move he planned to make. "I hope you have a goodly supply of rice powder, Your Grace."

"If not, I'm sure I can borrow some from your lovely wife," the duke drawled, not removing his gaze from Alex's.

Alex didn't so much as blink. "My wife doesn't use rice powder. I'm afraid you'll have to make do without." Alex threw a left-handed hit to draw the duke.

"That won't serve!" crowed Algy.

The duke placed a jab to Alex's jaw, causing Alex's head to snap back. He quickly recovered and returned with a left-right punch to the duke's nose.

"Hah!" cried Barney. "That's altered his weathercock and shifted his wind!"

The duke and Alex backed off and circled each other, watching for an opening.

Alex kept his guard high. "You've improved, Your Grace. I suppose you must have ample opportunities to practice."

In spite of the blood oozing from his nose, the duke smiled. "Yes. Foolish brothers and husbands abound in this world. It's no wonder their women seek to escape from them. I, of course, feel obligated to help any lady in distress."

"If only you would wait until the ladies ask for your help," Alex said, shaking the sweat from his eyes.

The duke was quick to take advantage with a punishing left to Alex's jaw, followed by a blow to his stomach.

"Ho, ho, ho, a home hit to the breadbasket!" cackled Algy.

"My dear boy," the duke drawled, "certain ladies *beg* me to take them away from their dreary husbands."

Alex, still wheezing from the force of the last blow, straightened, a hot red mist rising in front of his eyes. Rushing the duke, he grappled with him. The duke managed a blow to his shoulder before Alex, with a violent swing, threw him to the ground. Dropping to his knees, Alex captured the duke's head in a vise with his left arm, while serving out a series of blows with his right.

"That's the ticket! Peppermint his upper story but good now!" Barney encouraged Alex.

With one last punch, Alex let go of the duke. Staggering, Alex rose to his feet and leaned against the wall, watching as the duke slowly sat up and wiped the blood from his nose and mouth.

"Had enough?" Alex panted.

"Yes, I think I have. More than enough." The duke made no move to rise from the floor.

The two onlookers hurried over to congratulate Alex and clap him on the shoulder. Ignoring his wince of pain, they complimented him on his "science" and went into a blow-by-blow analysis of the bout.

"Great fight," Barney concluded. As he and his friend walked out the door, he said, "Algy, pay up."

Alex straightened and started pulling on his shirt and waistcoat. When he had completed this amazingly difficult process, he noticed that the duke, who had managed to get to his feet, had already finished dressing. The duke looked up and met Alex's gaze.

In a deadly cold voice, Alex said, "Stay away from her."

"My dear boy." The duke lifted his quizzing glass to his

one good eye. "Don't be foolish. I have my reputation to think of."

With that enigmatic statement, the duke gathered up his belongings and limped out the door.

Alex did not waste much time pondering the duke's words. Various parts of him were beginning to throb in a most unpleasant manner. Just the effort of getting on his horse caused a shaft of pain to shoot through his shoulder; and as he rode at a snail's pace back to his lodgings, the cold breeze stung the raw skin of his jaw like a thousand nettles.

After what seemed like an eternity, he entered the building where his lodgings were and paused at the bottom of the stairs. Looking up the steep ascent, he groaned. At this moment, Mount Olympus could not have been more daunting. He lifted one foot up to the first step, then stopped to rest, leaning heavily on the railing.

Eventually, he managed to limp all the way up the stairs and hobble down the corridor. Like a weary pilgrim, his destination finally in sight, he walked a little faster.

He reached the door and opened it, wanting to do nothing more than fall into bed and rest his aching body.

"My lord, thank heaven you're back!" his valet said in greeting. Then after taking a good look at his master he gasped. "What happened?"

"Never mind." Alex tried to shrug out of his coat, but his shoulder was too stiff. "Help me with my coat."

"Of course, of course, my lord," the valet said. "Er, but you might want to look at this first."

"This" was a sealed document. Alex took the heavy piece of parchment and studied the judicial seal. Slowly, almost reluctantly, he broke the sealing wax and unfolded the document.

The first sentence made him forget about his stiff shoulder

and his aching jaw. He read the rest of it, and then reread it to make sure he had understood correctly.

There was no mistake.

Within ten minutes he was out the door and on his way to Grosvenor Square.

24

Dusk was falling, but Miranda did not light a candle. She lay on her stomach, fully dressed, across her bed. Her chin rested on one hand, while the fingers of the other played with a loose thread on the coverlet. Her tuggings on the string wreaked havoc with the blanket's pattern, but in her distraction, she did not notice.

Belle Hastings.

How beautiful she was. How . . . liquid. Every motion she'd made had been boneless, beckoning. Miranda had seen the curious manner in which the duke had watched Belle. He liked the way the woman moved, she could tell. She had a feeling most men would like it. Including Alex.

Alex and Belle Hastings.

Miranda's throat tightened, squeezing unpleasantly. From anger, of course. Anger at Alex. She didn't really care about what he had done—she was going to divorce him after all—but what gall to complain about her taking a lover when he'd had one all along! She was so angry, why, she could feel tears burning behind her eyes.

Someone knocked at her door, but she didn't answer.

She continued to pluck at the string, trying to will away the foolish tears.

"Lord Huntsley is below in the library, my lady," Bomford called through the door.

She tensed, her fingers growing still on the string.

"I told him Lord and Lady Briarwood were out for the evening, but he requests the pleasure of your company for a few minutes." Bomford sounded a little doubtful as he relayed the message.

Alex probably had not couched it in such polite terms, Miranda thought angrily. "Tell him I don't want to see him ever again."

There was a short silence. "Are you certain that's what you desire me to say?" Bomford asked uneasily.

Miranda thought of Belle. "Yes, I'm certain."

She heard Bomford's footsteps retreating. Angrily, she yanked at the string. Alex had a lot of nerve coming here. She wished she'd never married him. From the beginning there had been something about him that made her uneasy. Mr. Pelham had tried to warn her, but she had been too innocent to understand. Now, she did.

All Alex understood or cared about was carnal lust. He had no appreciation for the finer emotions. He was like the brute beasts—

The door crashed open.

Gasping, Miranda rolled over and sat up.

Alex stood in the doorway, a piece of paper clenched in his upraised fist. There was a scratch by one glittering blue eye and his jutting chin sported a bright purple bruise.

She gasped again.

Before she could gather her wits to speak, he slammed the door shut, strode over, and waved the piece of paper in front of her nose. Through clenched teeth he demanded, "What the hell is the meaning of this?"

With an effort, she tore her gaze away from his face to

glance at the paper. His furious movements prevented her from reading it, but she could see that it was some sort of document. She opened her mouth to say she hadn't the least idea when enlightenment dawned, and she realized exactly what the paper was.

She straightened her spine. "It's a court order prohibiting you from doing me bodily injury. It is obtained through a process called 'swearing the peace.' I applied for it through the courts."

He stared at her uncomprehendingly.

"If you strike me, I can have you thrown in jail," she explained kindly.

"I know what it means," he snapped, crumpling the paper in his fist. "What I want to know is, Why? I have never struck you. I have never so much as lifted a hand to you. Was a court order necessary? Was it?"

"You threatened to beat me," she reminded him. "I didn't want to take any chances."

He glared at her. "I would never strike you—or any woman—whether you have this silly piece of paper or not." Bending over her, he shook the mangled document in her face. "Do you realize that if the newspapers get hold of this, I will be a laughingstock? Do you?"

Miranda eased to one side and rose to her feet, facing him haughtily. "Judging by your uncontrolled manner—not to mention the condition of your face—I would say the newspapers will have a field day."

He raised a hand to his swollen jaw. "Men like the duke de Morieux can only understand something if it's pounded into their heads," he said grimly.

She stuck her nose in the air. "Men like the duke and *you*, apparently."

"I'm nothing like the duke," he snapped. "I don't lie or cheat or steal, and I certainly don't take young women to gaming halls and let them lose three hundred pounds."

She gasped. "How did you find out about that?"

"My mother's spies are everywhere."

His momentary wryness was lost on Miranda. "How convenient for you," she said waspishly. "I suppose you keep a green bag like the king's, filled with all the gossip about me. Tell me, do you and His Majesty compare notes on your wives' misbehavior?"

"If we did, I'm sure Caroline would be a model of propriety compared to you," he said coldly. "What possessed you to go to such a disreputable place? No decent woman would be seen there."

"Perhaps that's why I went. Perhaps I wanted to see an *in*decent woman. Perhaps I wanted to meet Mrs. Belle Hastings—your mistress."

For a fraction of a second, he met her gaze. She stared into his eyes, and she knew it was true.

A shiver coursed through her. She wrapped her arms around herself, trying to ward off the chill.

"Belle is nothing but a friend," he said, his face coolly composed now.

Her shivers increased. A small corner of her brain noticed that the shadows in the room were lengthening. She walked over to the fireplace, took three candles from the mantel, and stared down at them. "But once she was something else?"

"This is irrelevant." His voice was full of impatience. "You sound like a jealous wife."

"*I* sound jealous?" She laughed bitterly. "You can say that when you've waxed so indignant about my mythical lover?"

"Hardly mythical when the fruit is so abundant." His laugh was equally bitter. "I didn't come to you with a child in my belly."

Her fingernails sank into the soft wax of the candles. "So, if I hadn't become pregnant, everything would have been fine? You wouldn't have cared if I had a lover?"

"It's different for men." The dimness of the room obscured his features. "Men expect their wives to be chaste."

She stared down at the candles again. "And shouldn't wives expect the same from their husbands?"

"It helps if the man has some experience." He moved slowly forward. "It increases the woman's enjoyment."

"Hah. There's not that much to it."

He stopped in the middle of the room. Then he continued forward until he was standing beside her and staring down at the fire. When he spoke, there was a curious bleakness in his voice. "Perhaps you are right—there is no logic to it." Quietly, he added, "But it still eats at me to think of you in another man's arms."

A candle slipped through her fingers and fell to the floor, but she made no move to retrieve it. Was he trying to tell her that he cared about her? A tiny spurt of joy flickered inside of her. She stared at his profile, at the firelight limning it, and wished she could see his expression. Perhaps . . . oh, perhaps they *could* work everything out.

"Alex . . ." She placed her hand on his arm. "It never happened."

His arm stiffened under her touch. "What never happened?"

"I never had a lover."

He turned to look at her, the firelight casting deep shadows on the planes and angles of his face. "Miranda, you told me so yourself."

"I did no such thing!"

"What nonsense is this?" He sounded inexplicably angry. "Do you honestly expect me to believe that you never had a lover?"

She nodded.

He laughed harshly. "Are you saying your child is the result of an immaculate conception?"

His question confused her. "I don't think so," she said cautiously.

"What *are* you saying, Miranda?"

"I'm saying that *you* are the father of the baby. At least, you were. I mean, I thought you were. I find I'm not increasing after all."

His head turned toward her sharply and he stared at her through the shadows for a long moment. Abruptly, he took the two candles from her hands and lit them in the fire. A soft light spread through the room. He put them in their holders and then turned back to her again.

She expected to see signs of relief in his face, but instead he was staring at her strangely.

"Miranda," he said, watching her closely, "how could I be the father of a baby when we never consummated our marriage?"

Miranda stepped back in astonishment. "But we did! Don't you remember? At Ribblebank Manor, you kissed me, and you . . ."

She paused, a slight blush rising in her cheeks. Her voice dropped to a whisper.

"You touched my breasts."

25

No.

It wasn't possible. No one could be *that* innocent.

Alex stared at the blush rising in Miranda's cheeks. No. It couldn't be true. Perhaps some girls went to their marriage beds completely ignorant of what was going to happen to them, but surely not Miranda—not his bright, impudent, capable Miranda.

He stared at her puckered brow, her wide, confused, *innocent* green eyes.

Dear Lord above.

He stumbled over to the bed and sat down, elbows on his knees, his hands shielding his face.

How could he have been so *stupid?*

His shoulders began to shake.

"Alex?" Her voice was tentative, and he felt her gentle hand on his shoulder.

He gasped for breath.

"Are you all right?" she asked.

It was too much.

He inhaled a lungful of air, then released it again in a great guffaw of laughter. Miranda, her eyes widening, pulled her hand away from him as if he'd bitten her.

Alex, holding his aching shoulder, laughed until tears ran down his face.

"Why are you laughing, you cad?" she snapped. "Stop it at once."

He laughed harder.

Her mouth tightened. "Very well, you overgrown hyena. Go ahead and laugh. You can laugh yourself into the grave for all I care!"

Crossing her arms over her chest, she turned on her heel and presented him with a view of her slender back.

Alex closed his eyes, trying to check a fresh wave of laughter. He shouldn't be laughing at her. And he wasn't. Not really. If anything, he was laughing at himself for being such a fool.

If he wasn't a viscount, he would surely qualify for the position of village idiot.

He opened his eyes. Miranda stood in front of him, her back rigid. He sobered as he remembered the hurt that had flashed in her eyes before she turned around. He thought of what she must have endured these last weeks. No wonder she had been so angry.

He would make it up to her, he promised himself. He would make it up to her.

Starting right now.

Miranda was biting back tears as she stared down at the carpet. She trembled angrily as she thought of his laughter. She had held out an olive branch, and he had laughed at her! He really was a beast—

She jumped when his arm slid around her waist and pulled her down. Plopping down onto his lap, she glanced up, startled, to see that his blue eyes were still gleaming with laughter but also with regret—and something else.

"Miranda," he said, lifting her hand to his lips, "can you ever forgive me?"

A tiny quiver shot through her hand and along her arm and up to her heart where hope flickered anew. "If you will explain the joke, I might find it amusing, also."

His eyes gleamed brighter. "I would be delighted to. But first I must apologize for misjudging you."

"Oh!" She wriggled a little on his lap. "Then you believe me that I didn't have a lover?"

He nodded. "It was stupid of me to think you did. I should have known—but I'm afraid I haven't been thinking very clearly ever since I met you." He brushed a loose strand of her hair back from her face. "Will you forgive me?"

Happiness bloomed in her heart and she smiled at him. "Of course, I will. But tell me, whatever made you think such a thing about me?"

"Are you certain you want me to explain?"

"Of course."

He lowered his mouth to hers and kissed her—very thoroughly.

She was gasping for breath when he finally lifted his mouth. "Wh-what are you doing, Alex?"

His tongue explored the corner of her mouth and traced up over the bow. "I'm attempting to explain. But in order to do so, I must explain the meaning of 'consummation.'" His tongue continued down to her full lower lip and gently caressed it.

Pleasure curled through her, making it difficult to think. She forced herself to pull her mouth away. "What do you mean?"

His hands stroked her waist. "I mean, dear innocent, that our marriage has not been consummated."

"What?" Miranda nearly fell off his lap. Only his hands tightening on her waist prevented her. She grew very still at his grasp, and suddenly the warm fluttering in her heart moved down to her stomach and turned cold.

There must be more to this consummation business than she had thought.

She looked into his dark blue eyes uncertainly, trying not to panic. "What else is there?"

"I would be glad to show you," he offered.

"Right now?"

He nodded.

"I don't know . . ." The cold flutters in her stomach increased. She tried to stand up, but his hands tightened around her waist.

He pressed her head against his shoulder. She held herself stiffly, but he stroked her back gently and after a few minutes she found herself relaxing.

"Miranda," he asked softly, "why are you so frightened?"

"I'm not frightened exactly," she lied. She groped for the words to explain her vague fears. "It's just that I worry that you are allowing your carnal lust to corrupt you."

His shoulders shook for a moment. "I don't think you need to worry about that. There's nothing wrong with a little bit of lust between husband and wife. Don't you remember the marriage ceremony? 'With my body, I thee worship.'" He kissed her ear, his tongue tracing the curves. "Let me show you, Miranda."

She hesitated, wanting to say no. The cold flutters were still in her stomach, and she was afraid.

But at the same time she wanted to say yes.

She was tired of being afraid. It seemed she had been fighting her fear ever since she married him. And the worst of it was she didn't even know what she was afraid of or why.

Perhaps it was time to find out.

She squared her shoulders. "Very well. I am ready."

He choked a little. "You are?"

She nodded, studying the lapel of his coat. "Will you tell me what to do?"

"Of course, I will. First, I must take off your dress."

"Take off my dress!" If she did that he would see her petticoat. The idea was shocking. Her petticoat was fairly modest, true, but still . . .

She bit her lip. "Does everyone do that?"

He nodded solemnly.

"I see." She bit her lip again, then straightened her spine. "Very well, go ahead."

She looked down as he tugged at the top bow of her gown. His large, masculine hands seemed alien against the white cotton and blue satin ribbons of her dress. He untied the next one, too, his fingers brushing against her breasts through the material as he did. She wondered if he could feel her heartbeat. Surely he must. It was pounding under his fingers like a kettledrum.

He continued to untie the ribbons all the way to the hem, the material parting slightly to reveal her petticoat beneath, and then stood up, bringing her with him. He pulled the dress off her shoulders and tossed it on the floor. Then he stepped back to look at her standing there in her muslin petticoat.

She blushed as his gaze roved over her. She wished he wouldn't stare at her so blatantly. She was relieved when he turned her around so that her back was to him.

Her relief evaporated, however, when she felt him undoing the tapes of her petticoat.

"Alex!"

But it was too late. The petticoat gaped away from her shoulders. She reached up to hold it in place, but his hands came around to cover hers and his lips were against her ear. "You have to take off your petticoat, too, Miranda."

Her petticoat, too! She had nothing on underneath, except her corset and her garters, stockings, and slippers.

She wasn't even wearing pantalettes–a lapse in proper behavior she now regretted.

He would see . . . he would see . . . *everything.*

She stood there frozen, tremors coursing through her. "Is that necessary?" she asked.

"It's very necessary." His voice sounded husky. "Let go of your petticoat, Miranda."

She clutched the material more tightly.

"Miranda . . ." His lips traced down her neck and shoulder. "Let go."

Squeezing her eyes shut, she obeyed. She felt his hands at her shoulders, pushing the material down until it pooled at her feet. She felt a draft on her naked bottom and on her bare breasts where her corset pushed them up.

There was a long silence.

She peeked through her eyelashes. Alex stood in front of her, staring at her, his eyes so dark they looked black.

He glanced up and met her gaze. "Miranda," he said hoarsely, "take down your hair."

She hesitated a moment, then raised her arms to pull the pins free.

His gaze immediately fell to her breasts again.

She felt as though her cheeks were on fire as her hair fell around her shoulders.

Without looking away, he shrugged out of his coat and waistcoat and stripped off his cravat. He pulled his shirt loose from his trousers and pulled it over his head.

Involuntarily, she stared, unable to tear her gaze away from his chest. It was very broad and muscled, with small flat nipples and a light dusting of hair. He was very different from her. He was all rough planes and hard angles where she was soft, smooth curves—

His hands went to the buttons on his trousers and her eyes widened. Then she squeezed them shut again.

A minute later, she heard the clunk of his boots hitting

the floor. A few more seconds passed, and she felt him untying the strings of her corset, but by this time she wasn't really surprised. The garment fell away.

He pushed her gently down onto the bed. She lay there stiffly, afraid to open her eyes. He removed her slippers and rolled down her stockings. The mattress sagged and she felt the full length of him against her—his hot bare skin pressing against her and the rough hair of his chest scratching her breasts. His mouth covered hers again, and his hands caressed her curves.

Shock and pleasure intermingled. His tongue plunged into the inner recesses of her mouth while his fingers cupped and stroked and teased her breasts. Then his lips slipped down to kiss the pulse in her neck.

He lifted his mouth and blew gently on the spot, then kissed the pulse again. Her blood heated and rushed through her veins. His mouth moved to the hollow of her shoulder, and his fingers traveled down to her navel to lightly trace circles on her skin. Her stomach muscles quivered.

His mouth moved lower and covered her breast. Gasping, she slid her fingers into his dark, crisp hair. His tongue flicked against the peak of her breast and she tightened her fingers in his hair. His mouth suckled gently. She arched her back, gasping again with the sweet pleasure of it.

She was almost too dazed with the sensations his mouth was creating to notice that his fingers were creeping down to her thighs and slowly insinuating themselves between. Her first real awareness was when she felt his finger stroking the moist folds between her legs.

She stiffened and pressed her legs together, but he kept kissing her breasts and teasing the soft inner skin of her thighs, until helplessly she allowed him to do what he wanted.

His fingers stroked her again and again until she was slick with wetness. She was embarrassed by the odd moisture, but she heard Alex make a soft sound of satisfaction. Slowly, carefully, he eased his finger into her.

Her eyes flew open and she yanked her hips away, trying to pull back from him. He responded by covering her mouth with his and moving on top of her.

She felt something pressing against her. Something big and strange and hard. She tried to keep her legs together, but one of his knees pressed between hers, spreading them, and he settled himself right up against the most intimate part of her.

Some of the pleasure faded, and fear streaked through her as a hazy idea formed of what he was going to do to her. "Alex. Alex!"

His body grew still for a moment. He lifted his mouth from hers and looked down at her. "Shh," he whispered. "Don't be frightened, Miranda. Please don't be frightened. Do you want me to stop? I will if you want me to."

She opened her mouth to say yes, but the word stuck in her throat. In spite of her fear, she didn't want the warm tingling in her blood to stop. Part of her couldn't bear to let it stop. Her body wanted the feeling to continue and grow. But her brain was reeling from shock.

She stared up at him. He was holding himself very still, and the muscles in his face were taut as though he was under a great strain.

"Miranda?"

He wanted very much to finish this, she realized hazily.

Her arms crept around his neck. "I . . . I don't want to stop," she whispered.

His mouth softened and curved upward. Then it covered hers and she felt him probing between her legs. He slipped inside her. She held her breath.

Nothing happened.

It did not hurt or feel good. It just felt odd—very odd—to have part of him inside her.

He kissed her ear and murmured, "I am going to have to hurt you a little, Miranda. But it will only be this one time."

"Oh." She bit her lip. "Very well. Go ahead."

He kissed her cheeks, her eyebrows, and her eyelids as he slid deeper inside her and pressed against the barrier there. She felt as though he was stretching her, splitting her skin in an effort to fit into a place that was too small for him. The pressure increased and intensified until suddenly something broke and he plunged through.

She bit her lip harder until she tasted blood in her mouth.

He grew still again. "God, I'm sorry, Miranda."

"Never mind. I'm glad it's over with." She felt strangely disappointed. "It really wasn't so bad."

His mouth paused against her forehead. "It wasn't?"

"No. Although to be perfectly honest, I don't know why you were so eager to do it."

His shoulders shook. "We're not done yet, Miranda. Is the pain fading?"

The pain had indeed faded. She frowned up at him, wondering what on earth he was going to do now. Wondering what else he possibly could do.

She soon found out.

He withdrew a little, then pushed into her again. To her surprise, a tiny frisson of pleasure pulsed through her. He repeated the motion and the sensation increased.

He continued to move over her and the pleasure grew stronger and stronger. Her earlier excitement returned and intensified as he continued to stroke the direct source of her pleasure. She grew accustomed to the rhythm and began, awkwardly at first, then with greater skill, to return his thrusts, meeting and matching his movements, seeking the ever-increasing pleasure.

Her blood learned the cadence also, and pulsed faster and faster. She wanted something, something she couldn't identify. Clutching Alex's shoulders, she strained toward it, arching her back and lifting her hips. Suddenly, a great burst of spiraling pleasure soared through her, making her gasp and cry out. Bright rainbow colors flashed behind her eyes, and her blood raced as if she were riding on the tail of a shooting star.

At almost the same moment, she felt a matching pulsing in him. He tensed. "Dear heaven!" he gasped, then collapsed against her.

Her blood slowed and cooled, but she lay shaking. Her brain began to function, and she was aware of a strange jumble of emotions: pleasure and happiness, but also embarrassment and shock. How wrong, how *very* wrong she had been about consummation!

Alex eased himself off of her and she felt his fingers in her hair, gently stroking, smoothing it back from her face. With exquisite care, he bent over her and kissed her brow, following the line of it, murmuring unintelligible, soothing words. Gradually the trembling in her limbs ceased, and she felt the warm comfort of Alex's hands caressing her arms and shoulders.

He raised himself on an elbow and leaned over her to inspect her face. Whatever he saw apparently satisfied him, for he smiled wickedly, then turned onto his back and pulled her to his side.

As she lay in the crook of his arm, a warm glow spread through her. She felt so close to him—closer than she'd ever felt to anyone. She felt as though she would never be unhappy, or confused, or uncertain again.

"Do you understand what consummation is now, Miranda?" he whispered into her ear. "Or would you like me to explain again?"

26

"I think you've managed to explain consummation very thoroughly," Miranda said primly, turning her face to hide her smile.

Alex lifted a handful of her hair to his nose and inhaled, then spread it out over the pillow. "Actually, I did leave out a few details."

She looked at him suspiciously. "I don't believe you."

His brows rose and the familiar gleam lit his eyes. "I can see I'm going to have to prove it to you."

He leaned over her, but she laughingly evaded his kiss. "Stop it, Alex. I want to talk to you before you leave."

"Leave?"

"Yes, leave. Lord and Lady Briarwood will be home soon. You're going to have to go."

His lips drifted lazily down her throat. "Hm. I suppose you are right. I doubt Lady Briarwood would appreciate an unshaven, uninvited guest at her breakfast table."

"I don't think she would mind." Miranda tried to control her breathing. "But I would be very embarrassed. I think

Lady Briarwood will be happy for me. She's been so kind, helping me with divorcing you. She is the one that told me about 'swearing the peace,' and she even used her acquaintance with one of the judges to have the order rushed through the courts."

His lips paused at the juncture of her neck and shoulder. "How generous of her," he said, a trifle sardonically.

"Yes. She's been the greatest support to me, and so understanding. . . . Oh, good heavens!" Miranda sat straight up in bed, holding the sheet to her breasts.

He leaned on one elbow, watching her. "What's wrong?"

"Alex, I just remembered. I told Lady Briarwood that we consummated our marriage in the library at Ribblebank!"

Alex's eyebrows rose nearly to his hairline before he started to shake with laughter. "Perhaps she just thought I was extremely impatient."

"I'm certain she must," Miranda said shamefacedly. "Because I told her it only took a few moments."

Alex shouted with laughter.

"Hush!" Miranda said, trying to control her own laughter. "No wonder she looked at me so strangely."

"So I would think. She must have a very strange idea of me indeed." He swung his legs over the edge of the bed.

"I think everyone has a strange idea of us." Discreetly, Miranda studied his broad back. "But I suppose that's to be expected since *you* had some very strange ideas."

Alex looked over his shoulder at her. "*I* had strange ideas? What about you?"

She scooted back against the headboard, still holding the sheet in place. "Never mind about me. How could you possibly think that I had done *that* with someone else?"

He picked up his drawers and stood up. "What else was I to think when you said you were pregnant?"

She stared at his firm buttocks in fascination. "I did not actually *say* I was pregnant," she murmured. She caught a glimpse of his front as he pulled on his drawers. She frowned. She could have sworn that his . . . his instrument of carnal lust was much larger than that.

"Don't quibble. It's lucky Pelham went to America or I would have throttled him."

Miranda looked up from his whatever it was and gaped at him. "Pelham! You thought Mr. Pelham was my lover?"

Sitting back down on the bed, he nodded and pulled on his knee-high stockings.

"But he only loved me in a very *pure* way."

Alex snorted and picked up his shirt. "If you still think that, then you are hopeless, Miranda."

A small frown knitted her brow as she watched him raising his arms to pull on his shirt. For some reason, his words disturbed her, but she couldn't quite figure out why—

"Ow," he groaned, lowering his arms again. "I hurt like the very devil."

The niggling unease retreated to a distant corner of her brain. Grasping the sheet tightly, she rose onto her knees and touched his arm. "Where does it hurt?"

"My shoulder." He rotated it slowly, as if trying to ease the discomfort. "I think it may be sprained."

"Did your valet look at it?"

"No, I was too eager to visit my impudent wife."

With a tsking noise, she bent down and retrieved her petticoat from the floor. She managed to pull it on without releasing her hold on the sheet in spite of his amused gaze.

"Haven't you lost your modesty yet?" he drawled, watching her with blatant interest. "I'm going to have to cure you of that.

Blushing, she climbed out of bed. With as much dignity as she could muster, she went over to the wardrobe and withdrew a roll of bandages and a jar of liniment.

She returned to Alex's side and applied a liberal amount of the strong-smelling ointment to his shoulder.

She frowned as he groaned. "Did the duke do this to you?"

He nodded.

Her frown deepened. "Why were you fighting with him, anyway?"

"I was trying to redeem your gambling debt."

She stepped back to stare at him. "It so happens I took care of that myself!"

"So I understand. I'm still curious to know how."

She rubbed some more of the ointment onto his shoulder, her fingers not so gentle this time. "The duke gave it to me."

She felt him stiffen. "Oh, did he?"

"Yes, and you needn't look like that." She stepped closer to him to wrap the bandage around his shoulder. "I'm convinced he had no ulterior motive."

She leaned forward, and he placed his hands on her hips, steadying her. "That only shows how little you know the duke," he murmured.

"That only shows how little you trust my judgment," she retorted, leaning forward to wind the bandage around him again.

"Mmmmm."

Thinking she had hurt him, she glanced down in concern, only to see him staring at her barely concealed breasts, which were bobbing very close to his face.

She frowned and finished tying the bandage, pulling on it with a sharp tug that made him groan in earnest this time. "You didn't answer me, Alex."

He sighed. "Let's not talk about de Morieux," he said, pulling his shirt on and reaching for his boots. "I can think of a hundred topics more interesting."

She picked up his cravat. "I think we need to talk about the duke."

He tugged on one of his boots. "If you insist. But not

now. I have to go. You can talk all you want once we move into my parents' house."

"Move in with your parents!" Her hands tightened on his linen cravat. "Why must we do that?"

"Renting a house during the Season is very expensive," he said, tugging on his other boot. "After the mess my granduncle left, I can't afford to waste money on trifles."

She folded the length of linen between her fingers. "Perhaps we could borrow some money from my father."

"We don't need to borrow money from your father." He pulled on his waistcoat.

"But if my dowry wasn't enough—"

"Your dowry was very generous. It would have helped the estate considerably if I had chosen to use it."

Her fingers grew still on the cravat. "You didn't use my dowry? But why?"

"I have no desire to live off my wife." He shrugged into his coat. "The money is in trust for you."

She brightened. "If the money is in trust for me, then I will use it to rent us a house."

He shook his head. "It would be irresponsible of me to allow you to spend your money on frivolities."

"I thought you said the money was for me."

"It is. But I control it."

"So it is really *your* money."

"Miranda, let's not argue about this. We will only be staying with my parents for a few weeks. Will that be so horrible?"

"Yes, it will. Your mother makes me nervous."

Alex laughed rather callously, Miranda thought. "You'll grow accustomed to her. She's not so bad. And it will relieve my mind considerably to know she's watching over you when I'm not around."

Miranda stiffened. "What do you mean by that?"

He gave her a sardonic look. "You know exactly what I mean."

"You still don't trust me, do you?"

"Of course I trust you. I don't trust *him.*"

"There's nothing wrong with the duke."

"That's a matter of opinion. His dissipations are legendary and he's nearly run off his legs. He is so in debt, he had to sell his horses and carriages and now has to hire out from the jobmaster. De Morieux is an unsavory character, and everyone in town knows it—except you. There's only one thing he's interested in from you, Miranda."

His words reminded her of his similar comment about Mr. Pelham. "You seem to think that every man who is friendly to me is driven by his carnal lusts."

"Most of them probably are," Alex agreed.

"It would seem men are quite indiscriminate about such matters," she said quietly.

He was silent a moment. Then he said gently, "You don't understand, Miranda. Men are different from women."

"You said that before."

"It's true. A man sometimes needs a physical release. It means nothing."

She crumpled the cravat into a tight ball. "So what we did tonight meant nothing to you?"

"Of course it meant something. You are my wife."

That was not what she wanted to hear. She wanted to hear him say that he felt something for *her*, that he felt more for her than just lust, that what they had shared tonight meant as much to him as it did to her. She handed him his cravat. "I think you'd better go."

He frowned at the wrinkled piece of linen. "Miranda, I don't want to argue with you. We are going to my parents' house."

Her lips tightened. "And I have no say in the matter?"

"You've had your say." He moved over to the dressing table mirror.

"That's not good enough, Alex. I don't want to move in with your parents."

"You have no choice. You are my wife." Bending down, he looped the wrinkled cravat around his neck and tied a simple knot.

She glared at his back. "If you cared for me at all, you wouldn't insist on something that you know will make me unhappy!"

He straightened and turned to stare at her, his eyes narrowing. "You are beginning to sound quite childish."

"I'm only trying to make you listen to me."

"I have listened. But the fact remains, we are moving in with my parents."

"Perhaps *you* are." She lifted her chin. "*I* am staying here."

He grew very still. "What did you say?" His voice was dangerously soft.

She quailed a little under his stare, but she refused to look away. "If you move in with your parents, I am going to stay here."

His jaw tightened. "If that's the way you want it," he said quietly. "Let me know when you come to your senses."

She watched in disbelief as he strolled out the door and shut it softly behind him.

27

Miranda woke up slowly the next morning. She kept her eyes closed, hoping the stabbing pain behind them would go away. It didn't. Hoping to fall back asleep, she rolled over and buried her face in her pillow. The smell of leather and tobacco assailed her nostrils.

Her breath caught and she started to roll away, but then, almost convulsively, she pressed her face to the pillow and inhaled deeply.

Instantly, memories floated through her brain. Memories of kisses and touches and pain and pleasure. Wondrous pleasure.

And then pain again.

Tears stung her eyes as she remembered the sharp words they had exchanged. But even worse than the words was the realization that he didn't care for her. He never had. All he cared about was carnal lust.

She understood now why she had been so afraid. She had opened herself to him in a way that made her completely vulnerable, and she had given him something that

was an expression of a much deeper emotion on her part.
And he had taken it. But he had given nothing in return
except lust. Last night she had risked everything—and lost.

Now she had a difficult decision to make, and she knew
what she must do.

She dressed and went downstairs to look for Lady
Briarwood.

She found the older woman in the breakfast room, dining on ham and eggs.

"Good morning, Miranda," the countess said in greeting.
"Would you like some breakfast?"

"No, thank you. But I would like to talk to you."

Lady Briarwood studied Miranda's face for a moment,
then said gently, "Sit down my dear and tell me what's on
your mind."

Miranda seated herself on one of the hard, straight-
backed chairs and stared down at the lace tablecloth. "I
spoke to Alex last night."

The countess cut off a bite of ham. "I take it you and
Huntsley did not reconcile." She placed the ham in her mouth.

Miranda shook her head. "We did clear up the misunderstanding about my having a lover. But there are other things
that we can't seem to settle."

"Such as?" The countess took a bite of eggs.

Miranda traced a tiny embroidered flower on the tablecloth with her finger. "He doesn't trust me, for one—he is
quite unreasonable about the duke de Morieux. And he
won't let me spend my own money, for another. And he
wants us to live with his parents."

"Gracious me." Lady Briarwood ate some more of the
eggs. "Anything else?"

Miranda put her hand back in her lap and bowed her
head. "He doesn't . . . care for me."

The countess set down her fork. "Nonsense, girl, of
course he does."

Miranda shook her head. "It's hopeless. So I've come to a decision about what I must do. I am going to go back to Black Down Abbey. I think my father will take me in. I really can't impose on you any longer."

"You're not imposing," Lady Briarwood said. "I love having you here. And besides, hasn't your father remarried? I doubt his new wife will enjoy your company as much as I do."

That was certainly true, Miranda thought, remembering the tense atmosphere at Black Down Abbey before she had married Alex. She had been very uncomfortable watching her father with Thelma. The two of them had always seemed to be holding hands and looking into each others' eyes.

Miranda's throat tightened.

Lady Briarwood leaned forward, her gaze intent. "You can't turn tail now, my dear. Not when you've finally figured out what the real issue is."

"I have?" Miranda said.

"Love," Lady Briarwood said simply. "It always comes back to love. I suspect you two stubborn young people haven't admitted you love each other."

Miranda stiffened. "What makes you think I love him?"

Lady Briarwood rolled her eyes. "You do, don't you? You must tell him so."

"I would never tell him any such thing!" Miranda traced the embroidered flower again. "Unless he said it first."

Lady Briarwood smiled. "Then we must convince him to say it first," she added.

Miranda stared at her. "But how?"

"That's an excellent question. We're going to have to bring the two of you together somehow." Lady Briarwood tapped her finger on the table. "I will invite him to go to the opera house with us next week. That will give both of you time to cool your tempers."

"Do you think he will accept?" Miranda asked doubtfully.

"No, he will most likely refuse. But since he is so concerned about the company you keep, I do think he will want to attend the opera to keep an eye on you. Once he sees you again, I have no doubt he will contrive to have a few words with you. And then you are going to *talk* to him and *not* argue. Do you understand?"

Miranda nodded. Lady Briarwood's plan seemed farfetched, but the older woman was so confident that Miranda felt a faint flicker of hope. Perhaps, just perhaps, the countess's plan would succeed. If it didn't, she would have to return to Black Down Abbey. But if the plan did succeed . . . "You've been so kind, Lady Briarwood," she said, a catch in her throat as she thought of everything the countess had done for her. "How can I ever repay you?"

The countess snorted. "By making up with that husband of yours, of course!"

One week later, Miranda was sitting in her seat at the opera house peering tensely through her opera glasses at the other boxes.

So far, she had seen no sign of Alex.

She sighed. As expected, Alex had refused the invitation to the opera. Lady Briarwood was still confident, however, that he would be present.

Miranda wasn't so sure.

The Briarwoods' box was in an excellent location, on the second tier, immediately to the right of the stage. Their party consisted of Lord and Lady Briarwood; Sara and her aunt; a Mr. Constantine, who was a friend of Lord Briarwood's; and Mr. Hamilton-Smith. Miranda chatted politely with everyone, but mainly she searched the pit and the other boxes for a certain dark-haired gentleman.

"Isn't this exciting?" Sara perched on the edge of her seat, raising her voice slightly to be heard over the babble of voices and the tuning of instruments. "This is the most beautiful theater I have ever seen. Aren't the boxes elegant with the gilt and red velvet curtains? Oh, and look at the ceiling, Miranda!"

Miranda peered through her glasses, glancing at the painting of a charioteer driving two white horses in the clouds while angels hovered above. Pretending to study the painting, she angled the glasses so she could see the occupants of the boxes high up under the domed ceiling.

Still no sign of Alex.

Sara bounced in her seat. "Look down there, Miranda! Are those two men fighting?"

Indeed, two men in the pit appeared to be arguing over a seat. They both swayed unsteadily on their feet, and their altercation grew louder and louder until an usher came and attempted to hush them. When one of the men took a swing at the usher, a great deal of shouting and shuffling ensued. In the end, four ushers removed the two troublemakers from the theater.

Miranda searched the crowd in the pit and then trained her glasses on the other side of the theater. She scanned past a box on the fourth tier, then stopped and returned her gaze to the box.

Alex!

He was seated in a box with Petronella and Preston. Through the glasses, she could see almost every detail of his face. Her heart flipped over in an odd little somersault. How handsome he looked in his stark black-and-white evening clothes! She wished he wasn't so far away. She wished she could reach out and touch him—

He turned and seemed to look directly into her eyes.

Her breath catching, she dropped the glasses. They tumbled to the floor.

"Miranda," Sara said, "you are very quiet tonight."

"Am I?" Miranda bent down to pick up the glasses. "I'm sorry. I don't mean to be."

Sara stared at her. "You sound rather strange. Is something wrong?"

Miranda hesitated, clutching the glasses in her lap. "I talked to Alex last week," she finally admitted. "We discovered that everything had been a misunderstanding."

Sara sat up straight. "Miranda! That's wonderful!"

Miranda looked dreamily across the theater. "Yes. It was." Her gaze returned to Sara. "You won't *believe* . . . I will have to call on you soon and explain something to you. But anyway, everything was perfect until we argued again."

Sara's eyes grew round. "You argued *again*? Good heavens, I didn't realize marriage was so difficult!"

"I don't think it is for everyone." Miranda stared down at the gold filigree opera glasses. "Mama and Papa certainly never fought the way Alex and I do. But they loved each other very much." She sighed unhappily. "Oh, Sara, I wish things could just be *simple*, the way they were before Mama died."

Sara clasped her hand comfortingly just as a loud burst of music boomed from the orchestra. Ushers with long-handled candlesnuffers doused the lights in front of the boxes. Sara gave Miranda's hand a final squeeze as the opera began.

Il Flauto Magico had received good reviews, but Miranda could not concentrate on the trials of Tamino, as he fell into scrape after scrape. Even when the serpent threatened Tamino, and the audience gasped with delicious horror, Miranda failed to take an interest.

She was wondering if Alex would try to approach her.

During most of the first act, she stared blindly at the stage. But every so often, her gaze strayed across the theater to the boxes on the other side.

Did he regret their quarrel also? She hoped so. And she hoped that Lady Briarwood was right, and he would try to talk to her. If he did, she would have to remember to stay calm as Lady Briarwood had directed.

She risked another peek at him. He was watching the performance, apparently enrapt. Then, as if he felt her eyes upon him, he turned and gazed broodingly at her.

She lowered her glasses quickly and pretended to watch the opera. Pamina had just finished an aria, but Miranda had no idea which one. She imagined she could feel Alex watching her, studying her.

The first act ended, and a general exodus began from all the boxes. For many, this was the best part of attending the opera, the time when one could meet a lover in the corridor, or have a discreet conversation in the privacy of the dim boxes.

"I think I'll go blow a cloud," the earl said. "Will you join me, Mr. Constantine?"

Mr. Constantine agreed and the two men left the box.

Mr. Hamilton-Smith bowed to Sara and Miranda. "Would you two ladies like to take a turn in the corridor?"

Miranda glanced at Alex's box.

It was empty.

"I think I'll stay here," she said, trying to sound nonchalant even though her heart was quivering like all the violins in the orchestra. "I want to see the ballet."

Neither Mr. Hamilton-Smith nor Sara looked disappointed at her refusal.

The countess and Mrs. Waterton sat huddled in the opposite corner of the box, exchanging gossip. They completely ignored the opera.

As did Miranda. She waited.

A knock sounded at the door. Her pulse raced in an aria of its own as the door opened. She glanced up, smiling, and saw the duke de Morieux.

The music fell sadly flat.

Looking at her, he raised an inquiring brow. He didn't say anything though, turning instead to greet the other ladies.

That taken care of, he sat down next to Miranda, taking great care not to wrinkle his coat. She couldn't help but smile at his exaggerated efforts.

When his coat was arranged to his satisfaction, he leaned toward Miranda and whispered, "A gentleman can never be too careful of his appearance, my dear. There are too many horrors that can befall the unwary—a spot on the breeches, a scuff on the boots."

Her smile widened. "I shouldn't think you need to worry. I am sure I have never seen you look less than immaculate."

The duke inclined his head as if accepting his due. "Thank you for your kind words. They almost make up for your earlier cruelty."

"I, cruel?"

"Oh, yes. I was crushed, my dear, absolutely crushed just a few minutes ago. I have never seen such an expression of keen disappointment as when I entered this box. Am I so lowly rated?"

Miranda's smile faded and she looked down at her hands. "Oh, no. I'm sorry. It's just that I thought it was someone else."

He was silent for a long moment. "That husband of yours no doubt."

Surprised by the tone of his voice, she glanced at him quickly. There was an expression in his eyes she had never seen before.

Involuntarily, she shivered.

He leaned toward her immediately. "Are you cold, Lady Huntsley?" he asked. "These boxes can be so drafty."

"No, no. I am fine." She searched his face, wondering if she had imagined the look in his eyes.

For the first time, she noticed that his nose looked slightly swollen and there was a faint discoloration under his eye. She met his gaze and saw the expression once more—a hardness, a coldness that had not been there before tonight. She had to restrain herself from shivering again.

Lowering his eyelids, he pulled out a handkerchief and polished his quizzing glass. "I have a favor to ask of you." He raised the glass and looked through, then polished it again. "Next Tuesday is my birthday. It occurred to me that the greatest gift I could receive would be the pleasure of your company. Would you accompany me to Vauxhall that evening? I would be most honored."

"I don't know," she said uneasily. "Alex would not like it."

He glanced up, his eyes glittering. "Huntsley is incredibly dull. I don't know how you tolerate him, my dear." Placing his hand over hers, he spoke persuasively, insistently. "It is so lowering to be alone on such a day, knowing you are growing older, with no friends to cheer you up. Don't condemn me to such a dismal fate, Lady Huntsley. Please say you will come."

"I . . . I—"

Another knock sounded at the door. Relieved, Miranda turned to see who entered.

It was Alex.

He halted, his eyes narrowing as he stared at Miranda's hand under the duke's. Quickly, she pulled it away. A muscle in Alex's cheek quivered.

Leisurely, the duke rose to his feet. "My dear Huntsley. What a pleasure to see you again. Are you enjoying the opera?"

Alex's deadly gaze moved to the duke's face. "It has its moments."

"Ah, how I admire your perspicacity. You noticed that

Sarastro's priests were just a trifle off-key, didn't you? An offense to the ear, I agree."

"Not nearly so offensive as the scum that attends the opera these days. One would think the management would be more particular."

The blatantly insulting words hung in the air for a long tense moment.

"I agree wholeheartedly," the duke finally replied, swinging his quizzing glass. "I see the curtain is about to rise, but I hate to end this fascinating conversation. Would you consider meeting at a later date to continue it?"

"I would be delighted. At an earlier hour, if that will suit you."

"Let us step out into the corridor and discuss the time and place. Little as I care for Sarastro's priests, I do not wish to interfere with the less discriminating's enjoyment of their singing." After nodding to the two older women who were unabashedly listening, the duke lifted Miranda's hand and kissed it lingeringly.

"I will call on you tomorrow," he murmured.

Alex, his mouth a tight line, held the door open for the duke to saunter through.

Scarcely had the door closed behind them, than it opened again, and a bewildered-looking Sara came in.

"That's odd," she said, staring back over her shoulder. "Miranda, your husband and the duke look as though they're planning someone's funeral. Lord Huntsley grabbed Mr. Hamilton-Smith and pushed me in here."

Sara looked inquiringly at the three women, who were sitting with blank expressions on their faces. No one spoke or moved.

The countess broke the silence. "I wonder where Lord Briarwood and Mr. Constantine are. They will miss the beginning of Act Two if they don't return soon."

As if they had heard her, the two men entered.

"What's toward?" Mr. Constantine asked. "Huntsley and the duke de Morieux are standing in the corridor, and they look devilish serious. Has something occurred?"

"Please hush, Mr. Constantine," Lady Briarwood said. "The music is about to begin. Gentlemen, please take your seats."

The curtain went up. When the priests had finished their chorus and Sarastro was praying for virtue and wisdom, Mr. Hamilton-Smith reentered the box.

"Pardon me," he murmured as he slipped into his seat.

Miranda stole a glance at him over her shoulder. His gaze was fixed on the stage, but he did not appear to be enjoying the opera. In fact, he looked exceedingly grim.

Miranda raised her opera glasses and trained them not on the stage but on the box across the theater. Preston and Alex were whispering. After a few minutes, Alex left, and Preston leaned over to whisper something in his wife's ear. Petronella nodded, not removing her gaze from the stage. Alex did not return.

Miranda lowered her glasses and stared blindly at the stage, where three of the Queen of Night's attendants had appeared before Tamino. They begged him to flee, warning him that his life was in danger. Tamino would not listen to them.

How foolish, Miranda thought dazedly. Such witlessness deserved to reap its bitter reward.

Miranda's worst fears were confirmed when Alex's sister called early the next day. Highly agitated, Petronella burst out, "Miranda, I think Alex and the duke are going to fight a duel!"

Miranda sank onto the sofa, feeling oddly stiff all over. "What makes you think so?" she asked through lips that could barely form the words.

"I heard them whispering in the back of the box last night. Alex said something about pistols and the duke de Morieux. I asked Preston about it later. He denied it, but I don't believe him. He had an odd look in his eye. Oh, Miranda, if anything should happen to Alex, I would never forgive myself." Petronella burst into noisy tears.

Miranda stared at her, not moving. Then a deep tremor coursed through her and she clenched her hands into fists. Pistols. Alex was going to fight a duel with pistols. He might be injured or maimed. Or killed.

A loud wail penetrated her daze. The noise pounded at her eardrums until she glanced up. Petronella was still sobbing.

The fog in Miranda's brain cleared a little. "This situation is hardly your fault," she managed to say. "If anyone, I am to blame for continuing to see the duke when I knew how it infuriated Alex."

Petronella sobbed louder.

Miranda fought the urge to cover her ears with her hands. "Whatever is the matter, Petronella?"

"I c-c-can s-s-see you haven't heard the story," Petronella said, sniffling loudly. "I thought Alex might have told you . . . but no, I suppose he wouldn't. He's always been the b-b-best of brothers, and he knows how deeply humiliating the tale is to me."

Petronella groped for her handkerchief, then blew her nose and dabbed at her eyes. She pulled a small mirror from her reticule and checked her appearance. Apparently satisfied, she took a deep breath. Miranda waited, trying not to reveal her impatience.

"Nine years ago," Petronella began in a barely audible voice, "or was it ten? Yes, it must have been ten, because Preston and I were married that same year—ten years ago, I was here in London for my first Season. I was very giddy, I confess, for the men swarmed around me, and I was a tremendous success. How wonderful that was, all the men vying for my favors, pledging their undying love for me, composing poems to my beauty."

Petronella sighed deeply.

"But anyway, one night, Papa, Mama, Alex, and I went to the opera. Thomas refused to go because he detested the opera. I was very upset with him, because it was my first visit, but Thomas was like that sometimes. Usually he was the sweetest brother, but he could be horrid. As it turned out though, he was very right, because the opera was terribly tedious, and I wished I could leave. But I was not *serious*, you understand. When Mr. Overfield—as the duke was then called—asked me to walk with him in the corridor, of course I accepted. No sooner were we out of the box, than Mr. Overfield—the duke—forced me outside and into his carriage. He ordered his coachman to drive us over the border to Scotland where he intended to compel me to marry him!"

Miranda frowned. "But, Petronella—"

"It was perfectly horrid!" Petronella interrupted, her voice increasing in pitch. "The carriage was such a shabby affair—he had hired it!—and the horses were the worst slugs you ever saw. Which turned out to be very fortunate, because as soon as Papa and Alex realized I was missing, they followed. Some friends had seen me leave with the duke, so Papa and Alex guessed we were headed for Scotland. They caught up to us, and oh, Miranda! The look on Papa's face! I was so ashamed to be in such a fix!"

Petronella twisted her handkerchief. "Alex challenged the duke to a duel, but the duke refused to fight him. Alex called him a coward and knocked him down, but still the duke would not fight."

She looked down at her hands. "I returned home with Papa and Alex, but I had been alone with the duke for hours, and several people had seen me leave with him—

including that busybody Mrs. Hurley. There was bound to
be the most dreadful scandal, Mama said. She was terribly
upset, and glared at me as if it were my fault, even though I
told her the duke forced me to go with him. There was
nothing for it but to marry immediately. Fortunately,
Preston was devoted to me and didn't care about the duke.
So we were married, and of course I have been *very* happy
with him and I don't regret it at all, but Alex and the duke
have hated each other ever since. I kept hoping their hatred
would die a natural death, but even though they avoid each
other, it seems to increase. And now—" She burst into tears
again.

Miranda sat quietly for a moment, absorbing this
startling story. Finally she nodded slowly. "Now I am the
bone of contention between them. Or perhaps I should say,
the excuse for them to vent their hostilities."

Tears rolled down Petronella's cheeks. "We must stop
them, Miranda. Alex loves you, I can tell. If you talk to him,
he might listen to reason."

Miranda bit back a bitter laugh. Alex didn't love her. He
would no more listen to her than he would listen to a
grasshopper. "I've already tried talking to him. He is impossibly stubborn. But perhaps there is another way," she said
slowly. "The duke is supposed to call on me today. Perhaps
I can appeal to him."

Petronella stopped crying. Hastily, she rose to her feet
and pulled her gloves on. "I must go. Appeal to the duke, if
you like, but I doubt it will do any good." Quickly, she was
gone.

Miranda did not try to stop her. She needed to think and
Petronella's wailing made that difficult.

She pressed her fingers to her temples. Petronella had
made the duke sound quite wicked. Was he really so evil?

Miranda wished she'd had a chance to ask Petronella a
few questions. Namely, why would the duke do such a

thing? Petronella had not been wealthy. He would have gained no great material benefit from marrying her. Even if there had been something to gain, Miranda would not have believed him capable of so dastardly a deed.

He must have been very young. Had he perhaps been suffering from unrequited love, despairing of ever winning Petronella from her numerous suitors?

Miranda sighed. It didn't really matter why he had done it. All that mattered was that she convince him to call off the duel. But how?

"His Grace, the duke de Morieux," Bomford announced.

The duke entered and bowed deeply over her hand. "My dear Lady Huntsley."

Miranda stared at him. His usually pale cheeks were slightly flushed and his eyes glittered strangely. She swallowed. Looking at him now, she could almost believe he had abducted Petronella.

"Have you decided about Vauxhall, Lady Huntsley?" He toyed with his quizzing glass. "I have been in an agony of suspense all night, wondering what your answer will be. It is to be a masquerade, and should be most diverting."

"I am afraid I must decline," she replied.

His fingers stilled on the quizzing glass. His face turned hard and cold as marble. "I am sorry to hear it." He rose to his feet. "Forgive me for cutting my visit short—"

"Wait. Please." Miranda rose also, putting a hand on his arm. "I understand you are to meet my husband in a duel."

The duke looked down at her hand. "My dear, I'm afraid I can't discuss the business between your husband and me."

Her hand tightened on his sleeve. "Can't you refuse to fight him? Is your silly honor worth risking your life?"

"Really, Lady Huntsley—"

"Please. I consider you my friend."

He grew still. He stared at her, some of the coldness leaving his eyes.

Encouraged, she said, "Please don't fight this duel. It is too dangerous. I don't want to lose my husband."

The duke's lips curled back from his teeth. She drew back, startled, but then she saw he was smiling charmingly. Feeling foolish, she said again, "Please don't fight this duel."

He stared at her for a long moment. Then his eyelids drooped. "I might be persuaded to sprain my arm or have some other such accident that would prevent my fighting, but I feel I must have some compensation for the damage my pride would suffer. Perhaps if you would reconsider your decision to attend Vauxhall with me?"

Miranda's stomach sank. "You will call off the duel immediately?"

The duke laughed. "My dear, it's not that I don't trust you, but I don't want you to be tempted to break your word. I will insist that the duel be delayed until after Tuesday. Say, Thursday. If you keep your engagement with me, then I will endeavor to suffer some trifling accident."

Miranda turned slightly away. She didn't want to go. She wasn't sure if she quite trusted the duke. She wished she could say no. But how could she? Alex's life was at stake.

"Very well," she said quietly.

A blaze of triumph burned in the duke's eyes.

"You will need a mask and cloak. Beyond that, you may wear whatever costume you like. I will call for you at seven." With a bow, he departed.

She stood very still for a moment, feeling decidedly uneasy. Then she jumped up and rang for Bomford.

"Send Samuel to me. Quickly, if you please." In a few minutes the boy appeared, his head cocked inquiringly.

"Can you do something for me and not tell anyone?" she asked the red-haired urchin.

He nodded vigorously.

"Very good." She smiled. "Now listen. . . ."

*　　*　　*

The duke de Morieux drove directly to his town house. Once inside, he summoned his secretary.

"Knowles, I want you to arrange for the house in Kent to be opened up. I am going to have a guest, a lady, and I want to ensure her every comfort." He flecked a speck of dust from his sleeve. "I also want you to hire a closed carriage for Tuesday."

"Yes, Your Grace," the man said, his face impassive. "Er, begging your pardon, Your Grace, but how shall I pay for it? Your credit with the jobmaster is overdrawn."

"Use whatever means are necessary," the duke snapped. He wished he hadn't given Miranda her note back. Three hundred pounds would be very useful right now. "Rob someone if you must, just get that carriage."

"Very well, Your Grace. Who shall I send down to Kent?"

"How should I know? Send anyone. Send that footman you hired last month."

"He left, Your Grace. He hadn't been paid since he was hired. None of the staff has been paid." Knowles's gaze drifted to a spot above the duke's head. "Including myself, Your Grace."

"Damn your eyes," the duke snarled. "You'll be paid when I'm ready to pay you and not before. You're welcome to look for another position any time you like. If you wish to keep this one, I suggest you go hire that carriage immediately."

"Yes, Your Grace," Knowles said woodenly. "Will a week be sufficient time for the carriage?"

"Yes," the duke said. "It will be more than sufficient."

28

Bomford had tried to heed Figgley's lessons, he really had.

He had learned the trick of standing in a dignified manner with his arms close at his sides. He had mastered the art of speaking without stuttering, in haughty and/or respectful tones, depending on whom he was speaking to. He pretty well had the knack of exhibiting no emotion, he thought, except for one or two slips.

But Figgley's order to stay aloof from the aristocracy's doings was beyond him.

He felt it was his duty to watch over his master and mistress—someone certainly needed to. Especially since Lady Huntsley was living apart from her husband, and the duke was calling on her regularly. That duke, he was a real ugly customer.

Her ladyship was too easily taken in. The boy, Samuel, was another perfect example. Why her ladyship wanted to bring home such a wretch was a mystery, but to take him into her confidence!

Bomford still felt the raw indignation he'd suffered this

morning when the brat was summoned into Lady
Huntsley's presence. When Samuel came out, his pasty little
face had an expression of smug superiority. He had slipped
away before Bomford could collar him.

Bomford's hands clenched and unclenched. How he'd
love to get his hands on that miniature fiend!

Out of the corner of his eye, he saw a shadow slinking
across the floor. It was Samuel, heading for the drawing
room with a package under his arm. Bomford grabbed him
by the ear.

"Ow, ow, ow!" Samuel yowled.

Bomford pulled harder. "Where are you going, brat?"

"I 'ave to see milady."

"Her ladyship never would want to see the likes of you."

"Huh. Lot *you* know."

Bomford glared at this impertinence. "What have you
got there?"

"Ain't none of yer business."

"Everything in this house is my business, you little imp of
Satan. Now tell me what it is, or I'll—"

"What's going on here?" a smooth, haughty voice interrupted.

Bomford whirled around, although he kept his hold on
Samuel's ear.

"Lady Briarwood! I, er, I beg your pardon, your ladyship.
I, er, I . . ." He glared down at Samuel. This was all *his*
fault. Taking a deep breath, he regained control of his
tongue. "I suspect the boy has stolen this package." He
smiled maliciously at Samuel.

"H'ain't never stolen nuthin' since I bin here," Samuel
retorted indignantly. "Milady gave me some money all right
n' tight. H'ain't stolen nuthin'"

"What is in the package, boy?" the countess asked.

Samuel hesitated.

Her expression grew severe. "Well?" she said.

Bomford wasn't surprised when Samuel answered. His own knees were knocking at the tone of Lady Briarwood's voice.

"H'it's jist a cloak an' mask, yer ladyship." He threw a furious glance at Bomford.

"I will take it in to her. She is in the drawing room?" Samuel nodded reluctantly and placed the package into Lady Briarwood's outstretched hand. "Bomford, will you please bring some tea into the drawing room?"

Bomford gloated silently as he hurried down to the kitchen. That would teach the imp to be more respectful of his betters. When Cook had prepared the tray, Bomford took it upstairs and entered the drawing room just as Miranda was speaking.

". . . call on Sara tomorrow and talk to her. I will find out if she is free on Tuesday."

Lady Briarwood looked very serious, Bomford noted as he began setting out the tea things.

"Is this wise, Miranda? The duke is very unpredictable." Bomford stood back a discreet distance.

"What else can I do?"

"I don't know. Perhaps this ball will be the answer. I just hope—" The countess stopped speaking and picked up the teapot. "Thank you Bomford. That will be all."

Greatly disappointed, Bomford was about to leave when Lady Briarwood said, "Wait."

He turned eagerly.

"Send that boy—what's his name?—Samuel in here."

Really, it was too much. And although he relayed the message with as much dignity as was his to command, Samuel's cheeky grin was almost more than he could bear.

Bomford's wounded dignity was still throbbing the next day, when Lord Huntsley called.

"Her ladyship is not at home," he told the viscount.

Lord Huntsley slapped his gloves against his thigh. "Where the devil is she now?"

"I believe she went to visit Miss Rowan."

"Damn." When Lord Huntsley started to turn away, Bomford saw his chance. He coughed gently.

"Excuse me, my lord, but may I speak to you, just for a moment?"

"I'm very busy, Bomford."

Bomford waggled his brows up and down in a significant manner. "It concerns her ladyship."

Lord Huntsley paused, his boot tapping impatiently. "Well, what is it?"

"I chanced to overhear—I couldn't avoid it—that she is planning something involving the duke de Morieux."

Bomford had the viscount's full attention now. He puffed out his chest. Certainly that brat, Samuel, would never elicit such interest.

Lord Huntsley's brows drew together. "What the devil is she up to now?"

"I don't know precisely. Lady Briarwood spoke of a ball they all plan to attend on Tuesday night."

"Hm. She should be safe enough with the Briarwoods. But perhaps I had better make certain I attend that particular ball also. Who are the hosts?"

"I don't know, my lord. This is the first I've heard of it."

Lord Huntsley pulled on his gloves. "I'll check my own invitations. Likely, I have received one. Thank you Bomford. I appreciate your concern for my wife."

Bomford beamed as he watched Lord Huntsley walk down the stairs and take the reins of his horse from Samuel. Samuel made a most impudent face, but Bomford, his pride restored by Lord Huntsley's words, haughtily ignored the boy.

*   *   *

When Alex arrived at his lodgings, he found Daniel Hamilton-Smith about to go up the stairs.

"I think your wife is up to something, Alex," Daniel said by way of a greeting.

"Miranda is always up to something," Alex said sardonically. "Come up, though, and tell me what makes you think so."

Once inside, Alex immediately picked up a stack of mail lying unopened on a silver salver. He started to leaf through it, ignoring anything that looked like a bill.

Daniel paid no heed to Alex's preoccupation. He poured himself a brandy and spoke as if he had his host's undivided attention.

"Miss Rowan invited me to escort Mrs. Waterton and her to a ball next week."

"Nothing unusual in that," Alex said distractedly. He opened one invitation that looked promising. It was an invitation to a musicale, featuring one of Mrs. Hurley's daughters. He crumpled it up and threw it in the fire.

"No, but she also wanted me to invite *you*. Made some nonsensical excuse about being worried that you were lonely."

Alex's fingers paused in the act of opening another invitation. "How strange."

"Very." Daniel sipped his brandy. "What's more, we're both invited to dinner beforehand at her aunt's house."

"Where is the ball?"

Daniel frowned. "I don't know. Miss Rowan didn't say who the hostess is."

Alex dropped the mail and pushed the salver aside. "When exactly is this ball?" he asked intently.

"Tuesday evening," Daniel replied.

"Ah."

"What do you think, Alex? Does it sound like a conspiracy?"

"Definitely. But to what end?"

"You said Lady Huntsley knows about the duel." Daniel studied his sleeve. "Do you think she might be planning something to convince you to withdraw?"

Alex's jaw tightened. "If that's her game, she's wasting her time."

Daniel shrugged. "She may not think so. But what concerns me more is the duke's part in all this. He may have some mischief planned."

Alex nodded. "I wouldn't be surprised. He did ask for the duel to be delayed until Thursday." Frowning, he tried to guess what lunacy Miranda could have cooked up. He couldn't come up with a logical answer, but he was certain of one thing—he'd better find out.

He remembered that his sister had mentioned at the opera that she intended to call on Miranda. He decided to check with Petronella and see if Miranda had told her anything. In the meantime, he would play along with Miranda's game—whatever it was.

"Tell Miss Rowan I accept her invitation." Meeting Daniel's gaze, he added, "And bring the pistols. We may settle this situation once and for all on Tuesday night."

29

Lady Briarwood completed her toilette by picking up a black lace fan shot with gold. She walked into her husband's dressing room where he was in the final stages of tying a cravat.

"Hurry, Henry, we can't be late." She opened the fan and plied it against the uncomfortably warm and sultry air.

"I'm doing my best, my dear. This damn heat is making the linen go limp. Whoever heard of such weather in May?" He finished tying the cravat and studied it closely. With a sigh, he yanked it loose and turned to his wife. "Go on down. I will be only a few minutes more."

Downstairs, Lady Briarwood said to Bomford, "Have the carriage brought around, Bomford."

"Yes, my lady." He went off to do her bidding.

She waited in the hall, tapping her toe and glancing frequently at the watch pinned to her emerald silk gown.

Just as the earl appeared at the head of the stairs, the butler returned.

"The carriage is ready, my lady."

"Thank you, Bomford." Lady Briarwood inspected her husband's cravat.

"Will I pass?" he asked with mock anxiety.

She laughed. "You will be the most handsome gentleman there, I vow."

"And you the most beautiful lady." He took her shawl from her maid and held it out, but she shook her head.

"No, it's much too warm."

Offering her his arm, he said, "Then let's be off."

She rested her hand lightly upon his sleeve, and they started toward the door.

"Lady Briarwood!"

She turned to look at Bomford. His eyes were almost popping from his head.

Her brows rose. "Yes?"

"I, er, I beg your pardon, my lady, but isn't Lady Huntsley accompanying you?"

"No. She and the duke de Morieux are going to Vauxhall. He should be arriving for her in another half hour or so."

"Let us go, my love," Lord Briarwood urged.

They left and Bomford goggled after them. He wasted almost five minutes with this exercise. Then, coming abruptly to his senses, he quickly found paper and pen. He wrote a note and summoned a footman.

"Take this to Lord Huntsley, at once!" Bomford said. The footman nodded and set out.

Bomford paced around the hall. What a disaster! How could he have made such a mistake? He prayed the footman would reach his lordship before—

The knocker sounded.

It was the duke de Morieux.

*   *   *

Miranda stared in the mirror while Alice tied the strings of the black silk mask.

In spite of the lightweight fabric, the mask felt heavy against her face. She could feel beads of perspiration starting to gather where the material touched her skin. Abruptly, she pulled on the strings and removed the mask.

"I think I will wait to put it on," she told Alice.

A knock sounded at the door. While the maid answered it, Miranda studied her reflection. She looked very pale, like a wraith with wide eyes.

"He's here," Alice said.

The duke, resplendent in dark blue and yellow, waited at the bottom of the stairs, watching as she slowly walked down each step. As she drew closer, she could see the strange glitter in his eyes.

"Good evening, Lady Huntsley." He bowed deeply over her hand, his lips touching her skin. His mouth was hot and dry, and the hand holding hers was tense. "You look more radiant than the moon and the stars." In spite of the fulsome words, his tone was perfunctory, as if his mind were otherwise occupied.

"You look very handsome also," Miranda replied distantly.

For an instant, he looked surprised. Then, he laughed. "Why do I always forget what a delight you are?" His eyes caressed her. "I am going to enjoy this night."

She smiled uncertainly.

They went outside. She paused when she saw the plain, black traveling carriage.

"My own vehicle is being repainted and refitted," he said smoothly, pulling her forward and handing her up. Vaulting in behind her, he took the opposite seat and rapped on the ceiling.

Miranda heard the coachman shout at the horses. The carriage set off with a lurch, bumping and rattling over the cobblestones.

It was dark and uncomfortably warm inside the box. With the windows tightly closed and the curtains drawn, she could only see a dim outline, a sort of black presence, where the duke sat.

"Tell me about Vauxhall, Your Grace." Her lips felt stiff.

His voice came out of the shadows. "It offers several amusements. There is a concert early in the evening, which you may enjoy."

"It sounds pleasant enough."

"The musicians are of indifferent quality. Truth to tell, I find the concert unbearably tedious."

"That is unfortunate, Your Grace."

"Yes. After the concert, there is an illuminated scene, called the cascade. It features some thirty-seven thousand lamps—if you can believe the advertisements—of multitudinous colors arranged in various fashions."

The carriage turned sharply, and Miranda grabbed a strap to hold herself upright. The noises outside diminished. She could hear the wheels crunching over rocks, and she guessed they were now on one of the macadamized roads. Their speed increased and she retained her hold on the leather strap.

"It sounds perfectly lovely."

"Actually, it's a bit tasteless. But then there are the fireworks, at the end of one of the grand walks," the duke said. "You will not find a more magnificent display anywhere in Europe. Of course, many couples get lost on the way. There are many dark footpaths where they can be private, if they so choose."

"How tawdry."

He laughed. "How perceptive of you, my dear. In truth, the place is not as fashionable as it once was. The guests can be a trifle uninhibited."

"You are making it sound less and less appealing."

"Depending on the company, it can be very appealing

indeed." He paused. "But you are right. Vauxhall is not a suitable place for you. Which is why I hope you will not be upset when I tell you that the location of my birthday celebration has changed."

"Oh?"

"Yes, to my house in Kent."

She stiffened. "I hope all of your guests were informed."

She saw a shadow of motion as he clapped a hand to his forehead. "How careless of me. I do believe I forgot."

She did not reply. A thick, heavy silence fell, and she could hear her own breathing. It sounded unnaturally loud. She peered through the dark, trying to see the duke's face.

"Is something wrong, Miranda?"

Her spine stiffened at his use of her first name. "Not at all, *Your Grace.*"

He laughed at the edge in her voice. "Come, come. Surely we've known each other long enough to warrant a little friendliness."

"I'm afraid I dislike all forms of familiarity."

In the close, dark confines of the carriage, his laughter seemed to ebb and flow around her.

"I cannot agree. You must know that I long for an even closer relationship with you."

"You become incredible, Your Grace."

He laughed again. When he spoke, his voice was intimate. "You are a very beautiful woman, Miranda. Do you doubt your attraction for me?"

She ignored his question. "It's a trifle warm in here, don't you think? Do you mind if I let down the window?" Without waiting for a reply, she reached up, feeling for the catch. But before she could undo it, he seized her hand in his.

"I don't think so, my dear."

He lifted her hand, turning it so that the palm was upward. She shuddered as she felt his mouth touch her skin.

"I find I can no longer control my ardor." His voice was thick with passion.

"What do you mean?"

"My dear Miranda, surely you must have guessed. I am abducting you."

30

Lady Thurlow did not appreciate the interruption of her dinner. She surveyed the Briarwood footman disapprovingly, wondering what could be so important that it warranted delaying the sweet course.

"Beg pardon, your ladyship, your lordship, but can you tell me the whereabouts of Lord Huntsley? There's no one at his lodgings, and I have an urgent message for him."

"I have no idea," snapped the countess. "I am only a poor mother."

"What is this urgent message?" asked the earl.

"I do not know, your lordship. Lady Huntsley's butler asked me to deliver the letter."

There was a small silence.

"Could something have happened to—" Petronella did not complete the unthinkable thought.

"Is Lady Huntsley at home?" the earl asked.

"No. She went out with the duke de Morieux."

"Good heavens," Lady Thurlow said faintly. "Charles, do you think . . . ?"

"We must do something," cried Petronella.

"Perhaps we should drive over and talk to Bomford," Preston said. "After all, we can't be sure anything is wrong until we speak to him or Alex."

"But where is Alex?" The countess looked around the table as if she expected to see him sitting there.

"He's at Mrs. Waterton's, I believe," Petronella said suddenly. "He told me this morning he was having dinner with her tonight."

"Go to Mrs. Waterton's," Lord Thurlow instructed the footman. "If he is not there, return to the Briarwoods' and wait for us."

The servant nodded and left.

The countess laid her napkin on the table.

"I think we will have to forego the sweet," she said.

The footman's timing was more propitious at Mrs. Waterton's. The ladies had already withdrawn and Alex and Daniel had just poured the brandy, when he was announced.

"I have a message from Bomford for you, my lord."

Alex set his glass down carefully, a premonition of disaster sweeping over him. He took the message and ripped it open.

"*There is a Certain Matter here which requires your urgent Personal Attention,*" he read. *Urgent* was heavily underscored. It was signed "Bomford."

"What has happened?"

"I'm not sure," Alex replied. He rose to his feet. "Forgive me, but I must go."

"Of course. Is there anything I can do?" Daniel spoke to Alex's retreating back.

"I doubt it," Alex said grimly. With a curt nod, he strode through the doorway.

Daniel frowned. Slowly, he sipped his brandy, delaying the moment when he would have to rejoin the ladies and make some excuse for Alex's absence.

When Alex arrived at the Briarwood town house, he found his family there before him. They were standing around Bomford, bombarding him with questions. Bomford's elbows were flapping, he was stuttering, and he greeted Alex's arrival with palpable relief.

Lady Thurlow rushed to Alex's side. "Thank heaven you're here!"

Alex did not feel a similar gladness as he gazed at his family. "What the devil are you all doing here?"

"Well!" The countess drew herself up in affront. "If that's your attitude—"

"Please, my dear." The earl rested a hand on his wife's arm, and she subsided.

Petronella answered Alex's question. "We want to help, Alex. We think the duke has abducted Miranda!"

"Is this true?" Alex said fiercely to Bomford.

"I'm afraid so, my lord. Lady Briarwood said the duke and Lady Huntsley were going to Vauxhall."

Alex frowned. "Vauxhall? You told me they were attending a ball with the Briarwoods."

"I don't understand it, my lord." Bomford's forehead wrinkled and he sounded perfectly wretched. "I wasn't aware of the change of plans until Lord and Lady Briarwood left. The duke arrived shortly afterward with a closed traveling carriage."

"He would hardly have a closed traveling carriage to go to Vauxhall," Preston said.

"He has abducted her!" Petronella cried.

"Let's not be hasty," the earl said calmly. "We don't know that for certain. I have sent a servant to the duke's residence to see what he could discover. He should be back shortly. Let us see what he has to say."

"Thank you, Father," Alex said, silently blessing his father's cool head. "Bomford, have the fastest horse in the stables saddled and ready at the door."

"Very good, my lord." The butler looked glad to escape.

"Surely you're not going to ride in those clothes?" exclaimed Lady Thurlow.

Alex glanced indifferently at his elegant evening attire. "It won't be very comfortable, but I certainly don't want to take the time to go home and change. If the duke does have Miranda, I can't waste even a minute."

"Do you have any idea where he might have taken her?" the earl asked.

Alex shook his head. Restlessly, he paced about the room. "There are a hundred disreputable inns where he could carry out his purpose."

"Oh, Lord, the scandal!" moaned Lady Thurlow, sinking into a chair.

Alex abruptly stopped pacing. "Is that all that concerns you, Mother?"

"No," she shot back. "I am concerned that my daughter-in-law will be ravished and my son will be killed!"

Alex frowned. "You are being melodramatic."

Lady Thurlow grew rigid. "You and the duke are going to shoot each other full of holes and *I* am being melodramatic? Oh, how did I ever bear such an unnatural child?"

To Alex's relief, the earl's servant returned at that moment, preventing the necessity of a reply. The footman was a big brawny individual and looked more like a prize-fighter than a servant.

"Were you able to learn anything?" Alex demanded.

"Aye," the man said morosely. "The duke's servants are a loose-mouthed bunch. I didn't have to so much as threaten to darken their daylights—they just gabbed away."

"What did they say?" Alex asked impatiently.

"The duke is taking a lady guest down to his Kent estate for a week. Chelsfield it's called."

"I know it," Alex said, his face grim. He pressed a coin in the man's hand, and without even a pretense of a farewell to the other people standing in the hall, he strode out of the house.

"Charles, we must do something," Lady Thurlow said, watching her son striding away. "The foolish boy will challenge the duke to a duel. I couldn't bear it if . . ." Painful, unaccustomed tears welled up in her eyes as she contemplated the unthinkable.

"We must follow him," Petronella said in a decisive voice. Everyone looked at her in surprise. She continued quickly. "Alex will not fight a duel if we are there."

"You're right, dear," the earl said. "But there is no need for your mother or you to go. Especially in your condition. You can both wait here."

"Certainly not," said Lady Thurlow. "I have waited before, and it is not good for my nerves."

"I want to go, too," Petronella said. "Miranda may need a friend." Her face crumpled. "This is all my fault."

Preston spoke briskly. "Don't be silly, my dear. You could not help it that the duke abducted you. Nor could you foresee that he would do the same to Miranda."

Petronella bit her lip, but she only said stubbornly, "I must go."

"Very well, then, we shall all go," the earl said. The carriage is right outside. It is not a long journey to Kent, after all perhaps one or two hours at most."

Thus agreed, four more travelers headed south out of London.

31

Miranda clutched the carriage strap until the leather cut into her flesh.

"Why?" she asked quietly.

"Your dear husband reminded me, my dear, that I have a reputation to live up to, or down to, if you prefer. He made me realize that mere mischief-making—such as taking you to that gaming hell—is really not worthy of my disreputable nature. An abduction is so much more iniquitous. And it has a certain poetic justice about it."

"Because of Petronella, you mean."

"Ah, so you know about that. Yes, my dear. It all boils down to that most mundane of reasons: revenge. Your husband spoiled my, er, elopement with the beauteous Petronella some years ago. I will spare you the details. Suffice it to say, it was quite a blow to my pride."

"But why did you abduct her?"

There was a silence. "I was in love, of course. Hard to believe now that I ever made such a fool of myself over a woman."

"Then why repeat your mistake?"

"I have tried to forget the incident. I have tried to forget how my pride suffered. But your husband's deplorable manners every time we meet has kept the wound raw, the desire for revenge ripe. Did you know he was instrumental in having me blackballed from several clubs? Before I came into my title, that is. Once I was able to call myself the most noble duke de Morieux, not even Huntsley's influence could keep me out."

She wished she could see his face. The dark was beginning to wear on her nerves. "Would you mind lighting the lamp?"

"Of course not. Your wish is my command." Suiting his action to his words, he quickly and efficiently lit the lamp.

A faint light spread throughout the carriage. The heat from the lamp made the enclosed carriage even hotter, and the smell of the burning oil was unpleasant, but it was better than sitting in the dark, unable to see.

"You must have been very young," Miranda said.

"When I eloped with Petronella? Barely twenty-one." The motion of the carriage caused the shadows to dance around in crazy patterns on his face, obscuring his expression. "But already set on the road to no good and the despair of my poor mama."

"What will your mother think of this particular escapade?"

He laughed an ugly laugh. "She will moan and sigh, but little else. She is well used to my vices."

Miranda was silent.

The duke remained quiet for a moment also, then said, "What, no hysterics? No swooning or pretty pleadings?"

"Would they help me?"

"No." His voice hardened. "No, my dear. This particular form of revenge will be especially pleasant for me." His pale green eyes caressed her. "We could deal very well together. I actually have something of a fondness for you."

"I also considered you a friend."

"Then what do you say? Will you throw your lot in with mine? Leave your husband, and we will fly for the Continent."

Surprised, she stared at his face for a moment, trying to read his thoughts. She shook her head slowly.

Anger flashed in his eyes. He laughed again, but shortly, without amusement. He reached across the coach to caress her shoulder.

She shrank away, and for the first time she felt truly afraid of the duke.

He smiled that nasty smile and said, "You wound me, my dear. But perhaps you prefer the comfort of a bed? So do I. We will be arriving shortly. I suppose I can wait."

As soon as he finished speaking, the carriage slowed, and then stopped. The duke opened the curtain and let down the window, then leaned out to listen to what the coachman was saying.

"There's a carriage on the road ahead, Your Grace. Appears to have broken a wheel."

The duke peered through the dark. A thin man, holding a lamp, was standing by the disabled carriage.

"Joplin! What the devil is he doing on this road?" The duke looked at Miranda for a moment, then grasped her face between his long fingers. He squeezed tightly before releasing her and gently tracing the outline of the red marks that appeared. He spoke quietly. "Joplin is a friend of mine. He won't help you, even if you are foolish enough to try to ask."

Their carriage inched forward until it reached Lord Joplin. Quickly the duke hissed, "I don't want to hurt you, my dear. Please don't do anything rash. It will take me less than a second to silence you if you should try."

She shrank back against the squabs. The duke leaned out the window again. From her corner, Miranda caught a glimpse of Lord Joplin looking eagerly toward the carriage. When he saw the duke, however, his expression abruptly changed to one of dismay. He ducked behind his carriage, as if trying to conceal himself from view.

"What is that idiot doing?" the duke murmured. Then more loudly, "Joplin, is that you?"

With obvious reluctance, Lord Joplin reappeared. "Why, Duke. Fancy meeting you here."

"Yes. A startling coincidence," the duke said ironically. "I see you've suffered a mishap."

"Er, yes. A wheel came off my carriage," the other man said inanely.

"I regret I cannot offer to take you up, but I have a . . . companion."

"Of course, of course. No problem. I understand. I'll wait for the next carriage."

"It's unlikely there will be another at this time of night. I live nearby, though, and I will send the carriage back, if you like. The coachman can take you to your destination."

"Capital idea. Very generous of you."

The duke nodded, and the carriage continued on its way. He sat quietly for a moment, frowning over the strange encounter. Then he shrugged and looked at Miranda.

"Very wise, my dear. I would have hated to mark that pretty face."

She faked a yawn. "Do you mind if I sleep until we arrive, Your Grace? I find I am very weary."

He leaned back, laughing with genuine amusement. "So calm. So cool. I truly admire you, my dear. Go ahead. You will get little enough sleep later."

Making no response to his ominous statement, she closed her eyes and feigned sleep. She consciously relaxed her body, to perpetuate the ploy.

Silence filled the carriage as it moved swiftly through the dark. In all too short a time, it turned sharply. The new road had ruts, and the carriage bounced about, making it difficult for Miranda to continue her charade.

A shot rang out. Miranda sat up and gripped the window ledge tightly. The duke stiffened and drew a pistol out from under his cloak. He waited, the pistol cocked, but there was no further noise.

"A poacher perhaps." The duke frowned, carefully uncocking the pistol. "How odd." To Miranda, he said, "I suppose you thought it was Huntsley, riding to the rescue."

She tore her gaze away from the gleaming pistol and looked into his mocking eyes.

His gaze held hers for a long moment. "It's too late, my dear, we have arrived."

The carriage stopped.

He handed her out of the carriage, and she paused to stare at the crumbling edifice before her. It was old, probably Tudor, and covered with ivy. Untrimmed hedges and lawn and overgrown beech trees gave the place a desolate air. No gleam of light showed through the windows to relieve the dark facade.

The duke frowned. "That damned servant had better have followed my instructions, or I'll cut open his windpipe for him." His voice turned sardonic. "I should hate for our night of love to be marred by cold sheets and an unaired room."

She turned her back to him.

Ignoring her for the moment, he strode to the front door, which stood slightly ajar. His face growing blacker by the second, the duke pushed it open and stepped into the darkened hall.

"Knowles," he shouted. "Knowles, where the devil are you?"

A door at the back of the hall opened, revealing a bright luminescence. From the doorway spilled a steady stream of people, including Lord and Lady Briarwood and several other prominent members of the *ton*. They were all laughing and exclaiming, "Surprise!" "Surprise!"

The duke gripped the doorway until his knuckles shone whitely. His eyes widened, then closed. When he opened them again, he put his hand to his forehead as if questioning the soundness of his reason.

A figure at the front of the group moved forward. It was Mrs. Overfield, his own mother, her smile not quite reaching her eyes as she walked up and kissed him on the cheek.

"Many happy returns, my son."

He suffered the embrace, his arms automatically coming up to return her hug. She stepped back and stood quietly, watching him. Turning away from her, he looked at Miranda, who was also watching him steadily. Seeing her calm expression, sudden comprehension lit his face.

"Is this your doing?" His voice was incredulous.

Miranda barely inclined her head. Her gaze was unwavering. "Happy birthday, Your Grace."

32

The duke's shoulders started to shake. He began to laugh. He laughed until he was gasping and wheezing. Unaware of the undercurrents, the people gathering around him laughed also. The crowd moved back into the great hall, sweeping the duke and Miranda along with them. A dusty chandelier, lit by over two hundred tapers, cast a warm glow over the scene. The shabby furniture had been moved back and the carpet rolled up to permit dancing. When they saw the duke, a string quartet in the gallery started to play a lively waltz. Over one hundred gaily dressed guests broke into applause.

The duke flashed a brilliant smile and bowed deeply. Then he turned to Miranda and held out his hand. For the first time that evening, she smiled. She took his hand and accompanied him to the dance floor. Other couples followed.

"How?" The duke asked.

"I have to confess, Your Grace, I suspected your motives might not be of the purest. I have in my employ a servant,

Samuel by name, who is most adept at gathering information. Perhaps you remember him? The child you almost knocked down with your curricle?"

"Ah yes. I think perhaps I should have run over the brat."

She ignored his callous remark. "It was not difficult for him to discover that you had hired a closed traveling carriage and ordered your Kent estate to be readied for a visitor on this night."

"Ridiculously simple." He paused and looked down at her, his eyes curious. "I find I must echo your earlier question—Why? Why go to all this trouble? Why not simply refuse my invitation?"

"You made it difficult to do so, Your Grace. I did not care to be widowed or forced to live on the Continent because Alex had killed you."

"Ah yes, the duel," he said. "I suppose you are expecting me to withdraw now."

"You did promise." Her clear gaze met his shielded one. "In fact, I think I know you well enough to know that your heart was not really in this abduction. I don't think you are as evil as you like to pretend, although"—her brow darkened as she remembered his behavior at the gambling house—"I know you do like to cause mischief."

Her face cleared and she looked at him steadily. "I am now counting on your honor not to cause any more trouble for my husband and me. Tell me now, please, will you give up this feud and let bygones be bygones?"

The music stopped, and he led her to the edge of the dance floor. "Dear lady, I would not dare to abduct you again. I would be terrified that I would find myself at a party with psalm-singing Bible-thumpers or rabid reformists or some other such horrific bores." His lips twisted. "As for your husband . . ." He looked into her eyes. Something he saw there seemed to decide him. "I believe it will not cause me too much distress to avoid him. It should not be difficult."

"Thank you, Your Grace." She smiled radiantly at him.

"Then again," said the duke, looking at something behind her, "perhaps it will be more difficult than I think."

Turning her head, Miranda saw Alex standing in the doorway, looking stunned. As she watched, his gaze met hers, and he started across the room.

"What the *hell* is going on?" Alex asked in a low voice as he reached her side.

"Alex, what a surprise." Miranda looked uneasily from him to the duke. "Er, didn't Sara explain about the duke's ball?"

"Perhaps I can explain," the duke said. "Your charming wife and my mother arranged this soiree as a surprise for my birthday. Lady Huntsley very graciously agreed to—" the duke coughed a little into his sleeve, "to act as a decoy."

Alex turned a freezing stare on the duke. "I hope you are not planning to leave any time soon, Your Grace. After I finish talking with my wife, I would very much like to speak to you."

The duke shrugged. "As you wish," he said. With a bow to Miranda, he strolled off.

Alex turned back to her. "Would you like to explain?"

Seeing his cold eyes, Miranda felt her heart sink. Something had gone wrong. He knew about the abduction. She tried to think of some story to tell him but finally had to settle for the truth. "I knew the duke intended to abduct me."

His brows snapped together. If possible, he looked even angrier. "You *knew?*"

She clasped her hands tightly together. "Yes. I'm not stupid, you know."

"That is a matter open to debate."

Miranda laughed nervously. "Alex, be reasonable. I

couldn't let you fight a duel. The duke agreed to call it off if I would come with him."

"And you believed he would keep his word?"

"Well, yes. He is not *dishonorable*."

"Of course not." His voice was ominously quiet. "And when were you planning to tell me what was going on?"

"I don't know what went wrong. You weren't supposed to know about the abduction."

"I see," he said coolly.

She looked at him uncertainly. "Alex—"

A commotion at the front door interrupted her. She turned around to see his family entering. Her heart sank lower. Did they know what had happened, too?

"What the devil?" Alex muttered before crossing the room.

Reluctantly, Miranda trailed after him.

The new arrivals were gazing about in a bewildered fashion. When they saw Alex and Miranda, identical expressions of relief showed on their faces.

"Alex, thank God!" Lady Thurlow rushed to his side and subjected him to a fierce hug.

Alex gripped her shoulders. "Here, Mama, what's this?"

"Oh, nothing," she replied, trying to compose herself.

Preston stepped forward. "Don't keep us in suspense. What on earth happened? Didn't the duke abduct Miranda after all?"

Alex's jaw tightened. After a slight pause he said, "Apparently it was a misunderstanding."

Lady Thurlow frowned. "A misunderstanding? What does that mean? Tell us plainly, Alex. Was she or was she not abducted by—"

"Excuse me for interrupting," the duke de Morieux drawled. "My mother has instructed me to inform the guests that dinner will be announced shortly."

Lady Thurlow gaped at the duke, and the earl studied

him with cool eyes. Petronella blushed fiery red, then grew pale as wax. Preston moved protectively to her side. Alex stiffened and Miranda held her breath, wondering what would happen next.

Lady Thurlow broke the silence. "The nerve!"

The duke arched an eyebrow, then bowed. "Forgive me. I did not mean to intrude."

He started to move away, but Petronella cried out, "Wait!"

Everyone stared at her with varying degrees of astonishment, except for the duke, who looked suddenly wary.

"I—I have something to say," Petronella stammered, clutching convulsively at Preston's sleeve. "Ten years ago I claimed that the duke de Morieux abducted me." All eyes swiveled toward the duke. He was engrossed in polishing his quizzing glass.

Petronella took a deep breath. "The truth is, I went with him willingly."

Lady Thurlow gasped and swayed, leaning against the earl for support. "Petronella, how could you?"

Petronella hung her head. "I was so ashamed when Papa and Alex caught up with us. I just couldn't confess, so I made up that story about the duke's abducting me." She looked at the duke directly for the first time. "I'm sorry, Your Grace."

"No apology necessary, my dear." The duke returned his handkerchief to his pocket. "Now if you will please excuse me, I see someone who has just arrived. Joplin! Joplin, you sly dog. You knew about this . . ." Languidly he strolled away.

Petronella peeked at her father. He frowned at her with unusual sternness. "If you were still under my care, Petronella, I would take the rod to you until you couldn't sit down."

Tears slipped down Petronella's face. Preston put his arm around her, and she huddled against him.

"I'm so sorry," she whispered. "I've regretted it ever since, but I've never had the courage to speak up."

"It's over with, Petronella," Preston said, handing her a handkerchief. "You've told the truth, and we all applaud you for that, at least."

She turned her teary eyes up to him. "Do you hate me, Preston?"

The corner of Preston's mouth curled up in a half smile, and he said tenderly, "Hate you? Of course not. You know I've loved you ever since we were children. And if your elopement hadn't caused such a scandal, you might never have married me."

"Oh, you are the best husband anyone could wish for. I love you." Arm in arm, they wandered away, whispering in each other's ears.

Lady Thurlow watched them go. "Unbelievable!" She turned to Alex. "When will you and Miranda be moving in with us? Alex? Alex!"

Alex stood rigidly. He had not moved since Petronella's revelation and it took a moment for Lady Thurlow's voice to penetrate his reverie.

He answered her question bluntly. "I'm afraid Miranda and I are not going to be able to stay with you this year, Mother."

Lady Thurlow frowned and opened her mouth, but the earl said quickly, "I believe I am in need of sustenance, my dear. Would you care to go in to supper?"

Lady Thurlow's gaze moved back and forth between Alex and Miranda. Then a heavy sigh escaped her. "Yes, thank you, Charles." To Alex and Miranda she said, "You will have to come visit us in Northumberland soon."

"I doubt we will be able to do that, Mother," Alex said in a pleasant tone, "since Miranda is going to be locked up in her bedchamber for the rest of her life."

Miranda's eyes widened and she darted a quick glance at Alex's face. What she saw there made her swallow.

"Alex!" Lady Thurlow said. "That's no way to speak to your wife!"

Lord Thurlow took hold of her elbow. "Let's let Alex and Miranda handle this themselves, my dear." He steered her away toward the dining room.

Reluctantly, Miranda glanced at Alex. To her surprise, he wasn't looking at her. He was staring at something across the room.

"Stay here," he said brusquely. "I will be back in a moment."

Her brow wrinkling, she watched him thread his way through the crowd. Where could he be going? She scanned the other side of the room where he had been looking, pausing when she saw a familiar face with pale green eyes and stiff curls.

Fear gripped her. Was Alex going to challenge the duke after all?

Gathering her skirt in her hand, Miranda hurried after Alex.

She caught up to him just as he reached the duke. His mouth tightened when he saw her, but he ignored her as he spoke to the duke.

"De Morieux," Alex said stiffly, "it seems I have misjudged you."

The duke fingered his quizzing glass. Then, with a sigh, he said, "I don't think so, dear fellow. I have not been a saint. Oh, perhaps I am innocent of abducting your sister, but I certainly have done other things worthy of your odium." He looked at Miranda, his lips strangely twisted.

"Nonetheless, I owe you an apology." Alex's voice was cool.

"Very well. I accept. I also apologize for those times that I have been . . . less than gracious."

Alex nodded curtly, his gaze fixed searchingly on the duke. "Why didn't you ever tell the truth?"

The duke looked down and adjusted the set of his sleeve. "I have a peculiar dislike of calling a lady a liar, even if you would have believed me."

A slight grimace curled Alex's lips. "No doubt I would have called you out for maligning my sister."

"Just so."

"Then again, I apologize." Alex's face had a strange expression. "If things had turned out differently, you and Petronella would have been married."

"No need to apologize," the duke replied. His gaze drifted to where Petronella sat a short distance away, talking animatedly to Mrs. Overfield. Miranda could hear snatches of the conversation.

"And Edward is *much* taller than other boys his age. He already has his own pony, he has been riding since he was two! And he is intelligent, also. Why, just the other day . . ."

"In fact," continued the duke, his face perfectly straight, "I thank you from the bottom of my heart."

33

"You could do me an enormous favor," the duke said, glancing back at Alex and Miranda. "I have decided not to return to town. I have a yearning to enjoy the bucolic pleasures of Kent, and I believe it will be most beneficial to my health. I was wondering if you would be willing to drive the carriage I hired back to town."

Alex nodded. "I would be happy to do so. I'm intending to leave shortly."

"Ah, excellent. And perhaps you will not mind paying the jobmaster? I shall reimburse you, of course."

"Of course," Alex said dryly.

"Dear boy, you are as generous as ever. If you will come with me, I will inform the coachman of the change in plans."

"I will be with you in a moment." Alex waited until the duke had strolled out the door, before turning to Miranda. "What are you going to do now?"

Miranda looked at him uncertainly. What did he mean? Was he asking her to come with him or telling her to stay?

She swallowed. "I will come with you, if I may. I just need to say good-bye to Lady Briarwood first."

Evidently not caring one way or the other, he turned and strolled out the door after the duke.

Miranda, biting her lip, watched him go, then she glanced about the ballroom for Lady Briarwood.

She spied the countess sitting on a sofa on the other side of the room, talking to Mrs. Overfield. She hurried over to them.

The countess smiled when she saw Miranda approach. "You pulled it off, girl."

"Thank you for your help, Lady Briarwood," Miranda said. "And yours, Mrs. Overfield. I couldn't have organized everything without your assistance."

"It was a pleasure, dear," the duke's mother said. "And I think perhaps it will make that son of mine take a hard look at himself." She smiled. "I really should be thanking you. You are a very brave girl."

Blushing, Miranda shook her head.

Lady Briarwood waved her fan languidly. "So have you and Huntsley finally settled everything?"

Miranda's smile faded. "Alex and the duke have agreed not to fight the duel, but I think Alex is very upset with me. We're leaving in a few minutes. I don't know what he will say."

"I am sure you can talk things out. Just remember—stay calm."

Miranda nodded.

The countess closed her fan and said quietly, "I'll miss your company, dear."

Miranda gave her a fierce hug. "Thank you for everything, Lady Briarwood."

She turned and made her way back across the ballroom. She was about to go outside when a whirlwind of skirts dashed up to her.

"Miranda!" Sara cried. "We lost Lord Huntsley! He just disappeared after dinner. I was forced to confide in Mr. Hamilton-Smith, and we searched for him, but he was nowhere! I'm so sorry!"

"Sara," Miranda said, grasping her arm, "calm down. Alex is here."

"Here! How did he end up here?"

"The duke's servants told Alex that the duke was coming here. He arrived shortly after the duke and I did."

"Well! And after all we went through!"

Sara looked so indignant Miranda couldn't help smiling. Sara frowned ferociously, but she could only maintain it for a few seconds before she smiled also. "So, have Lord Huntsley and the duke agree to call off the duel?"

Miranda nodded. "Alex and I are leaving in a few minutes and I don't know what will happen, but I want to thank you for your help." She hugged Sara tightly. "And for being such a dear friend."

Sara hugged her back, a suspicious moisture in her eyes. "You're welcome, Miranda. Good luck with Lord Huntsley." She dashed the tears away with the back of her hand. "I'd better go find Mr. Hamilton-Smith and tell him everything."

She wandered away, and Miranda stepped to the door just as the duke entered.

"Huntsley is waiting for you outside," he told her.

"Thank you." Miranda hesitated, looking up at him. His pale green eyes were remote, revealing no trace of emotion. "What will you do now?" she asked slowly.

He swung his quizzing glass idly. "Rusticate here for a while. Then perhaps go on a visit to the Continent. France has had a peculiar appeal for me lately. I have relatives there."

"Good luck." She searched his face. "I had better go now."

"Good-bye, Lady Huntsley."

She smiled a little. "You may call me Miranda. I think we've known each other long enough to warrant a little friendliness."

A glimmer of an answering smile lit his eyes. He bowed low and kissed her hand. Then, he walked away.

She gazed after him, a slight frown between her eyes. Shaking her head, she walked out onto the portico.

She stood there for a moment in the fragrant darkness. Wild rosebushes nearby released a sweet scent. Closing her eyes, she took a deep breath, the air sweet after the stuffiness of the house. A pleasant breeze cooled her cheeks.

"Are you ready?" a harsh voice asked.

34

Miranda's eyes flew open.

Alex stood on the bottom step of the portico, looking up at her coldly.

She swallowed and nodded.

Silently, he led her to the carriage and handed her in. He climbed in after her and seated himself opposite. The lamp he had lit swayed as the carriage set off, its light playing on his face. His expression was cool and remote—so remote that she wondered if she could ever bridge the distance.

The silence was oppressive. She wanted to say something, but she couldn't think of anything. She was more afraid of him than she'd ever been. She had to break the silence.

"Wasn't Petronella's confession a surprise?" she asked brightly. "I always thought there was something odd about her story, but I never guessed—"

"Miranda," he interrupted her quietly, "we can't go on like this."

His words were like a blow to her chest. Her throat tightened and tears blurred her eyes.

So he wanted the divorce after all.

She ought to be relieved. This marriage had turned out nothing like she had expected. She had thought marriage would be a pleasurable friendship between two people who lived in a nice little cocoon. She had never expected to be caught up in such a whirlwind of unfamiliar emotions.

Their marriage had been a disaster from the beginning. She should be glad to be out of it—so why did his words make her heart ache with such unbearable regret?

Fighting back tears, she said, "You're right, Alex. I think a divorce is the most sensible solution."

She sensed, rather than saw him stiffen. When he spoke, however, his voice was still cool. "A divorce may be the only solution if you ever do something as incredibly stupid as you did tonight. Do you know what could have happened?"

Miranda twisted the cloth of her skirt. "There was no risk. Lady Briarwood and I planned everything most carefully."

"Oh?" His fingers gripped the window ledge. "What if the carriage had broken down? What if the duke had decided to take you somewhere else? What if a hundred other things had gone wrong?"

Remembering the moment when the duke had caressed her shoulder in the carriage, Miranda bit her lip. "Perhaps there was some slight danger, but I was willing to take that chance." She looked down at her lap and whispered, "I was afraid you might be killed."

There was another long silence.

"Miranda," he finally said, leaning toward her, "I am glad you are concerned for my health, but you never should have attempted such an insane scheme. You could have saved both of us a great deal of trouble if you had only heeded my warnings about the duke."

"That's true. We don't seem to listen to each other very well."

His brows rose. "I have always listened to you."

She smiled, a trifle sadly. "Have you, Alex? Have you really?"

Frowning, Alex sat back in his seat. What the devil did she mean by that? He thought back over the last few months. There had been some conflict over the house, he remembered. She had wanted to make changes and he hadn't really listened to her then. But his behavior was perfectly understandable, he assured himself. Any man would have reacted the same way to being unable to touch his wife.

They had gotten along very well once he figured out what the problem was. Or at least they had until the absurd misunderstanding about her pregnancy. That hadn't been his fault, either. What else could he have thought with Bomford congratulating him on his impending fatherhood and Miranda blushing so guiltily? But he hadn't even given her a chance to say anything. He had stormed out of the house like a character in an Italian opera.

She had definitely been in the wrong with the duke, however. He had specifically warned her about de Morieux.

But if you hadn't driven her away, she never would have gotten tangled up with the duke.

Alex tried to ignore the accusing inner voice, but it was impossible. He leaned his head back against the carriage panels and closed his eyes, the truth slowly seeping into his brain. If anything had happened to her tonight, it would have been *his* fault, not hers.

He opened his eyes and looked at her. She was sitting very still across from him, her hands twisting in her lap, pale shadows beneath her eyes—eyes that were full of wary uncertainty. He remembered how she used to look at him when they first met, when she was so full of trust.

Guilt and despair gnawed at him. Would she ever trust him again?

"Miranda," he said slowly. "I owe you an apology."

She lifted her head, her eyes widening. "You do?"

"Yes, I do. You're right, I haven't listened to you and I've failed you because of it." He put his hands in his pockets to hide his clenched fists. "Can you ever forgive me?"

She shook her head. "You haven't failed me. I realize now I had an unrealistic view of marriage. That our marriage will never be like my parents'. But I'm glad. You've taught me about something that I never knew existed."

"You're very generous." He eased his hands out of his pockets. "Much more generous than I've been. I had unrealistic expectations, too. I thought that loving you was all that was required of me, but now I see that there is more."

Miranda, her heart thumping, grew very still. "You love me?" she whispered.

Frowning, he cast her a quick glance. "Of course, I do. Did you ever doubt it?"

She lowered her gaze to his crumpled cravat. "You don't only want me to slake your carnal lust?"

He stared at her incredulously. "I don't only want you for *what?*"

She blushed. "Well, Mr. Pelham did warn me."

"If Mr. Pelham ever shows his face in England again, I will skewer him and spit-roast him." He leaned forward and tipped up her chin, his gaze dark and intense. "If that was all I cared about, I wouldn't have to marry to do it, and I certainly wouldn't have chosen a bride with some very peculiar ideas about how children are conceived. And I certainly wouldn't have agreed to wait *three months* to 'slake my carnal lust,' as you so quaintly put it. I've loved you from almost the first day we met, and I expect I will until the day I die."

Miranda stared up into his eyes and saw something there she had never seen before. Her heart swelled and the tears she had been fighting earlier suddenly returned and spilled over.

Agony flashed across Alex's face. He grasped her hands. "Don't cry, Miranda. I'm sorry. God, I'm sorry—"

"Alex," she said. "Please be quiet and kiss me."

His grip on her hands tightened until he was almost crushing them.

She smiled at him through her tears.

His eyes blazed with happiness. With a sudden tug, he pulled her across the carriage onto his lap and wrapped his arms around her. Then his mouth covered hers and he kissed her very thoroughly indeed.

Nearly an hour later, Alex watched the brilliant pink, red, and gold sunrise through the window, with Miranda's head resting against his shoulder. The carriage struck a particularly deep rut, and he tightened his arm around her waist as his stomach bounced with the coach.

She snuggled closer. "Where are we going?"

"To Ribblebank Manor."

"Oh, Alex, yes! It will be so nice to be home." She plucked at a button on his coat. "Would you mind if I invited my father and Thelma to visit us?"

He glanced down at her in surprise. "What made you think of them?"

"I don't know. I was thinking of how much my father loved my mother. I think it was very hard on him when she was ill for so long. Much harder than I realized. I don't think I was very fair to him. Or to Thelma."

"You are welcome to invite them any time." He paused, then added, "Of course, we will have to invite my parents, also."

Her gaze flew to his; then she hung her head. "I'm sorry, Alex. I didn't mean to be so rude about your mother."

"She is really not so bad. I know she is not easy to live with, but she means well, and we will have to visit her and my father on occasion."

"Yes, Alex."

His brows shot up. "Heavens, that was remarkably easy. Does this mean we aren't going to argue anymore?"

"I doubt it." She reached up to kiss his chin. "I think it's impossible for two people always to agree. But if we make an effort to understand each other, and if you listen to me—"

He put a finger to her lips. "I swear, I will listen to you. Frankly, I am quite weary of finding dogs in my bed, of planning ways to murder vicars, and of challenging dukes to duels. If listening to you will prevent all that, then I will gladly do so."

He took his finger away from her lips, and she said in a meek voice, "Thank you, Alex."

He looked down at her suspiciously, just as the carriage bounced over another rut.

His stomach bounced, too.

Then he noticed that the golden flecks in her eyes were glowing and she was smiling up at him with a familiar sweetness that made his breath catch.

"I love you, Alex."

Alex forgot about the carriage, the ruts, and his stomach. He forgot about everything as he tightened his arms around her and demonstrated his love in a most satisfying way— and taught her a few new things about carnal lust.

Let HarperMonogram Sweep You Away!

Touched by Angels by Debbie Macomber

From the bestselling author of *A Season of Angels* and *The Trouble with Angels*. The much-loved angelic trio—Shirley, Goodness, and Mercy—are spending this Christmas in New York City. And three deserving souls are about to have their wishes granted by this dizzy, though divinely inspired, crew.

Till the End of Time by Suzanne Elizabeth

The latest sizzling time-travel romance from the award-winning author of *Destiny's Embrace*. Scott Ramsey has a taste for adventure and a way with the ladies. When his time-travel experiment transports him back to Civil War Georgia, he meets his match in Rachel Ann Warren, a beautiful Union spy posing as a Southern belle.

A Taste of Honey by Stephanie Mittman

After raising her five siblings, marrying the local minister is a chance for Annie Morrow to get away from the farm. When she loses her heart to widower Noah Eastman, however, Annie must choose between a life of ease and a love no money can buy.

A Delicate Condition by Angie Ray

Golden Heart Winner. A marriage of convenience weds innocent Miranda Rembert to the icy Lord Huntsley. But beneath his lordship's stern exterior, fires of passion linger—along with a burning desire for the marital pleasures only Miranda can provide.

Reckless Destiny by Teresa Southwick

Believing that Arizona Territory is no place for a lady, Captain Kane Carrington sent proper easterner Cady Tanner packing. Now the winsome schoolteacher is back, and ready to teach Captain Carrington a lesson in love.

And in case you missed last month's selections . . .

Liberty Blue by **Robin Lee Hatcher**
Libby headed west, running from her ruthless father and her privileged life. Remington Walker will do anything to locate her, as long as her father keeps paying him. But when Remington does he realizes she's worth more than money can buy.

Shadows in the Mirror by **Roslynn Griffith**
Iphigenia Wentworth is determined to find her missing baby in West Texas. She never expected to find love with a local rancher along the way.

Yesterday's Tomorrows by **Margaret Lane**
Montana rancher Abby De Coux is magically transported back to the year 1875 in order to save her family's ranch. There she meets ruggedly handsome Elan, who will gamble his future to make her his forever.

The Covenant by **Modean Moon**
From the author of the acclaimed *Evermore*, a spellbinding present-day romance expertly interwoven with a nineteenth-century love story.

Brimstone by **Sonia Simone**
After being cheated at the gaming tables by seasoned sharper Katie Starr, the Earl of Brynston decides to teach the silly American girl a lesson. But soon the two are caught in a high stakes game in which they both risk losing their hearts.

Echoes and Illusions
by Kathy Lynn Emerson

Lauren Ryder has everything she wants, but then the dreams start—dreams so real she fears she's losing her mind. Something happened to Lauren in the not-so-distant past that she can't remember. As she desperately tries to piece together the missing years of her life, a shocking picture emerges. Who is Lauren Ryder, really?

The Night Orchid by Patricia Simpson

In Seattle Marissa Quinn encounters a doctor conducting ancient Druid time-travel rituals and meets Alek, a glorious pre-Roman warrior trapped in the modern world. Marissa and Alek discover that though two millennia separate their lives, nothing can sever the bond forged between their hearts.

Destiny Awaits by Suzanne Elizabeth

Tess Harper found herself in Kansas in the year 1885, face-to-face with the most captivating, stubborn man she'd ever met—and two precious little girls who needed a mother. Could this man, and this family, be her true destiny?